GOLD BRICK RANGE

GOLD BRICK RANGE

ALLAN VAUGHAN ELSTON

CUTTING EDGE

ISBN-13: 978-1-954840-00-3

Published by
Cutting Edge Books
PO Box 8212
Calabasas, CA 91372
www.cuttingedgebooks.com

CHAPTER ONE
THE AUCTION

S TANLEY COGSWELL elevated his long, lean legs to the balcony railing and lighted a cigarette. For a week now, although he was still twenty pounds underweight, they had allowed him to smoke.

He gazed off toward twin cone mountains. "I'm tired of this coop," he told them. He threw the cigarette distastefully to the lawn. "For a plugged nickel I'd walk out of this coop, right now."

He couldn't imagine, though, where he would go. Not back to New York. He'd lost his engineering practice there, after the infernal grind of it had wrecked his health. For almost a year he had been shelved at this Western sanatorium.

"You're lookin' good, Mr. Cogswell," spoke a voice at his elbow. "I guess maybe you'll be outa here soon. Yep, it's prepaid. Just sign for it."

It was the little nut-brown messenger boy who on numerous occasions during recent months had delivered telegrams to Cogswell. He now delivered another one, and Cogswell tipped him.

When the boy was gone, Cogswell opened the message and observed that it was from Luther Hayes in New York. He read:

Stanley Cogswell,
San Isabel Sanatorium,
Trinidad, Colorado.

Am informed property known as Pauly Horse Ranch near Trinidad is about to be sold under foreclosure stop Have investigated and believe it good speculation if buyable at lien figure stop Acting for me please bid lien figure plus one dollar stop Do not go higher.

Luther J. Hayes.

Cogswell read the message twice and smiled.

"Just like old Luth!" he thought aloud.

Due to precedents, the request was in no way extraordinary. In the first place, Cogswell and Hayes had always been on terms of extreme intimacy. Moreover, Hayes was a man of wealth and an inveterate speculator in realty of all kinds. His judgment was usually sound. Whether he bought a Manhattan lot or a coal mine in West Virginia, Hayes usually managed to turn it at a profit.

Cogswell, sitting there with the telegram in his hands, recalled that Hayes had made a trip west a few months ago, stopping over a week-end here at Trinidad. While calling on Cogswell at the sanatorium, he had advised Cogswell to buy an option on a certain Jersey shore tract. A week later Cogswell had decided to do so, wiring Hayes in New York to make the buy for him. Hayes had complied, with a resultant quick profit for Cogswell.

Here was a chance, therefore, for Cogswell to return such a favor.

He arose from the balcony chair and, using the cane they had given him, went to the sanatorium's office. There he telephoned the Public Trustee, at the county courthouse. His inquiry was, "Is a property known as the Pauly Horse Ranch to be sold at foreclosure?"

2

The reply was, "Yes. Are you interested?"

"I might be. What does the mortgaged property consist of?"

"Three thousand acres of improved land along Rincon Creek. Also three hundred head of horses."

"And the amount of the lien?"

"Thirty thousand dollars."

"When and where is the sale?" was Cogswell's final question.

"The east door of the courthouse at eleven o'clock this morning," the Public Trustee said. Cogswell thanked him and hung up.

His watch told him that it was now ten-fifteen. Forty-five minutes was pretty short notice. And thirty thousand dollars, Cogswell reflected, was a lot of money. On the other hand, three thousand acres of improved land and three hundred head of horses was a lot of property. Luther Hayes, Cogswell knew, often made his realty speculations by buying at foreclosure auctions, dropping out if he failed to purchase at the lien price plus one dollar. In general the practice was sound; realty loans being usually made only up to half value, buys at such minimum bids were likely to be bargains.

Cogswell realized that he'd have no time to get in further communication with Hayes. If he bid, he must use his own checkbook and let Hayes later reimburse him. Consulting his checkbook, he saw that his private balance in the Thirty-Fourth Street Bank of New York was a trifle over thirty-five thousand.

"And about all I have," Cogswell reflected wryly. His affluence in no way compared with that of his friend Hayes. Barring that one deal in Jersey shore, for more than a year now everything had been going out with nothing coming in. "Still," he further reflected, "I wouldn't even have made that profit on the Jersey option if Luth hadn't stood by me in a deal just like this."

His decision was to attend the sale and make a bid for Hayes. Quite likely someone would bid higher than the minimum figure plus one dollar, which would let him out. On the way to his room for his cap, he saw the superintendent conversing with Vera Grady. Miss Grady was the nurse who had been especially assigned to Cogswell's case. Sight of the pair made him feel a little guilty about going out. He knew he should ask permission, but decided he wouldn't.

He passed unseen downstairs and out into the street. He still carried the cane, but found no need to use it as he walked briskly toward the business district. The fresh air brightened him. It was June in Colorado. He hadn't walked a block before he decided to cut loose from the sanatorium the very next day. This was what he needed, exercise, action. He'd quit letting people in white uniforms tell him he was sick. The devil take them all, anyway, Cogswell thought, as he flicked at a weed with his cane.

Midway between the hospital and the courthouse he met a man of the range, a cowboy if one judged by peaked hat, high-heeled boots, spurs, and batwing *chaparejos*. The man had a homemade cigarette between his lips and was fumbling through his vest for a match.

"Got a light, mister?" he asked as the two came elbow to elbow on the walk.

As Cogswell affably produced one, it occurred to him that here was a chance for a little free information. This bechapped citizen might know something about the Pauly Horse Ranch.

"Do you know the country around here?" Cogswell asked.

"Lived here all my life," the cowboy said, lighting the match with a black-bordered thumbnail.

"Ever hear of the Pauly Horse Ranch?"

"The Pauly Horse Ranch? Sure I have, mister." The rangeman cocked an inquisitive eye. He was a heavy-set man of middle age, with a hard, unshaven face. A rough customer, Cogswell thought. But no matter, as long as he knew the country. "Sure I know that Pauly place," the man repeated, squinting his eyes. "Worked there once. It's the sweetest layout in this county."

"A sound property, eh?" echoed Cogswell. He was distinctly relieved. The investment, of course, if unwise, would be Luther Hayes's funeral and not his own. Nevertheless, Cogswell would feel better about sinking his money even temporarily into the deal now that he had evidence that it was sound.

"If Bert Pauly's layout ain't a good one, I never seen no good grass and water," the cowboy went on. "He's got three thousand acres of the old Ramon Estabal place and his water holes control thirty-forty thousand acres more. An okay outfit, if you ask me, mister. You thinkin' of buying Pauly out?"

"I was just inquiring for a friend," Cogswell said. "Much obliged."

He passed on down Main Street toward the courthouse. En route he came to the entrance of the Picketwire National Bank. Here a thought struck Cogswell, and he paused. Foreclosure sales, he knew, are conducted on a strictly cash basis. It would do him no good to bid unless he could back his bid up with an immediately negotiable check. With this in mind Cogswell turned in at the bank.

"Glad to see you up and around, Cogswell." Cashier John Clarke himself greeted him heartily. The two were acquainted, because Cogswell had kept a small checking-account here for the past eight months in order to pay hospital and doctor bills. Also Cogswell's check on the Jersey shore deal had passed through this bank. Thus the local cashier had had occasion to look him up, had found him a man of substance, in good standing with the Thirty-Fourth Street National of New York.

Cogswell explained his errand. He was on his way to the courthouse, he said, to bid on a parcel of county property at a foreclosure sale. If his bid was successful, the Public Trustee would demand cash, and Cogswell requested Clarke to honor his New York check if presented for payment. He displayed his checkbook, which showed a thirty-five-thousand-dollar balance in New York. Clarke could, if he wished, verify that balance by telegraph.

Cashier Clarke, a shrewd judge of men, seemed to know immediately that he would be taking no chances in cashing a check of this customer. No doubt he saw a chance to get Cogswell's permanent account. If Cogswell bought a parcel of county property, that might lead to his residence here and make a profitable client for the bank.

"Glad to accommodate you," Clarke said heartily. "You and your checks are welcome any time. Is ft town property or ranch you're bidding on?"

"Ranch land," Cogswell explained hurriedly. A glance at the wall clock told him that it lacked only five minutes of sale time.

"Well," went on the friendly cashier as he took Cogswell's arm and accompanied him to the door, "you're not likely to go broke buying ranch acreage at lien figures."

"I'll make only one bid, Mr. Clarke. The lien figure plus one dollar. If the other fellow beats that, he can have it. Thanks a lot."

Cogswell found three men assembled at the east door of the courthouse. "Is this," he inquired, "where the Pauly property is to be auctioned?"

"It is, and in one minute by my watch," one of the trio responded genially. He was Ollie Bowman, Public Trustee, and immediately impressed Cogswell as a man of character. He had a round, frank face, was hatless and in coat sleeves. The visor of a green eyeshade was perched on his forehead. When Cogswell gave his name and errand, Bowman said, "Good! I was beginning to think we wouldn't get any bids except from the lien holder, who, dad blame him, has to bid to protect his own note. Step up, Prowers, and meet Mr. Cogswell. Cogswell, this is Milton Prowers, mortgagee, who loaned Bert Pauly thirty thousand on his land and stock. This other gentleman is Dan Yates, county sheriff."

Cogswell shook hands in turn with them. Yates, a rugged, wind-burned fellow, had no particular interest in the proceedings and was attending purely as a matter of form. The law required his presence at these dispositions at the courthouse door.

The more commanding figure was that of Milton Prowers, mortgagee. He was tall and burly, boldly good-looking, stood flicking the ash from a cigar with his left hand while his right closed in a hard grip on Cogswell's. Something about the man disturbed Cogswell. He was too well dressed, his hands were too white and well kept to match his big, burly build. His teeth, as he smiled a greeting, were too perfect and even. Upsetting all of Cogswell's preconceived ideas of a money-lending Westerner, this man seemed much better fit for the role of ringmaster at a circus. His eyes were black and darting; his voice came like the crack of a whip.

"Sit in, Mr. Cogswell. Competition is the spice of life, they say."

If not a master showman, then a gambler, Cogswell thought. His "Sit in, Mr. Cogswell" had a disturbingly familiar sound.

Bowman pushed his eyeshade back and faced the two prospective bidders, Cogswell and Prowers. "Now, gentlemen, I, as Public Trustee, have no interest in this transaction except that duty impels me to get the highest bid possible. The total amount in default, including unpaid interest, sale fee, and other minor charges, is $80,211.80. Any proceeds derived from the sale over that amount go to Bert Pauly, fee owner. Milton Prowers, mortgagee, is entitled to his principal and interest, no more.

"As auctioneer, I shall call attention to certain very remarkable excellences of the property being sold. First, gentlemen, this estate of Bert Pauly's is part of the original Don Ramon Estabal ranch, once the show place of this county. Second, each of its nineteen quarter sections of land either lies athwart Rincon Creek, a never failing stream, or includes a perpetual spring of water on the slope of Rincon Mesa. Many dry quarter sections lie between and among these nineteen watered half-mile squares.

They are government land. Thus the nineteen plots here to be sold control, for grazing-purposes, a vast range.

"Third, the realty here to be sold was, many years ago by Don Ramon Estabal, improved with buildings, fields, fences, and ditches, and these improvements, though old, are still on the property.

"Fourth, the three hundred head of horses included in the sale are all descendants of Ramon Estabal's famous stable of racing-stock. In their veins flows the blood of Estabal's nationally known stallion, Don Quixote. Ramon Estabal, in his day, was a great sportsman; in addition to cattle he raised purebred race horses."

Bowman then called upon Sheriff Yates to read aloud from a published advertisement a description of the chattel and realty. When Yates had complied, Bowman called for a starting bid.

Milton Prowers promptly made one. He bid $30,211.80, the exact amount due to himself. Such a bid was expected, and meant that if there was no other Prowers would get the property without the transfer of a cent.

"Thirty thousand, two hundred and twelve dollars and eighty cents," Stanley Cogswell offered, raising the bid exactly one dollar as instructed in the telegram from Luther Hayes.

He then looked hopefully toward Prowers. If Prowers bid again, he, Cogswell, would be out of it. But Prowers made no further bid. His big shoulders shrugged, and his white hands spread in a gesture of resignation.

"Can't you raise that figure, Prowers?" Bowman wheedled. "As it stands now Pauly gets frozen out with one dollar. Let's hike her up a few thousand."

Again Prowers's only answer was a shrug. It was the shrug of a gambler who knows when to lay down a hand, Cogswell thought.

"In that case," announced the Public Trustee, "the three thousand acres of land and the three hundred head of horses are hereby declared to have been purchased by Stanley Cogswell of—"

"Of New York," Cogswell prompted uncomfortably.

"Of New York, for the encumbrance plus one dollar. Step into my office, gentlemen, and we'll wind up the business with dispatch."

Bowman pushed through the swinging doors and led the way to his office. Cogswell, following close behind Prowers, noted that the man's tailor-made coat fitted him with neat perfection about the hips except at one spot. At his right hip there was a gun-shaped bulge.

A gun? More and more the role of a professional gambler seemed to fit Prowers. But why should a gambler loan money on a ranch?

The situation worried Cogswell. In defense of his position, he permitted himself a few arithmetical calculations. What was he doing? He was buying for his friend Luther Hayes three thousand acres of improved, watered land and three hundred head of horses. Swift calculations reassured Cogswell. The land would only have to be worth five dollars an acre and the horses fifty dollars per head to make it a safe buy. Those figures seemed to Cogswell conservative. As for the soundness of the title, on that score there need be no worry. He knew he would get a Public Trustee's deed with the Public Trustee himself back of it. He knew, too, that titles acquired at foreclosures are generally safe because the mortgage would not have been accepted in the first place had there been a flaw in title. Also his mind reviewed the fact that land loans are normally given only to half values; since Pauly had been able to borrow thirty thousand on the property, the true value should be more nearly sixty.

"I'm now ready to receive the amount of your bid in cash, Mr. Cogswell," Bowman was saying.

Cogswell, on the chance that he might get away with it, explained that he was bidding for a friend in New York. He asked a day's time in which to telegraph his friend and receive funds with which to cover the bid.

"Can't do that," Bowman said sharply. "This sale was advertised for cash on the nail. To grant a delay wouldn't be fair to the other bidder, or to bidders who may have stayed away for lack of ready cash."

"I only ask a day's time," Cogswell argued.

"No," the Public Trustee said with finality. "If you weren't bluffing, if your bid was sincere, please pay it."

Cogswell flushed. The suggestion of insincerity nettled him. "Very well, I'll pay cash," he said stiffly. He wrote a check in favor of the Public Trustee, for $30,212.80, and handed it to Bowman.

"You might cast your eye," Bowman said as he took it, "over this opinion of title dated this morning and rendered by Judge Lionel Southcutt. Southcutt is our leading attorney and looks up all titles for the Picketwire National Bank. Here is his statement as to Pauly's title. Over and above that, I myself have consulted the county recorder and made certain there's nothing against the property except the mortgage to Prowers, which this sale annuls. You get a Public Trustee's deed and are quite safe."

Bowman then called Cashier Clarke of the Picketwire National on the telephone.

"Is Stanley Cogswell's check, drawn on the Thirty-Fourth Street National of New York for $30,212.80, negotiable at your counter?" he inquired. The reply seemed to be satisfactory, for Bowman turned with an attitude of increased respect toward Cogswell.

In the meantime Cogswell had glanced through the opinion of title. "Let me have the phone before you ring off," he said.

Of Cashier Clarke he inquired, "Is Lionel Southcutt examiner of titles for your bank, and is his opinion the best obtainable in town?"

"Yes to both questions," Clarke affirmed. "When Southcutt says a title's good, it's good."

Cogswell hung up. "I'm satisfied," he told Bowman. "Give me a receipt for the money. When you execute the deed, please insert the name of Luther J. Hayes as grantee."

Bowman delivered an official receipt just as the courthouse bell struck twelve chimes. It reminded Stanley Cogswell that he, a patient, had now played truant from the San Isabel Sanatorium for an hour and a half, and that lunch was probably being carried on a tray to his room. So he picked up his cane and hurried home.

CHAPTER TWO

SOLD!

W HEN THE SUPERINTENDENT met Cogswell in the corridor, he mildly rebuked him for the excursion.

"Did me good," Cogswell defended. "I'm feeling fine."

"Well," the superintendent said, "you better not take chances. After lunch lie down and have a good rest."

A student nurse whom Cogswell had never seen before brought lunch to his room. Heretofore he had been served by the regular nurse, Vera Grady.

"Where's Miss Grady?"

"Miss Grady resigned this morning," the student nurse said.

The news did not impress Cogswell as important. If anything it was good news, for he hadn't cared much for Miss Grady. He was forced to admit, however, that she had been reasonably efficient. And willing. In fact, Vera Grady had served Cogswell even to the point of reading and writing some of his business letters, during that period when the patient had been confined to bed. Nevertheless he hadn't much liked her. Cogswell now dismissed her from his mind.

His appetite for lunch assured him that the morning's excursion had been distinctly beneficial. Therefore he took scarcely more than an hour's rest. Shortly after two o'clock he sallied forth, ignoring a remonstrance from the superintendent. This time not even taking his cane, he left the institution and walked briskly downtown.

At the Western Union office on Main Street he filed a message.

Luther J. Hayes,
Ambassador Hotel, New York.
Pursuant of your wired request I bid in Pauly Horse Ranch for $30,212.80 stop Please reimburse my account in the 34th Street Bank.
Stanley Cogswell.

"Rush that," he directed the clerk. "I'll wait next door in the lobby of the Arapahoe Hotel for an answer."

When he was seated in the Arapahoe's lobby, Cogswell noted that the hotel's dining-room was still open, though now nearly deserted by midday patrons. He saw, in fact, but two customers, a man and a woman seated facing each other across a table. The man's back was to him, yet somehow the short rear profile of him struck Cogswell as vaguely familiar. He was sure he had seen the man before. The woman he immediately recognized as Vera Grady, the nurse who this morning had resigned from the San Isabel Sanatorium.

It was not in any way strange that Miss Grady should be lunching with a man, and Cogswell's interest strayed to the street. He could see the length of it from his lobby chair. The pavement, in this important block, was brick. Posts or rails, provided for the tethering of horses, were in front of each building. Several mounts were now hitched across the street in front of another hotel, the Toltec. As Cogswell watched, two stockmen came out of the Toltec, mounted horses, and clattered away down the pavement. At least he got the impression that they were stockmen. They were dressed quite like various townsmen on the walks except that the riders wore half boots and spurs. The difference was in their faces. Their cheeks seemed to have been sandpapered and then blistered by a blow torch.

On Cogswell's side of the street a cab drew up in front of the Arapahoe. The Mexican cabman slumped into a doze, the two bony nags emulating his example.

Cogswell yawned. This range town, he decided, was about as exciting as a Boston suburb an hour before church time. Across the street he saw Sheriff Dan Yates walking along, in the company of a portly lady who was no doubt his wife. If the bundles heaped in Mr. Yates's arms were evidence, they had been shopping. The incongruous sight of the sheriff's revolver butt protruding from between two of the bundles made Cogswell smile.

"You can't ditch me like that, Bert. You promised to take me with you."

That shrill protest came to Cogswell from the diningroom and from the lips of Vera Grady. Turning his head, Cogswell perceived that the ex-nurse was considerably irritated. She was quarreling bitterly with her companion, the heavy-set man whose back was toward Cogswell. This man growled a response which Cogswell failed to make out. For a while the girl sulked, while the man argued persuasively. When he was done she waxed shrill again. She put no restraint on herself; obviously she didn't care whether the entire lobby heard her or not.

"You can't ditch me like this, Bert! You promised. I quit my job, didn't I? I'm going with you."

"Not a chance," the man retorted. "I'm pulling out of here right now, and I'm going alone."

Cogswell was startled. He'd heard that voice before and recently. But where? He could still see nothing of the man except his thickset rear profile.

The argument went on for another five minutes. Cogswell, idly interested, noted that the man was dressed in a loudly checkered suit whose color base was purple. Probably a small-town pool shark or a bartender off duty. Evidently he had been going with Vera Grady and was now about to get rid of her. More and more the man's voice struck Cogswell as familiar.

Finally the man tossed a bill on the table and stood up. He turned abruptly away from the girl and entered the lobby. Vera Grady followed, clutching his arm obstinately. She would not be put aside. The man shook her off. She was still trailing him, though, when they passed Cogswell.

Cogswell knew the man now, having seen him frontally. Here was the individual who this morning had accosted him midway between the hospital and the courthouse, and who had asked him for a match. He was the fellow who, during that brief sidewalk encounter, had given Cogswell a glowing recommendation of the Pauly Horse Ranch.

Yet except for his face and voice he was now totally different. This morning he had worn a peaked hat and batwing chaps. Incidentally, Cogswell realized that he hadn't seen anyone else wearing batwing chaps on the streets of this town. The fact was all the more remarkable because of the present loudly checkered getup of this fellow, and because of the brown derby hat he was now lifting from a lobby rack. Why should a man wear batwing chaps in the morning and a brown derby in the afternoon?

The only thing clear about it was that this fellow was in the act of breaking off an affair with a woman who had recently been Cogswell's nurse.

The couple were too occupied with their quarrel to notice Cogswell as they passed him. Repeatedly repulsed, the girl nevertheless persisted in clinging to the man's arm. Thus encumbered, the man picked up a grip and started for the street.

"You can't ditch me like this," Vera Grady shrieked shrilly. Cogswell felt ashamed for her. What could she see in that fellow, anyway? Why didn't she let him go?

The man, grip in hand, made his way to the cab parked at the curb. Presumably he had ordered it. The Mexican driver woke up, descended to the walk, and opened the cab door. Both cab doors were entirely devoid of glass.

"*Entré, señor*," the cabman invited.

The man got in with his grip and said, "Take me to the Rio Grande depot, and be quick about it."

"*Entré, señorita,*" the cabman repeated, addressing Vera Grady.

"She's not goin'," the man inside said harshly, and slammed the cab's door in the girl's face. The cabman shrugged, then climbed to the seat and took the reins.

Cogswell saw it all from the lobby window. He heard the girl plead once more, "Take me with you, Bert. You promised."

Bert said, "To hell with you!"

The woman said, "To hell with *you!*" In a fury she snatched a pistol from her dress and fired point-blank through the glass-less cab window. The range was scarcely a yard, the woman on the curb, the man seated within the cab. Cogswell saw the flash of flame as it leaped from the gun toward Bert's purple check-ered vest. The man fell forward across the sill, his head and arms drooping downward toward the curb.

By the time Cogswell reached the walk he was dead.

Although Main Street had been practically deserted an instant before, it now swarmed with the curious. Clerks appeared from the shops. The lobby of the Toltec, opposite, poured its life out on the walks. A policeman came around the corner and took the Grady woman, who did not run, by the arm.

"He double-crossed me," she was screaming.

"How?" the policeman wanted to know. He picked up her .32-caliber pistol which had fallen to the gutter.

"He was running out on me, the bum!" More than this Vera Grady would not say.

"We saw it," offered one of the two drummers who had been sitting in the lobby of the Toltec. "She tried to crowd into the cab with him and he wouldn't let her. So she pulled out a gun and gave him the works."

"It happened just that way," the clerk of a near-by store testified.

Cogswell said nothing. Had he been asked, he would have been forced to give the same testimony. It was a clear case against Vera Grady.

"There comes Dan Yates," someone yelled. "Hey, make way for the sheriff."

Yates, encumbered by neither wife nor bundles, made his way through the crowd. He took charge of Vera Grady. He examined the .32, saw that it had been fired once. He took the names of several witnesses. Cogswell kept out of it.

After he had heard the story several times, all versions agreeing in substantial details, Sheriff Yates saw a man approaching whom he recognized as the county coroner.

"Get busy, Jim," he said to the coroner. "This dame just plugged a hole through Bert Pauly. He's dead. Take him to the morgue."

Resigning the dead to the coroner, Yates ushered Vera Grady up the street toward the jail. Cogswell hardly saw them. Buzzing through his brain was the name—Bert Pauly! Could it be the same man?

Cogswell accosted a bystander. "Is the dead man Bert Pauly, who had a horse ranch on Rincon Creek?"

"He's one and the same gazabo," the bystander said. "Why?"

"I just wanted to know," Cogswell answered. He moved off in a daze.

It meant that he had asked Bert Pauly himself for information about the Pauly ranch. Pauly's natural reply should have been, "Why, I'm Bert Pauly myself."

But the fellow had given no such response. Instead he had given a glowing recommendation of the property, and then passed on.

A suspicion harassed Cogswell. Suppose that Pauly, having by some means foreknowledge that Cogswell would walk from sanatorium to courthouse at a certain hour of a certain day, had planted himself on the route! That the encounter had been the fruit of shrewd design! Pauly, knowing Cogswell's errand and that he was a stranger, might by comporting himself as a bechapped rangeman and asking for a match, have hoped to elicit a certain inquiry which at that instant would be dominating Cogswell's mind.

How natural the question! How innocently convincing the reply! Cogswell now knew that Pauly had been on familiar terms with Vera Grady. Vera Grady had read and written various business letters for Cogswell in past months. She had been present on the occasion of the call paid on Cogswell by Luther Hayes of New York. Therefore she would know about the relation of mutual confidence existing between the two men. Cogswell now recalled with chagrin that the nurse had written that later letter for him, the one in which he had asked Hayes to buy for him an option on a Jersey shore tract. Could that have planted the idea that Cogswell might be willing to return the favor? That he could be induced to make a similar purchase in response to a wire from Hayes?

Louder and more insistent these suspicions buzzed in Cogswell's brain. Suddenly they became definitely verified. His friend the little nut-brown messenger boy tapped him on the shoulder.

"Here's another one for you, Mr. Cogswell."

Cogswell knew dismally what he would read even before he opened the envelope. A fine fool he had been! A New Yorker trimmed neatly by a pack of small-towners! There were three of them in it, of course, Vera Grady, Bert Pauly, and Milton Prowers. The evidence revealed by the telegram read:

Are you crazy stop I never heard of Pauly Horse Ranch stop I sent you no wire about foreclosure bid stop Quit your kidding.

Hayes.

CHAPTER THREE

THE MAIN STREET MURDER

STANLEY COGSWELL KNEW that he had been duped. Pauly and Prowers had tricked him into buying a property which, whatever its value, he certainly did not want. Yet there was a way out. He could put a stop order on that check. Cogswell hurried up the street to do so.

Entering the Picketwire National Bank he saw Cashier Clarke, at his desk, engaged in talk with a bearded customer with the look of a stockman. Without waiting his proper turn, Cogswell interrupted them.

"Please stop that check I gave the Public Trustee this morning. The one for $30,212.80. Has it been presented here yet?"

"It has," Clarke said, "and we cashed it."

"But the deal was a swindle. Someone framed me with a fake wire from New York."

"You don't say!" Clarke whirled around in his swivel chair and stood up, concernedly. "Well, we've already cashed the check. Milton Prowers brought it in, properly endorsed by the Public Trustee. He wanted the money in thousand-dollar bills, but we gave him what we had and the rest in centuries."

"I can still get out from under, though," Cogswell insisted. His mind was so intent on his own predicament that for the moment he overlooked the viewpoint of this friendly bank. "All

I have to do is wire a stop order to New York. They can deny the check there. Isn't that right?"

"They could," Clarke admitted coldly. He looked Cogswell sternly in the eyes. "But that would leave us holding the bag. As an accommodation to you, we honored your check. You came in here and asked that service. We complied. We trusted you. Are you going to penalize us, Mr. Cogswell?"

Cogswell grimaced sheepishly. He could save himself, but only at the expense of innocent people. The money was gone with Prowers. Someone had to stand the loss, either he himself or this bank. No, he couldn't do it in honor. He admitted as much to Clarke.

Clarke commended his integrity. "If I hadn't had complete confidence in you, I wouldn't have cashed the check. What seems to be the trouble?"

Cogswell explained. He had been swindled by a fake telegram. He displayed the wire, as well as the genuine one from Hayes. Pauly and Prowers must have a confederate in New York whom they induced to file a message at a carefully timed hour, signing the name of Cogswell's most confidential friend. Everything pointed to a frame-up. "They used a woman named Grady as a cat's-paw," he concluded. "The situation is further complicated by the fact that the Grady woman has just shot and killed Pauly."

"What?" Both Clarke and his bearded customer were astounded. Cogswell had to expend more minutes to tell about the shooting. Then he returned to his own predicament. "Do you know anything about this horse ranch?"

Clarke didn't, but the bearded customer was well equipped with information.

"They's six thousand acres of deeded land in that layout," he said, "and it's stocked with six hundred head of horses. The water holes control the Rincon plumb to the rimrock, but the actual deeded land is only six thousand."

"Those figures are just twice what I bought at the sale," Cogswell protested.

"Simple," explained the informant. "Prowers and Pauly got the place ten years ago on a racing debt owed by Don Ramon Estabal. Estabal was a sport, always entering his horses at the tracks from coast to coast. Prowers was a bookmaker and Pauly a common tout. They took over this six-thousand-acre property and soon afterward Estabal died. Prowers took a deed to three thousand acres and Pauly took a like amount. Each took half the stock of horses. You, stranger, bought only Pauly's end. Your's title's good. I looked it up myself not long ago."

"Evidently Pauly had mortgaged his half of it to Prowers, and Prowers was foreclosing," suggested Clarke.

"That's it, and they framed you for a bidder," the stockman said to Cogswell. "Both Pauly and Prowers have been trying to unload for years. The ranch is run down, the alfalfa stands tromped out. They's other things about it that don't appear in the abstract, and which make it plumb unsalable. No, not the title. The title's okay. You bought a ranch, stranger, or half a ranch, and you got it."

"What do you mean by saying it's unsalable?"

"You'll find out soon enough. As for the six hundred head of broncs, of which you bought three hundred, they're no good. They'll run fifteen-twenty year old, all brood mares no longer able to foal. If they could give colts they'd be some account, because the blood's there. They survive from Don Ramon's old racing strain. Pauly and Prowers long ago sold the cattle they got with the ranch, and cashed in on all the young horse stock. The six hundred old mares left might bring, with luck, one dollar per head. Depends on the market for horsehides."

"And the ranch itself?" Cogswell asked dismally.

"In Don Ramon's day it was a beauty," the stockman said. "He had a sweet stand of alfalfa, surrounded by a two-mile race track. He built the track to try his colts out on, to pick the ones worth sending East. The race track is still there—but the two-mile circle of alfalfa is horsed out. I mean it's been tromped out by all-year-around pasturing with horses. It ain't been cut, neither, for ten year. Pauly and Prowers were plain con men, y'understand, not farmers. They never owned a mowin' machine in their lives, and wouldn't know what one was for. Alfalfa is a perennial crop, but it's gotta be cut, and you can't pasture it summer and winter with a big bronc herd without stompin' it out. So that big circle o' meadow has gone to pot; it's come up in thorns and briars, mostly wild roses.

"Wild roses?" Cogswell stared stupidly.

"This is getting us nowhere," Clarke interrupted. "Let's stick to the main issue. My advice, Mr. Cogswell, would be for you to get in touch with Sheriff Dan Yates right away."

Cogswell frowned. "You don't suppose," he inquired hesitantly, "that Yates and Bowman were wise to what Prowers was putting over? They were all at the sale, you know."

"Not for a minute," Clarke assured him. "Yates and Bowman are square shooters. They were fooled just the same as you were. Sheriff Yates will do everything in his power to recover your money for you. His hands will be tied, though, until you can establish the intent of fraud. Maybe that nurse will squeal and implicate Prowers."

Cogswell left the bank and hurried to the courthouse. He called at the jail in the annex there, just in time to see Sheriff Yates ushering Vera Grady into a cell. Cogswell followed down the corridor. He heard Yates, at the cell door, again interrogate the woman as to her motive in shooting Pauly.

"He crossed me up, the bum!" the prisoner shrieked.

"In what way?"

But the woman declined to make any further statement. Under more questioning her mood changed to sullenness. Yates gave it up, locking her in the cell.

Cogswell pounced upon him with his own tale of woe. Yates recalled having met him at the auction. The official was much more alert now than then. The proceedings of a routine sale had bored him, but this was different. The selling of Pauly's ranch had concerned him not at all, but the shooting away of Pauly's life was quite another matter.

Cogswell talking rapidly all the while, the two passed the front office. There Yates paced the floor while Cogswell gave him the rest of it.

"And the Grady girl was your nurse, huh?" the Sheriff prompted. "Well, I reckon maybe that links the swindle to the shooting."

"She helped me with my correspondence, coming and going. She knew all about my confidential relation with Luther Hayes."

"All right, let's get busy on that angle," Yates said briskly. He led the way from his office to the street. "Let's look up Prowers. We haven't a thing on Prowers, though, unless the girl squeals. The whole thing smells like a dead prairie dog in July, but there's no proof. It's even possible that Pauly alone ribbed up the fake wire, and Prowers knew nothing of it."

"Not likely," Cogswell objected. "There was nothing in it for Pauly unless he got a split from Prowers. And I've found out that the two were partners of more than ten years' standing."

"Your interest," Yates said thoughtfully, "is to get back your thirty thousand. No way to do that unless we can pin fraud on Prowers. Makes no difference how much we pin on Pauly. Pauly's dead. It's Prowers who got the cash. He got it at a legal sale, con-ducted according to Hoyle by a fair and square Public Trustee. Yes, sir, Prowers grabbed that coin at the courthouse door, in broad daylight. Not only that, but he made the sheriff and the Public Trustee help him take it. That's what riles me, Cogswell. It burns me raw."

"Where can we find Prowers now?"

"He generally hangs out at the Toltec hotel," Yates said. "I happen to know he's been there all this week."

At the Toltec they inquired for Milton Prowers.

"He checked out two hours ago," the clerk said. "Let's see, it was the one-o'clock Rio Grande he left on, wasn't it, Ed?"

Ed, who acted as both porter and baggage wrangler, looked up from his present occupation of shining a drummer's shoes and said yes. It was established that Prowers had, about twenty minutes after cashing the big check at the bank, left with his baggage to catch a northbound Rio Grande train.

"In a sweat to change his address, huh?" growled Yates. "Maybe he was in such a hurry he left some incriminating evidence in his room. Let's nosey up, Cogswell, and have a look."

The clerk gave them the key to the room recently occupied by Prowers. On the way up there, Cogswell said, "It was the Rio Grande depot that Pauly was heading for. I heard him tell the cabman to drive there, only a moment or so before the girl shot him."

"Chances are they planned to meet in Denver and split the thirty thousand," Yates said. "They were through with the girl, and tried to ditch her. But she wouldn't stand for that, and she cut loose on Pauly. That leaves Prowers with the total stake, and a better chance of getting away with it. Hello, the door's not locked."

The door of room 204 was indeed unlocked. Cogswell thought it in no way strange, since a man in a hurry to catch a train seldom locks a hotel-room door. Yates and Cogswell now entered the empty room.

"I wonder if he really did leave for that train?" said Cogswell.

"Easy enough to find out." Yates stepped to the room phone and called the Rio Grande depot.

"Do you know Milton Prowers?" he asked the agent.

In a moment he turned to Cogswell.

"Prowers caught that train all right. The agent sold him a Denver ticket at twelve fifty-five and saw him board the train."

"Look!" Cogswell exclaimed. While Yates was telephoning he had picked up a mutilated copy of the *Denver Tribune*. "I wonder why Prowers clipped out a half column from the front page of this paper?"

It was the *Tribune's* latest issue. A rectangle one column wide had been clipped from the front page.

"Won't hurt to look that up, either," Yates said. Again he used the room phone, this time calling the office downstairs. "Have Ed bring up a copy of this morning's *Tribune*," he instructed the clerk.

The porter appeared with a fresh copy of that journal. Comparing it with the mutilated copy, it was easy to locate the item in question. Cogswell read aloud:

"PROMINENT KENTUCKIAN DIES AT DENVER HOTEL

"Victim of a sudden heart attack, Colonel Sylvester Y. Claiborne of Lexington, Kentucky, passed away yesterday in his room at the Brown Hotel of this city. Colonel Claiborne was at one time well known as a racing patron, but of late years had devoted his attention to mining interests in the West.

"He is survived by an only daughter, Miss Elsie Claiborne of Lexington."

"That couldn't have anything to do with your thirty thousand dollars," Yates said as he tossed the paper aside.

"Not a thing," Cogswell agreed. "We know Prowers was once a race-track bookmaker, so he could easily have known this ex-turfman, Claiborne. That could have made him sufficiently interested to clip this item. But what's all that racket on the stairs?"

Men were taking the stairs two steps at a time. In a moment County Coroner Jim Ruxton and a deputy sheriff came rushing into the room.

"Hold everything, Yates," Ruxton announced. "Case against the Grady girl has blown up. She didn't kill Pauly, after all."

Yates and Cogswell stared.

"She didn't even hit him, boss," offered the deputy.

"Didn't hit him? You're crazy," objected Yates. "There were a dozen witnesses. The cab door and the curb was painted red with his blood. He was dead like a coffin nail before I even got there."

"He was dead, all right," the coroner admitted. "But from no bullet of Vera Grady's. Her gun is a thirty-two. Plenty of people saw her drop it. She shot once and must have missed, because there's only one bullet in Pauly. She was face to face with Pauly. But the bullet we dug out of Pauly is a forty-five. It entered his back and inclined downward. My hunch is that it was fired from the second floor of this hotel."

Cogswell and Yates whirled toward the front window of the room. It faced Main Street. The window was closed. On the floor beneath it, obscured from random sight by a chair, lay a heavy revolver.

Yates used his handkerchief to pick it up. He saw that it had been fired once, and recently. The used shell, a forty-five, was directly under the hammer, and the bore was fouled by powder.

When Yates said, "This here's the gun that killed Bert Pauly," no one doubted him.

"As sure as wind in March," the coroner agreed.

Cogswell, glancing across the street, saw that the window was exactly opposite that position at the curb in front of the Arapahoe where Pauly's cab had been parked at the time of the murder. From here any expert pistol shot could have picked off Pauly. The bullet, if it struck Pauly at all, must have struck him in the back, because at the moment the victim had been facing Vera Grady on the curb. Sight of her in the act of shooting Pauly might have inspired the sniper to his own act.

"As open and shut as a corral gate," Yates summed up. "He stood here watching the quarrel over there at the cab. When the girl fired and missed, the man up here opened his window and took a pot shot himself. It was Prowers who did the potting. Prowers, on a bet."

CHAPTER FOUR
THE COWBOY

"BUT PROWERS HAD ALREADY BOARDED a train," Cogswell objected.

"Maybe he pretended to leave town for an alibi," Yates said. "Or maybe he was trying to throw Pauly off his track, so he wouldn't have to split that thirty thousand two ways. Anyhow, he dropped off the train somewhere in the yards and came back to this room. There's an alley entrance and back steps. He could have got here without bein' seen by the clerk. After the shooting, he went out the same way."

"Sounds plausible," Cogswell admitted. "But to make sure let's send a wire to the conductor on that Rio Grande train. It left here at 1:00 p. m. If Prowers is still aboard, he couldn't have shot Pauly at two-thirty."

They repaired to the telegraph office. There Yates sent a wire to the conductor of the train, at Pueblo.

"The train's due at Pueblo in ten minutes," he said to Cogswell. "Let's wait next door for an answer."

They waited in the Arapahoe lobby. "We're equally interested," Yates reminded Cogswell. "You need your thirty thousand and I need Prowers on a murder charge. Looks like it'll be easier to prove the murder than the fraud."

"As it stands now," Cogswell admitted wryly, "I'm a partner with Prowers in the ownership of the Ramon Estabal ranch, a property I've never seen. I'm told it's no good. Anyway, I only bought half of it, the Pauly half. The other three thousand acres and the other three hundred head of horses still belong to Prowers. But here's our answer. That's quick service, Yates."

The Western Union boy was extending a message to the sheriff. Yates read aloud:

> *Yates,*
> *Sheriff, Trinidad.*
>   *Milton Prowers is aboard this train here at Pueblo having boarded at Trinidad.*
>
>   *Ames, Conductor.*

The sheriff's jaw sagged. Cogswell was no less astonished.

"Another good case gone up in smoke," Yates muttered. "Where do we go from here?"

Cogswell could suggest no new theory. Certainly Prowers, who was still on a train which had left town an hour and a half before the shooting, could not be guilty.

"He could have hired someone to do it," Yates pondered. "But we can't prove it. As for the Grady girl, all we got against her is a charge of shooting at a no-good lover and missing him. No jury'll blame her much for that. She'll be free in short order. In the meantime I'll try to throw a scare at her, hoping she'll pin some dead-wood on Prowers."

"Will you wire the Denver police to meet the train and detain Prowers?"

"Can't see where it would get me." Yates frowned. "He has a cast-iron alibi for the killing. As for the fraud against you, there's no evidence yet to implicate him. Arrest him, accuse him, or even embarrass him on that charge, and he'll pop back at us with a suit for defamation of character. Tell you what I'll do, though. I'll set my deputies to work here, trying to trace the forty-five gun and trying to talk a squeal out of Vera Grady. Then I'll go to Denver myself on tonight's train."

"You think you can locate Prowers in Denver?"

"Dead sure of it. There's a dive in Denver where sports bet on races by wire. Prowers, with a pocket full of cash, will likely head right for it. Then there's the clue of the newspaper clipping. He may drop in at the Brown Hotel where his old friend, Colonel Claiborne of Kentucky, died yesterday. He's interested there, or he wouldn't have clipped the item. I can inquire at all hotels. Prowers will be at one of them. He'd only weaken his case by hiding and he knows it. In fact, there's no case against him at all."

"Then what's the use of going up there?" Cogswell asked wearily.

"Oh, I can talk to him. I might get a break. The best of them slip, you know. In the meantime you send a wire to Hayes in New York. Ask him to set a detective on the job of tracing whoever filed the forged telegram."

Cogswell immediately went next door and sent a message to Hayes. Then he called a cab and was driven to the San Isabel Sanatorium. He told the cabman to wait.

"Pretty strenuous exercise for a convalescent, Mr. Cogswell," the superintendent warned him.

"It's cured me," Cogswell grinned. "Anyway, I'm leaving right now. I have to. I bought a ranch today at a forced sale."

"You mean the seller was forced to sell?"

"No. I mean the buyer was forced to buy. Please have someone come up for my baggage in ten minutes."

Cogswell went up to his room. There he packed hurriedly.

"You're a sucker de luxe," he said to his image in the mirror. "They saw you coming, and they took you for your roll."

He saw a six-footer reflected there, clothes hanging loosely on a frame twenty pounds underweight. Cogswell's face, too, never full in health, was now strikingly thin, making his forehead seem too high. His features indicated a capacity for concentrated thought. His eyes, brown and deep-set, carried out this impression. Crinkles at the corners, however, relieved their intensity and suggested humor. Cogswell was far from mirth just now. "You're the prize come-on of all time," he said again.

He returned to his packing. Fifteen minutes later he was being driven downtown to the Arapahoe. There he took a room. Soon after supper he went to bed.

A night letter from Hayes was awaiting him in the morning:

Stanley Cogswell,
Trinidad, Colorado.

I repeat I wired you no instruction stop Detective here easily traced forged telegram stop It was telephoned to local Western Union from booth in lobby of my hotel stop Knowing I live here they did not hesitate in handling it stop Bellboy reports having seen seedy slight hatchet-faced man with oval birthmark like splash of red ink on left cheek emerge from lobby booth about time message was phoned stop We cannot locate this person stop Since my name was used I offer to split loss with you.

Hayes.

"Darned white of him," Cogswell muttered. "But I can't decently let him do it. I was the chuckle-headed sucker. Can't penalize Luth. I'll stand the gaff alone."

He wired Hayes to that effect.

He next called at the jail, where a deputy told him that Yates had gone to Denver on the night train.

"We expect him back tomorrow," the deputy said. "In the meantime we've had no luck tracing the forty-five gun. Nor in quizzing the Grady girl. She knows by now that it wasn't her bullet that killed Pauly. So she's not afraid. Can't get her to say a thing."

Returning to his hotel, Cogswell reviewed the affair from start to finish. The more he thought of it, the more remote seemed the prospect of pinning a fraud on Milton Prowers. The unproven facts, as Cogswell saw them, were as follows:

First, Vera Grady had learned of his confidential status with Hayes. Second, she had revealed her knowledge to Pauly. Third, Pauly had given Prowers a mortgage, which may have been with or without actual indebtedness. Fourth, Prowers had pressed a foreclosure sale. Fifth, a confederate in New York had filed a carefully timed telegram. Sixth, Pauly had rigged himself as a rangeman and by design had met Cogswell en route to the sale, an encounter easily accomplished by watching for his exit from the sanatorium. Seventh, Cogswell had bit like a prime fish and bought the property. Eighth, Prowers had cashed the check and hiked for Denver to be joined later by Pauly. Ninth, an unknown assassin had shot Pauly from a room recently occupied by Prowers. The net result of it all was that Cogswell was stuck.

But how badly? Surely there was some salvage. Three thousand acres and three hundred horses were surely worth something—unless there was a flaw in the title.

Cogswell spent the rest of the day investigating this point. So many other elements of crookedness had entered the deal that he was rather surprised to discover that the title was absolutely flawless.

"What about filing a suit against Prowers?" he asked the best attorney in town, Lionel Southcutt.

"On the present setup of evidence, he'd beat you," the attorney said. "If you had proof that Prowers connived with Pauly to have a fake wire sent from New York, you could get a judgment. Even then the judgment wouldn't do you any good. You can rest assured that Prowers hasn't left anything lying loose in a bank where it could be attached under judgment. My advice to you, young man, would be for you to swallow your pride and make the best of the buy. There are great opportunities in this Western country. Why don't you take hold of the place, now that you have it, and whip it back into shape? It used to be a great ranch."

Cogswell left the office rather impatient with this advice. Under circumstances less grim it would have amused him. It was absurd to suggest that he, a consulting engineer and clubman of New York, should resign himself to the life of a back-range stockman. These fellows out here might chisel him out of his savings, but he'd be darned if they would put shackles on his career. A rancher! Cogswell's lip curved disdainfully.

Yet within the next twenty-four hours more than one local businessman made the same suggestion. Why not whip the old Don Ramon place back into shape? How did it get out of shape? Cogswell wanted to know.

To this he could get no clear answer. He tried in vain to locate the bearded stockman who had mentioned "thorns and briars—mostly wild roses." What did the fellow mean by that?

He wasted several days in these inquiries, and in fruitless communication with New York. New York was unable to turn up the seedy, slight, hatchet-faced man with an oval birthmark like a splash of red ink on the left cheek.

Cogswell fretted. He knew he ought to go out and look his property over, but delayed doing so because it would look like an admission of defeat. All the while he kept hoping that Vera Grady would give out information on which he could base a suit. He visited her at the jail, found her sullenly uncommunicative. She claimed that she didn't even know Prowers. She knew Pauly well enough, and he had promised to marry her. That was all she would say.

Cogswell was leaving the jail when Sheriff Yates came in. Yates had just returned from Denver.

Cogswell accosted him eagerly. "Did you see Prowers?"

"I sure did." Yates grinned wryly and led Cogswell into his office. "Fact is he saw me before I saw him. Hailed me from across the street like a long-lost friend. Came over, slapped me on the back, and gave me a cigar. Then he had the nerve to invite me to take lunch with him at the Brown Hotel."

"Did you go?"

"I did. What better chance would I get to look him over? I quizzed him, while we took lunch, about the whole deal from

A to Z. He answered every question as innocently as a school-girl. Claimed he loaned Pauly thirty thousand on his acreage and horses. Pauly gambled the money away and couldn't pay. So Prowers foreclosed. He thought he'd have to bid in the security himself, but luckily you came along and took it off his hands. He told me to tell you that any time you wanted the other three thousand acres and the rest of the nags for another thirty thousand, you could have 'em."

"The nerve of him!" Cogswell exploded. "I don't want any of that land and horses. A dozen people have told me they're no good."

"He's got nerve, all right," Yates admitted. "It's his stock in trade. He told me he never heard of Vera Grady, and that he didn't know a soul in New York. If a telegram was framed on you, it was Pauly's work and not his. While we were talking a young lady, a right pretty girl dressed in black, came in, and the headwaiter seated her at the next table. Prowers seemed to know her. He looked her way and smiled, and she nodded back. I asked who she was. He said she was the daughter of an old racetrack friend of his who had died recently while stopping at that hotel. The daughter had been summoned from Kentucky."

"Claiborne was the name, I think," Cogswell said. He remembered the item clipped from a Denver paper.

"We finished lunch, and Prowers left me in the lobby. Couple of hours later I saw him up in the balcony parlor. He was talking to the pretty girl in black. Prowers puts up a fair front, you know."

"Any connection there with our own troubles, you think?"

"If there is, I can't place it," Yates said. "Later I tried to shadow Prowers and find out what he's up to. He knew me, so I couldn't do much good. Next morning I ran into Dick Peters. Peters used to be a deputy under me here, and now's a plain-clothes flatfoot on the Denver force. I asked him to follow Prowers. He did. Later he reported that he'd seen Prowers go into the biggest bank in

Denver. He was standing by when Prowers asked the teller if he could change some money into ten-thousand-dollar bills. The teller didn't have any bills that big on hand, so Prowers left. Then Peters lost him."

"It means," Cogswell thought, "that Prowers is afraid of a judgment, so he doesn't want to bank or invest the thirty thousand. He wants to make a vest-pocket package of it—say, three ten-thousand-dollar bills. That would make it easy to carry around."

"And he'll do it, too," Yates agreed. "He failed at that particular bank, but some other bank will accommodate him. Well, that's about all. What are your plans?"

"All I can do," Cogswell said ruefully, "is to go take care of that horse ranch of mine till I can unload it on someone else. Which means I need expert help. Can you recommend a first-class ranch hand I could hire for a week or so, some dependable fellow who knows land and horses? I'd like to take him out there and have him show me the ropes."

Yates knew the very man. "Name's Steve Lacey," he said. "He's in town and out of a job."

"You're sure I can trust him?"

"With your shirt. Cimarron Steve, they call him sometimes. He was raised just over the mesa from your property, on the headwaters of the Cimarron. He knows all that country like a book. An all-round top hand, you can't beat him. And plenty of judgment. He's yours if you want him, on a long job or short, for forty a month and board."

"Sounds like a bargain," grinned Cogswell. "Send him around, and if he's willing to string along as a sort of consulting cowboy, I'll take him on."

Stanley Cogswell was seated in the Arapahoe lobby several hours later when a man approached and introduced himself as Steve Lacey.

Cogswell liked him on sight. Lacey was weathered, slender, about five feet nine inches in height, and as young as Cogswell himself. In a face as brown as the leather of a saddle the blueness of his eyes was almost startling. They were steady, clear eyes. When the man took off his tall, four-dented hat he displayed golden-blond hair, sleek and fine. "Yates told me about the auction, Mr. Cogswell. I got a line on it, too, from Clarke and Southcutt."

For a moment Cogswell wondered why he should be "mistered," while a banker and a leading attorney failed to receive that consideration. After he had talked with Lacey for a while, he understood. Cogswell was the employer, the boss; therefore he was Mr. Cogswell. Clarke and Southcutt and Yates were just men, like Lacey himself. Cogswell here got his first peep at the man-to-man democracy of the range. "So I savvy what you're up against," Lacey went on. "If I suit you all right, I wouldn't mind looking after that Rincon layout. Aimin' to stock it, are you?"

Cogswell laughed. "It's to find out what I'm aiming to do that I need you. I don't know whether your job would last a week or a year. I'm all in the air."

"If you'll take a chance, I will." The blue eyes were steady and convincing.

"On what terms?"

"Regular top pay, forty and found."

A feature of the situation seemed so ridiculous that Cogswell again laughed outright. Forty dollars *a day* and expenses had always been his own charge as a consulting engineer. Now he was employing the expert service of another man in a strictly consulting capacity, for forty a month. He shook hands with Cimarron Steve Lacey, giving him to understand that he was hired.

CHAPTER FIVE
THE LADY

H E MET STEVE BY APPOINTMENT early the next morning at Greenstead's livery barn. Steve, on coming to town, had left his horse, saddle, and bedroll at that place.

Cogswell now rented a stout team and buckboard. He was resolved to stay at least a week at the Rincon Creek property in order to study its possibilities.

"We'll cross no bridges farther ahead than that," he said to Steve. "In a week I ought to know whether I've bought a ranch or a gold brick."

With Steve's advice, he bought food supplies for a week. The Rincon Creek ranch house was furnished, he understood. Cogswell equipped himself, however, with new sheets and blankets.

By ten o'clock that Tuesday morning—it was just a week from the day of the Pauly shooting—they were rolling out of town. That is, Cogswell was, for he alone occupied the seat of the buckboard. Steve Lacey rode ahorse at the wheel.

As he drove along with the mid-June mountain air fanning his cheeks, a keen anticipation enlivened Cogswell. The piñon trees seemed to whisper assuringly that this affair might work out for the best after all. Mystery awaited somewhere over the hill ahead. A tangle of life challenged him, a thing which had to be met and whipped in the open. Success was bound to resist him; Cogswell could now feel that resistance symbolized in the taut reins he held. He could feel it in the bigness of the country around.

Lacey jogged silently at his right. He rode easily, yet strangely alert, Cogswell thought, as though even here on this peaceful trail they might encounter resistance. The man wore no gun. He had one, but at the moment it was wrapped in the bedroll now in the back of the buckboard.

In an hour they arrived at the summit of a minor divide. Ahead and below stretched a broad plain, still green because this was earlier than the season of cured grass. Thin lines of timber traversed it here and there, cottonwood creeks thrusting out from a long box mesa which lay ahead. The mesa was shaped like an Indian's drawn bow, a U, a rincon, a concave slope of grassy benches ascending to a steep bank of spruce, and thence on up to quaking-asp trimmed rimrock.

"That's your range," Lacey said. "The old Estabal property takes in every spring of water on the slope of yonder rincon. The buildings and the meadows are at the foot of the slope."

"I can't see any buildings," Cogswell said.

"Fourteen miles yet." Lacey spurred to a canter, the buckboard creaking along behind.

They had descended the slope and were making good time across a level plain when a rickety spring wagon, headed toward town, approached them. Cogswell saw that its single occupant was a dwarfed Mexican with squinty eyes and a flat nose. He had an unfriendly look, and was dressed shabbily except for his headgear, which was much like Lacey's and equipped with a wide buckskin band. A row of matches was stuck upright under the band. The man's reins were wrapped around his whip, and he was rolling a cigarette as the buckboard passed him.

"Howdy, Carlos," Steve Lacey greeted. But the man only scowled and drove on. Cogswell noted that the bed of his spring wagon was covered with a tarp. From this came a strong odor.

"Goat cheese," Steve explained. "That fellah makes a trip to town once a week with a load of cheese. He and his *compadres* make up one of the biggest goat colonies in this country, high up under the rimrock yonder."

"Goats?" Cogswell prompted.

"Yeh, they run thousands of 'em. It affects your layout, too. But I'll explain that later."

In two more hours they came to Rincon Creek. Its banks were lined with enormous cottonwoods. Its flow of water, though, was not much bigger than a man's leg. Lacey dismounted and opened a gate on that side of the road which was toward the concave box mesa.

"We're on the old Estabal ranch now," he explained. "This trail leads right to the house."

Having passed through the gate, they proceeded directly toward the mesa. Cogswell now saw what seemed to be a squat, tumble-down adobe town.

"It's what's left of the old Estabal building layout," Steve said.

They rode toward it. Cogswell counted twenty ramshackle adobe buildings set in parallel rows. Amazed, he saw a church with its rear wall caved in but with the cupola steeple still erect, and with a rusty bell. Opposite was a similar building, once a school. The main dwelling, he saw, was a sprawling one-story house in the shape of an H and surrounded by a dilapidated picket fence. Stunted hollyhocks peeped through the pickets. This main house, like all the others, was of adobe; but its roof was gabled and shingled. Winds had taken a sad toll of the shingles. There was a barn and many sheds, and a full street of one-room, flat-roof huts. There were acres of corrals, all surrounded by mud fences a foot thick. From one of these a buzzard flew. But for the buzzard and a group of bony horses grazing on a weedy meadow to the west, there was no sign of life.

It bewildered Cogswell.

"After we put up the broncs, I'll tell you what it's all about," Lacey said. He had dismounted by the barn and was already stripping the saddle from his horse. As he lugged the saddle into the barn he called back, "I'll see if there's any feed in the loft, while you're unhitching the team."

Cogswell grinned sheepishly. His top hand having practically ordered him to unharness a team, it occurred to Cogswell that he had never before performed such an act. But he wasn't going to admit it. Getting down, he unhooked the traces and unfastened every buckle he could find. When he was done he had the harness in more pieces than was necessary, but off. Steve came for the sack of oats they had brought along. "There's some old hay in the loft," he said. "With these oats, we can make out for a week." If he noticed the wreck of the harness, he was too polite to comment.

The three horses were soon stalled and fed. Steve then led his employer on a tour of inspection. Cogswell was more and more amazed at the extent of the improvements. They were hopelessly run down, though. Fully half the huts were roofless. The main house itself was barely habitable.

"Let's sit on the front porch, Steve, while you give me the lowdown." They found a pair of forlorn old rockers on the porch of the house.

"Any cow grazing between here and the rimrock," Lacey began, "has to drink your water or none. I mean either your water or Milton Prowers's water. I understand you bought only half the original Estabal ranch."

"But why so many buildings, and the school, and the church?"

"All the old Mexican ranches were *plazas*, Mr. Cogswell. Those fellows were a long way from town, so they built their own town right on the ranch. Estabal, in his day, kept at least thirty families of peons. That meant plenty of women and kids, which called for a school and a church."

"But what's that big circle out there in the meadow, on the other side of that old fence?"

"A two-mile race track," Steve told him. "Don Ramon made it to try out his colts. That fellah was the biggest runnin'-horse breeder in the Southwest."

"What are those weeds all over the big circle? They seem to be in bloom."

The circular area within the track was indeed a riot of blossoms, some pink, some white. Here and there among them an old horse stood cock-kneed and with drooping head. The horses were of sorrel color, suggesting a common blood strain.

"The big circle was sowed to alfalfa thirty years ago by Don Ramon," Lacey said. "But since the Pauly-Prowers combine took charge ten years ago, the stand has gone to pot. Too much summer pasturing and no regular mowing. You got to mow alfalfa; and you got to keep stock off it 'cept in winter. Right now that big circle's almost a solid stand of wild roses."

"Why roses?" Cogswell wondered.

"Wild roses are a native weed to irrigated meadows of this climate," Steve explained. "You notice that circular meadow is well graded and checkerboarded with lateral ditches. Every flood in the creek fills those laterals, and the water gets scattered all over the circle. So something has to grow. The alfalfa couldn't, because it was horsed out. Horses go after growing alfalfa like bears after honey. When they get hungry enough, they eat weeds. But they won't eat briars. So everything but stickered plants got horsed out."

"The survival of the stickerest," Cogswell said. "All right, Steve, tell me some more."

Steve rolled a cigarette. "When I was a boy," he explained between puffs, "I lived at the head of the Cimarron right over the top of this mesa. Our railhead then was El Moro, which was then the end of the Santa Fe, and to get there we had to pass right by this ranch. Which means I saw this layout in its prime.

"In those days that big circle was purple instead of pink. There were peons everywhere. Estabal ran plenty of cowstuff, but he was best known for his horse stock. He had a fancy sorrel stallion with a national rep, that won two or three big races back East. Don Quixote they called that stud. Don Ramon would bet his shirt or his ranch on a horse race. When he was cleaned out, two gamblers named Pauly and Prowers took the layout."

"And let it go to pot."

"Right. Estabal himself, of course, was a hundred years behind present-day methods of ranching, but he got results. He ran the place just like the old Spanish dons did, and like they still do in old Mex. It's a heap different from gringo style. Estabal never paid any wages in cash, yet he always had plenty help and everybody was satisfied. A peon would drift in with his family and move into one of those adobe huts. Then he'd loaf. When it came haying-time, or branding-time, Don Ramon's *segundo* would order the peon to work. If he did, he could stay. If he didn't, he was hustled off the place. As long as he stayed, he could get beans and clothing free at the ranch store. The result was that forty men did the work of about ten, but there was no overhead."

"What happened," Cogswell asked, "to that big colony of peons when Estabal died?"

"Now we're getting to the goats." Steve cocked an eye up toward the mesa rimrock. "Pauly and Prowers took charge and shut down the free store. In fact, they immediately skinned the place of everything salable. The peon colony pulled out from the row of adobe huts but not from the ranch itself. It was the only range they knew. Most of them were born right here on Rincon Creek. So they moved six miles up the mesa slope to an old summer cow camp just under the rimrock, and are still there."

"You mean they're still living on my property?"

"Not on your property but on your range. That old cow camp is on government land, although only a stone's throw from a big spring located on one of your deeded quarter sections. They have a legal right to squat at the cow camp. But they trespass every time one of them or one of their seven thousand goats wants a drink of water."

Cogswell whistled. "That's a lot of goats!"

"Too many," Steve agreed. "Well, thrown on their own resources those peons took to goats and goat cheese. The goats, with all that chinery brush to chew on, increased like rabbits. Carlos Estabal, the leader of the colony, now takes in a load of cheese every week."

"Is Carlos a son of old Don Ramon?"

"No relation. But a lot of those peons took the name of the master through pride, or ignorance, or anything you want to call it."

"The old plantation stuff, eh?"

"Point is," Lacey went on, "that those fellows are up there right now, goating out the water-controlled summer range of this ranch. They're spoiling the entire mountain slope for anything but goats. Worse, they're cutting off the flow of the creek down here at the house. You noticed the dinky trickle in it now? When I was a boy you could catch trout in it."

Cogswell was incredulous. "You mean the goats drink the water all up before it gets here?"

"Naturally not. But they dry it up. Water comes from the soil, from rain and snow meltings stored in the ground. For ten years thousands of goats have trampled your watershed and eaten away the shade. You savvy that goats live mostly on the twigs and leaves of brush. No brush, no shade. Nothing to hold the snow drifts in the spring. *También,* the feet of those goats pack the ground so hard that nothin' soaks in. Water runs off in big, short floods, gone in a few hours, instead of coming down in a steady flow all summer. Which reminds me, is the water right to the Rincon Ditch included in your deed?"

Cogswell took from his pocket the deed he had received from Public Trustee Bowman, consulted it, and found no mention of a ditch right.

"That leaves you in worse shape than ever," Steve said. "Pauly and Prowers each had three thousand acres. You got Pauly's end, which included the best meadowland and these houses. But the ditch right was left tied to Prowers's half. A tough break. With no ditch right you couldn't even reclaim the meadow if you tried. You're stuck."

"Looks that way," Cogswell said dismally. "I might as well walk off and leave it to those crowbait horses and the goats. Hello! Isn't that someone coming?"

A livery rig was in sight, coming from the direction of town. At any rate it seemed to be a rig similar to the one Steve and Cogswell had hired that morning.

The outfit came up at a smart trot. It halted in front of the picket gate. Cogswell and Steve, advancing to meet it, were amazed to observe that it was occupied by a livery stable hand known as Uncle Jack and two women. One of the latter, a Negress, occupied the rear seat with much baggage. A young white girl sat in front with Uncle Jack.

Uncle Jack, a grizzled veteran with gray, drooping mustaches and saddle-warped legs, assisted the young lady to alight.

The girl was uncommonly pretty, and not over twenty-three, Cogswell thought. The fact that she was dressed in black from head to foot made her face, at first glance, seem unnaturally pale. She had large black eyes, too. She was small but not frail. Most of all, she was a lady. Cogswell knew that from her voice, when she thanked Uncle Jack.

Steve Lacey opened the gate.

"Howdy, Steve," Uncle Jack greeted. "Meet Miss Claiborne of Kentucky. As I get it, Milt Prowers sawed off a limb and left her on it. She's stuck with three thousand acres of land and three hundred hosses. Let's see, your name's Cogswell, ain't it? Meet

Miss Claiborne. Yep, she got the other half of this layout, same as Pauly wished his'n on you."

The girl's rueful smile fascinated Cogswell. She was holding out her hand. "From what Uncle Jack told me as we drove along, I suppose we're partners, Mr. Cogswell."

CHAPTER SIX
TWIN DUPES

FOR A LITTLE WHILE Stanley Cogswell was so astonished that he hardly knew what was going on. There was much talking, some of it in facetious vein by Uncle Jack. There were details of self-introduction from Elsie Claiborne spoken in a voice of such culture and charm that Cogswell found himself attending its quality rather than the message. Steve Lacey was saying things, sensible things it appeared. For the young lady was now giving her full attention to Steve.

"I guess I'll unhook and give the team a little rest, afore we go back to town," Uncle Jack said. He drove his rig on to the barn.

The Negress, an immense person weighing well over two hundred pounds, had disappeared into the house with a bundle or two. Cogswell, Steve, and Miss Claiborne were still standing at the gate.

"You must be right tired, miss, after ridin' from town in one of Greenstead's springless spring wagons," Steve said. He ushered the visitor to the porch, where she sat down in one of the swaybacked rockers. Cogswell followed, abusing himself for having allowed his top hand to assume the honors of a host. The thought also struck him that Mr. Lacey was getting away with it in rather smart style.

The girl did not remove her hat. Cogswell came up and took the other rocker. Steve was seated on the railing, bronzed hands clasped around a knee.

He was saying, "So that's the game he worked on you, was it? It's not new, either. It's slick, but not new. They generally use it, I understand, to sell trick pencils and stuff costing, say, two to five pesos. First time I ever heard of it bein' used to unload land and horses."

Elsie Claiborne again smiled ruefully. Cogswell noted that she had extremely long eyelashes and deep dimples.

"I hadn't the faintest doubt that everything wasn't all right," she said to Steve, for the moment ignoring Cogswell, "until I arrived in Trinidad this morning. There I heard vague rumors that this same Mr. Prowers had been connected with the selling of an equal amount of land and horses under suspicious circumstances. On the drive out from town Uncle Jack told me more about it."

As she talked, the young lady had removed her hat and was now smoothing her hair with quick, unconscious gestures. The hair was black and abundant, the whole swirled close to her head and knotted low on her neck.

"Do you mean to say," Cogswell wondered, "that Prowers persuaded you to buy the other half of his broken-down horse ranch?"

The long-lashed black eyes shifted to Cogswell. Her black dress, he thought, was becoming; as yet it had not occurred to him that she was in mourning.

"Is it as bad as that?" she asked prettily.

"It couldn't be worse," he said.

"Oh, but it could," she argued. "For instance, I might have bought the same three thousand acres you did. But Mr.—"

"Lacey," Steve prompted. "Steve Lacey."

"But Mr. Lacey has just assured me that it's not the same. That you and I bought separate and distinct tracts."

"None of which is any good," Cogswell said. "Did Prowers lure you into bidding at a fake foreclosure, Miss Claiborne?"

"No. It was this way. My father died suddenly, nine days ago, while inspecting his mining investments in the West. It happened at a Denver hotel. I was notified and went immediately from Kentucky to Denver. After I had arranged to ship the casket home, I was confronted by Mr. Prowers. He showed me a contract of sale, on which I recognized my father's signature."

"You *thought* you recognized it," Steve Lacey corrected. "I'd bet a hundred dollars to an old cinch ring it was forged."

"No doubt of it," Cogswell agreed. "He knew of the colonel's death, all right. Before leaving Trinidad he had clipped an item about it from a Denver paper. Probably that was the first time he had ever heard of Colonel Claiborne."

"But if he hadn't known Father, how was he able to forge the signature?" the girl asked.

"Simply by arriving in Denver before you did," Cogswell suggested, "and looking back a few days on the hotel register. He could have traced your father's signature there while the clerk's back was turned. Or maybe he actually had known your father, distantly, and had contrived to receive a signed letter from him."

"Anyway, I thought the signature on the sale contract was genuine," she said. "And it was just like Father to have made such a purchase, because he always had a weakness for horses. Why, I've known him to pay that much money for just one race horse."

"How much money?" Cogswell asked.

"Thirty thousand dollars. According to the contract, father had agreed to pay that sum on the very day Prowers confronted me at the Denver hotel, in exchange for three thousand acres of land, a certain ditch right, and three hundred head of brood mares of racing strain. It seemed like a bargain, Mr. Cogswell."

Cogswell groaned.

"It'd sure strain 'em to do any racing," inserted Steve Lacey. "They're all of twenty years old."

"I tried to postpone the business," the girl explained, "because I had to go right back to Kentucky. Prowers was convincingly sympathetic. But he said he'd made certain business commitments on the expectancy of receiving the cash on that day, which would cause him, if he defaulted, to be sued by the other party. That in turn, he asserted, would force him to sue the heirs of Colonel Claiborne for breach of contract.

"I was horribly upset. Some of the considerations which influenced my decision might be hard for you to understand. In the first place, thirty thousand dollars did not seem to me to be a very large amount of money. I had known Father to pay that much for a single horse or to lose that much on a single race. I myself have always been allowed liberal sums to invest as I pleased. It happened that I had recently turned my investments into cash and the money was in a Louisville bank.

"In the second place, there has never been a lawsuit in the Claiborne family. I felt that a suit for breach of contract, especially if filed on the eve of Father's funeral, would be an insufferable disgrace. I was convinced that the contract was genuine. Viewed in one light, it pleased me. Father had been investing heavily in mining properties. Some of his advisers have been shaking their heads these last few years, warning that Father would do better if he stuck to the traditional investments of his line, land and horses."

Cogswell nodded sympathetically. The same sympathy stood in the blue eyes of Steve Lacey.

Elsie Claiborne looked bewilderedly out over the rundown acres spread before her, and concluded, "So I agreed to take up the contract provided title was sound. Prowers attended to this briskly. He produced an abstract which was quite up to date. He suggested I call the Denver Bar Association and inquire for a reputable attorney. The title was speedily examined and approved by expert counsel. That left me no further excuse. I accepted a deed and a bill of sale, giving Prowers my personal check for thirty thousand dollars."

"That makes two of us," Stanley Cogswell said. His lean features set grimly. Somehow the thing seemed a good deal more personal now. He felt for the first time a hot urge to get his hands on Milton Prowers. Robber of an orphan girl! A cheater of women! A ghoul reaching even into the grave to ply his trade of treachery!

"So after a trip back home," Steve Lacey prompted, "you came West again for a look at your land and horses?"

"That," she admitted, "was made more necessary than ever when Father's private bank box was opened for an inventory of the estate. It was thought to be large. But we found it wasn't; his mining investments had been unfortunate. Those certificates were worthless. In fact, the estate was quite wiped out—even our Lexington home was mortgaged to the shingles. There was nothing left, except—" The girl looked helplessly off toward the rimrock of Rincon Mesa.

She was destitute except for this buy she had made from Prowers. Cogswell saw the bronzed face of Steve Lacey harden, saw his hands clench. He knew that Steve was thinking of Milton Prowers.

"I thought perhaps," Elsie Claiborne said bravely, "that I might hold a sale and get something out of the horses. What do you think, Mr. Lacey?"

Cogswell was glad that she asked the question of Steve. Steve, he saw, winced at it. Nevertheless, Steve looked her squarely in the eyes and told the truth.

"The mares are worthless, miss. Racing strain, yes, but too stiff to run, too old to foal, too tough to skin. I know some horse peddlers who travel around the country and make a living trading. They generally start out with the worst stock they can find, so they can't possibly lose. Their racket is to call at some farm, look around until they see some old crowbait, or crippled young horse, and suggest a trade. The farmer is always dead anxious to get rid of his own no-good horse. So he overdoes himself. He trades crowbait for crowbait, giving five dollars to boot. These traveling horse swappers have made a living that way for years. They'll trade any horse in their string for any other horse, as long as they get cash boot."

"How does that concern us?" Cogswell wanted to know.

"This way. It's just possible we might unload our six hundred broken-down brood mares on the Tolliver brothers—that's the name of those professional horse traders—for, say, a dollar per head. They're not worth a dollar a head for anything except trade bait. The Tollivers might give that much, on account of their good colors. Mostly sorrels. You can see a few of them out there now, in that race-track meadow."

Elsie Claiborne turned to look as he pointed.

"Oh, how perfectly lovely!" There was genuine admiration in her voice and her cheeks flushed.

"That's because they're so far away," Steve said. "Close up they're all skin and bones."

"I don't mean the horses," she said. "I mean those beautiful flowers. Why, there's acres and acres of them! They're perfectly gorgeous. Who planted them, Mr. Lacey?"

Steve explained that they were wild roses.

Elsie was entranced. "I love roses," she said. She arose and walked to the porch railing. From there she gazed in growing fascination at the great circular meadow, two hundred acres rank with pink and white blossoms. "Do you mean they just grew?"

"They just grew," Steve said. "They're right nice to look at now, in the middle of June. But they're no good for anything else. That circle ought to be plowed up and re-sowed to alfalfa."

"It's too beautiful to plow up," she protested.

"Alfalfa's right pretty, too," Steve argued. "Nice purple blooms, and it makes three crops of fancy hay. It's the sign of a well-kept ranch, miss. Weeds, Russian thistles, wild roses—they're the sign of a run-down, tromped-out ranch. This place ought to be whipped back into shape. It ought to be made to pay, like it used to."

Abruptly Elsie sat down on the railing. She faced Steve with a bright interest, and seemed to have forgotten all about Cogswell. "Was it once a good farm, Mr. Lacey?"

"Yes'm." Sitting knee to knee with the Kentucky girl, Steve told her all about it. "It was a money-maker, once. Don Ramon Estabal was a dyed-in-the-wool stockman. He came from a long line of stockmen, reaching hundreds of years back and deep down into old Mexico. He knew a good horse and he knew a good cow. When I was a boy—"

He told her what he had told Cogswell, and more. He told it well. Either the man himself or his story seemed to charm the girl. She gave rapt attention. Cogswell felt out of it. He suddenly realized that his top hand possessed exceptionally good looks. Steve's hat was off, of course, had been ever since the girl had alighted at the gate. The blondish curly hair over indigo-blue eyes and the bronzed, clean-cut face were striking. The late-after-noon sun, shining brilliantly upon his face, gave him a fine, golden look, like the image of a Greek god.

At any rate that impression came to Cogswell, and it unex-plainably annoyed him. Or possibly it was Steve's present monop-oly of the consultation which annoyed Cogswell. The consulting engineer, Cogswell of New York, sat quite out of the picture; while the consulting cowboy, Mr. Lacey of the Cimarron, was expertly engaged with Miss Claiborne.

"And do you really think, Mr. Lacey, it could be made like that again?"

"It could," Steve said. "Get rid of the horses, get rid of the goats, get rid of the roses, and you've got a ranch."

"Oh, but I don't want to get rid of the roses!"

"There's things prettier than roses," Steve said, looking straight at her.

"You say we might get a dollar a head for the horses?"

"If we're lucky. If not, then the thing to do is to drive those six hundred head of old mares up some dry wash and shoot 'em."

The girl was horrified. "But I couldn't allow that! I'd rather give them away."

"Who to?" Steve challenged. "No stockman would let them have standing room in his pasture. Nothing quite so useless as an old horse that's unbroken to harness or saddle. Who'd take 'em as a gift? Don't forget that a horse eats as much grass as three cows!"

"Does it?" she asked.

"Yes'm. Every crowbait nag in a pasture crowds three, good money-makin' cow critturs out. Horses are harder on sod, too. They do more pawin' when snow's on the ground, to get at the feed. They graze on the move, and tromp more grass. A cow lays down once in a while to chew her cud, but a horse eats night and day. No, ma'am, you couldn't give those mares away, each with a pound of tea."

"That will be quite simple, I think," Cogswell said briskly. "If we can't sell them or give them away, we can just drive them a hundred miles away and leave them somewhere on the open range. That's more humane than shooting them, and quite simple."

Steve and the girl turned surprisedly, as though they had forgotten he was there. Little crow's-feet of amusement began to crack, then, at the corners of Steve's eyes.

"Make it two hundred miles instead of a hundred," Steve said, "and they'd beat you back home. An old mare will always come back to the range where she foaled her first colt."

Cogswell bit his lip.

"Isn't it splendid, Mr. Cogswell," Elsie said, "that we have someone to explain everything?" She turned confidently back toward Steve.

"This horse problem may look hard," Steve summed up, "but it's plumb easy compared to the goat problem. You could get rid of the horses by shooting them, but the only way you could get rid of the goats would be to shoot the head goatman, Carlos Estabal."

"Perish the thought!" Elsie protested. "There must be no shooting, please, either of horses, goats, or men."

The sun had now set behind the western horn of the long box mesa. In the growing dusk, Uncle Jack strolled up and leaned against one of the gateposts.

"Lady," he called out in a croaking falsetto, "ain't it about time we was startin' home? It's a good three-hour drive to town."

"Gracious, how time has flown!" Elsie cried. "Magnolia! I wonder where Magnolia is."

"Here I is, missy." The immense Negress came waddling out of the house. "Is we ready to lef' away from here, Miss Elsie?"

Cogswell and Steve stood up, presuming that the girl would do likewise. But she remained seated.

To the Negress she said, "Have you been through the house? What is it like?"

"It's like poor white trash been living here, all but one room." Magnolia was in high disdain. "Dere's one room where a gentleman's been hangin' out. Rest of the house is a mess, Miss Elsie."

Cogswell laughed. "She's not hitting at Steve or me," he explained. "We only blew in a little before you did and haven't even been inside. The one clean room she refers to must be the quarters occupied by Prowers. Prowers is a fastidious man, even if a scoundrel. On the other hand his partner, Pauly, was slovenly."

Again Uncle Jack called from the gate, repeating his advice that they start back to town.

"But we haven't settled a thing yet," Elsie protested. Cogswell and Lacey, each of them more than willing that the visit be prolonged, reseated themselves.

So there was more talk about horses and goats, of Pauly and Prowers and Estabal. The dusk became night. Stars grew in the sky. Uncle Jack came up and sat on the steps, while Magnolia withdrew into the house. When a glow appeared at a front window, Cogswell knew that the Negress had found an oil lamp.

"One thing is evident, Miss Claiborne," he said. "Your interests and mine are identical and we might as well pool them. It seems that you own the ditch right and I own the best acreage of meadow. So we might begin by assuming that it's all one ranch, of which we each have an undivided half interest."

"By all means," the girl said. "We'll pool our interests for better or worse, and maybe save something from the wreck." She turned impulsively and offered a slim white hand.

The touch of it sent a strange thrill through Stanley Cogswell. Of course they'd save something out of it. As far as he was concerned it was no longer a wreck. All of the dismal features were dissipated. With this lovely partner to share his ship of trouble, catastrophe became an alluring adventure.

CHAPTER SEVEN
INSOLENCE TO INJURY

"Pauly and Prowers," Steve told them, "finally got wise that the goatstuff was spoilin' their mountain pasture, so a year ago they started a war. They found one of Carlos Estabal's cousins herdin' goats on one of their deeded water holes, and shot him. Anyway, his body was found there, although Pauly and Prowers denied the killing. Carlos Estabal then proceeded to make it right warm and smoky for Pauly and Prowers. There was a lot of dry-gulching indulged in. No open fights, you understand; that's not Estabal's way. But whenever Pauly or Prowers took a ride up the mountain, a bullet would come whizzing mighty close. Finally they got scared and stayed off the slope. One day, while they were eating dinner, a bullet came jumping through the kitchen window. That was enough for Pauly and Prowers. They moved to town. All the ranchin' they did after that was to cook up these two schemes by which they unloaded on you."

Elsie shuddered. "And will Estabal be taking shots at us, now that we own the place?"

"Not unless we start something," Lacey said. "His grudge was personal against Pauly and Prowers."

"We can just let his goats alone and he won't bother us," the girl said relievedly.

"We could do that," Steve admitted. "But as long as we do that we haven't any ranch. We lose all our summer pasture. We let forty thousand acres get goated out, fouled for cattle by stinking goats. Even our meadows lose out because, as I explained to Mr. Cogswell, the goats harden the watershed and cut off the irrigation water. To reclaim the ranch the goats must go, which can't be accomplished without trouble with Carlos."

"I don't want any fighting," Elsie worried. "Maybe if we reason with Mr. Estabel he would be willing to herd the goats off our land."

"Where would they water?" Steve argued. "Every drop of water from here to the rimrock is owned by you or Mr. Cogswell. That colony shouldn't have squatted there in the first place, but it did. The job now's to get rid of it."

Elsie's brow wrinkled. She said she didn't like the idea of plotting to drive those poor people from their homes.

"Homes is the wrong word," Steve said. "They live up there like foxes, ignorant, raising their children without school or church. Carlos, who markets the cheese, is the only one who ever goes to town. They're simple folk, all except Carlos. I'm convinced Carlos is many times a murderer. My idea is that it was Carlos Estabal who shot Pauly from the hotel room. No need to pity him. The best thing that could happen to the rest of the colony would be for them to move some place where their children could learn something besides illegal goat-herding."

"Where," Cogswell asked, "would they go?"

Steve shrugged. "*Quién sabe?* Mebbe to old Mexico. Or maybe they could find a government arroyo somewhere with seepage in it, and file. They'd be a lot better off in either case. The one man to get rid of is Carlos. He's got the only savvy in the bunch. If he left, the rest would follow."

"You don't suggest shooting Estabal, do you?" Cogswell asked coldly. He was wondering if he had misjudged Steve.

"No. Instead of shooting Carlos, we might prove he shot someone else. Any one of his victims would do—say we take the case of Bert Pauly. Get proof that Carlos murdered Pauly and the goat problem is solved. He's human, he doesn't want to hang.

Get proof and he'd beat the fastest horse in this country to Old Mex. His dependent kinsmen would follow with every goat—this neighborhood would be shed of them for good."

"But why," Cogswell asked, "should we even suspect that Estabal killed Pauly? That's a brand new theory. First it was Vera Grady, then Prowers; now you say it's Estabal."

"Why not? First place, it was Estabal's style; that shot from an upstairs hotel window was the slickest bit of dry-gulching ever pulled off in this county. Second place, Estabal was known to be gunning after both Pauly and Prowers."

"Because of the goatherder killed a year ago," Uncle Jack wheezed from the porch steps.

"Third," Steve went on, "Carlos goes to town on schedule, once a week with a load of cheese. We passed him going in today. That means he went in a week ago today, the day Pauly was shot."

"Check," Cogswell agreed thoughtfully. It occurred to him that Sheriff Yates might do well to consult this clear-headed cowboy.

"All right. Being in town that day he hears about the auction sale. He figured Pauly and Prowers had cleaned up and were pulling out. It was his last chance to get them. So he ambled up to Prowers's room, we'll say, via the alley steps. He found Prowers gone. But from the window he saw Pauly over there, quarreling with a woman. He was out to get Pauly, too. So he took a pot shot, dropped the guilty gun, and left the way he came."

Cogswell conceded that it was a theory fully as tenable as the sheriff's—that Prowers, having prepared a personal alibi by catching a Denver train, had engaged an assassin to shoot Pauly.

"Especially," he reminded Steve, "since we now know that Prowers had another motive for the Denver trip. He had clipped the item from the paper and was scheming to swindle Miss Claiborne."

"If we don't start now," Uncle Jack said, "we'll be till daylight gettin' back to town."

"Gracious, it must be nearly midnight!" Elsie said. "You men are half starved, I imagine."

"Steve and I brought a supply of food. What about a little spread for all of us, here and now?" Cogswell suggested. "Also, you'll be interested in looking over the house. I haven't seen it, either."

They went inside. Magnolia was in the hallway holding a lighted lamp. Cobwebs were revealed dangling from the ceiling. From many spots on the walls the plaster had crumbled, exposing expanses of bare laths. The hall floor had no carpet, and the dust stood an inch thick. Threadbare furniture could be seen in the rooms on either side.

"Have you located the kitchen yet, Magnolia?"

"Yes'm, Miss Elsie. Right dis way."

"Come on, Uncle Jack," Cogswell called gaily. "Let's eat."

They followed Magnolia to a kitchen. Here there was a stove large enough to prepare food for a threshing crew, with some cut stove wood in a box behind it. There were two tables, one reasonably bare, the other heaped with unwashed pots and plates just as left by Pauly and Prowers at their last use of it. The chairs were homemade from quaking asp. Yet at one side stood a buffet of antique design, a thing carved from ebony and featured by ornate figures of sea serpents. This must have survived from the days of Ramon Estabal.

Steve made a fire, while Cogswell went to get cartons of food from the buckboard at the barn. When he returned, piñon sticks were crackling in the stove. Magnolia had found an oilcloth and spread it on one of the tables.

The Negress then proved that she was a prodigious respecter of human appetites. "With a fryin'-pan she's an artist," Steve said. In a very short time the three men and Elsie Claiborne were seated around a well-provisioned board. The odor of strong coffee filled the room.

Then came an inspection of the house. It was H-shaped, the two wings being connected only by the central corridor. The north wing was fairly well kept. A letter on a dresser there proved it to have been the residence of Milton Prowers. The south wing had been occupied by Pauly and was in ragged disarray. "Looks like a crew of half-breed sheepherders have been beddin' down here," Steve said.

Prowers had attached the best of the furnishings for his own use. He must have intended to come back when he had left the place, for several unused shirts laundry-marked *M.P.* were in the north wing. Steve also found there a pair of cuff buttons, silver and each with a tiny diamond set in its face.

"It's too late to go to town now," Cogswell suggested to Elsie Claiborne. "Why don't you and your maid take possession of this north wing, and stay all night? Not knowing what we'd find, Steve and I brought along fresh bedding."

It was so arranged, the three men retiring to the south wing.

There was a pink blossom in the girl's hair when Cogswell appeared for breakfast.

"I got up early," she said, "and went out to see if they were really wild roses."

After breakfast they went on a tour of the grounds. Stanley Cogswell and Elsie Claiborne walked like curious children through the ramshackle outbuildings; they passed through the ancient church, whose nave was festooned with cobwebs, and through whose remoter sanctums they could hear the scamper of rats. A fat bull snake hissed at them in the ruins of a hennery. In old adobe sheds they inspected an array of sorrowful vehicles, hay wagons, surreys, two-wheel racing-carts, all rusty and forlorn.

They strolled, finally, out upon the old race track which circled the great meadow. Originally it had been well graded and thus only in a few places had the rush of flood water from irrigation laterals cut gulleys across it. Cogswell and the girl wandered completely around the track, all the while in animated talk about their peculiar prospects, about old sorrel mares, goats, and wild roses. They talked at length but decided nothing—nothing except that here these things were and here, also, were they, Stanley Cogswell and Elsie Claiborne.

As yesterday, there was a score of the old mares standing within the big circle of roses. Others could be seen on the flat across Rincon Creek; still others were grazing on the lower slope of the mountain.

"Steve's prescription," Cogswell said, "is to get rid of the horses, the goats, and the roses."

"I think Steve is wonderful," she said. "But I don't like his idea of plowing up these roses. The place is big. Why couldn't we let this circle stay just as it is? We could plant alfalfa on that big flat across the creek, couldn't we?"

"Exactly," Cogswell agreed with enthusiasm. "Why should we plow up the biggest rose garden in the world?" What pleased him most was that Elsie was unconsciously taking a long-term view of the matter. Cogswell had arrived yesterday to stay only a week, the girl to stay only a few hours. Yet something about this old place had taken hold of both of them. It was firing their imaginations, appealing to their human sympathies, too, like a thing in distress.

Returning to the house, they met Steve at the door. Around the cowboy's slim waist was an article which Cogswell remembered seeing him unroll last night from his bedroll. A wide belt bristled with brass shells and was equipped with a holster. From the holster protruded the black butt of a forty-five.

"Not expecting any trouble, are you, Steve?" Cogswell inquired lightly.

"None at all, Mr. Cogswell."

"Then why the artillery?"

"So there won't be any trouble, expected or unexpected."

Elsie looked curiously at the gun and asked, "Is this range country really so full of bad men, like the books say?"

"There's bad men in all countries," Steve said. "There'll be fewer around here if we keep a gun or two loaded and handy."

"I've read books, though," Elsie insisted, "which made it appear that the old frontier ranches were always having wars with outlaws and neighbors and Indians. Was it really like that?"

"Those are just fairy stories," Cogswell laughed.

"I can't say," Steve answered, looking only at Elsie. "I've not read many books. There's other things to read, though. You might read that old pine door you've got your hand on, Miss Claiborne."

Cogswell and Elsie looked at the door. It was not only scarred and weather-beaten, but there were many small holes entirely through it. It was like a sieve, as though a flock of woodpeckers had pecked there. Not one, but more than a hundred holes were in and through the main entrance door of the house built by Ramon Estabal.

They were bullet holes. Decades ago those bullets had been fired; but they had printed an everlasting story on that door.

While Cogswell and Elsie stared at them, Steve became suddenly alert. In a moment the others also heard a galloping approach. A horseman was coming from the direction of town.

"Wonder who it can be?" muttered Cogswell. He was glad enough to change the subject from bullet-pitted doors.

The approaching rider, they could see, was a tall, broad man on an iron-gray horse. Not a rangeman, for he wore a narrow-brim velour hat and a well-fitting business suit. He wore gloves, and his face was boldly handsome. It was cast in lines of cocky assurance as he rode up to the gate. The way in which he pulled up short and made his horse rear gave Cogswell the impression of a showman. Still mounted, he tipped his hat to Elsie.

"Miss Claiborne! This is an unexpected pleasure."

Of all the nerve! Cogswell could hardly believe his eyes. Here was Milton Prowers! The same bold swindler who had cheated

ALLAN VAUGHAN ELSTON

both of them. Was the man crazy? How dared he call brazenly at
the very trap in which his victims were caught?

Cogswell flushed redly. This was heaping insolence upon
injury.

He advanced to the gate with his knuckles clenched and
his jaw set hostilely. He had been wanting to get his hands on
Prowers. And here was the chance. His fingers were itching to dig
deeply into the scruff of that fellow's neck.

Prowers dismounted, hitched his horse to the picket fence,
then stooped to remove a pair of bicycle clips with which, in lieu
of leggings or boots, he had secured the trousers to his ankles.
Then he advanced confidently to the gate, a towering man, erect,
his fine white teeth flashing a smile to Elsie Claiborne who still
stood on the porch.

He was ignoring Cogswell, would have brushed by him had
Cogswell not grasped his collar and spun him around.

"Of all the cheap nerve! You contemptible crook! What do
you mean by coming around here?"

Prowers turned, jerked away, then stepped back a pace. His
face darkened as he answered slowly, "You can't talk to me like
that, Cogswell. I won't take it. From you or anyone else. I'm no
more of a crook than you are. Why am I here? Merely to collect a few personals I left in my room—some cuff links and some
shirts."

"You're a liar and a blackguard," Cogswell said ragingly.
"That's not the real reason you came back, and you know it. You
could have sent for those things without the risk of getting beaten
to a pulp. That's what's going to happen to you right now."

"Mr. Cogswell!" Elsie Claiborne protested in alarm from the
porch.

Cogswell did not hear her. He was at white heat. He entirely
forgot that he was just out of a hospital and twenty pounds
underweight. His right fist shot out to the point of Prowers's jaw.
The man's head jumped back six inches, and Cogswell thought it

was from the force of the blow. It wasn't, though. The blow barely stung Prowers. He was measuring Cogswell. He stepped aside and neatly evaded the second punch.

The third came from Prowers himself. One of those gloved hands came up with paralyzing power under Cogswell's chin, lifted him from his feet. Cogswell hit a spinning earth, face down, and for a full minute was out.

He did not hear the cry of distress from Elsie Claiborne. He did not see Steve Lacey strip off his belt and forty-five.

Steve advanced to the gate and hung the belt on one of the pickets. "Fellah," he said, "what Mr. Cogswell called you was only a starter. I'm calling you a buzzard-livered bloodsucker. You got size, that's all. Mr. Cogswell, he's a sick man. If you're rested up after that one lick you hit, I'm ready to put you to sleep."

"Steve!" Elsie again protested from the porch.

Then Cogswell came to his senses, groggily. He saw Steve confronting Prowers. Steve's slim five feet nine was giving fifty pounds to Prowers.

"You're asking for it," Prowers said. He drove hard for the cowboy's bronzed face, but it wasn't there. Prowers stepped back, took off his right glove and tossed it aside. His bare fist swung a haymaker at Steve, but again Steve wasn't there.

Before he knew it, Steve was hammering at his midriff. Prowers grunted, then doubled. Before he could right himself Steve caught him in the jaw. Before he recovered from that, Steve was hammering once more at his ribs.

Cogswell was sitting up, staring in amazement when Steve Lacey drove home the knockout. The blow popped like a gun squarely into the white teeth of Prowers. Prowers went flat on his back.

The man was only out for a few seconds. Elsie cried a warning from the porch, and Cogswell himself wasn't too dazed to see Prowers, still on his back, pulling at something in his hip pocket.

Dizzily Cogswell remembered a certain gun-shaped bulge he had seen under the man's coat at the courthouse door.

That gun now appeared in Prowers's hand. From his neck he aimed it at Steve. But Steve's eyes were quick. He took a step forward and kicked with one of his trim half boots. The gun went spinning just as Prowers squeezed the trigger. The shot roared as the bullet flew wild, the gun itself landing ten feet away.

Prowers got slowly to his feet. His lip was cut and bleeding. Steve went to the fence and buckled on his own belt. Then he picked up Prowers's pistol and handed it to Prowers. He handed the thing butt first to its owner.

Was Steve crazy, wondered Cogswell, to give him a chance like that?

But Prowers did not again squeeze the trigger. The steady, blue gaze of Steve whipped him. Prowers faced it only for a minute. Then he restored the pistol to his hip and turned toward the girl on the porch.

Remembering that she had stood there all the while made Cogswell wince. She had seen his own defeat, and then she had seen Steve Lacey thrash Prowers. Was it always to be like that? The thought mortified Cogswell. His top hand had made him look like a weakling.

CHAPTER EIGHT
RUNAWAY ROGUES

Prowers recovered a semblance of poise sooner than Cogswell. The man produced a silk handkerchief and applied it to the cut on his lip. Then he brushed the dust from his clothes. He smoothed his wavy auburn hair and then looked up with an astonishing self-assurance at the girl.

"Two to one." He shrugged. Again his white teeth smiled. "I can't whip your entire army, Miss Claiborne. The truth is that this reception quite stunned me at the very outset. I can't understand it. Why the attack? Why the insults? I come here on a simple, peaceful errand and—"

"Please don't try to deceive us again, Mr. Prowers," Elsie said coldly. Then she came anxiously down the steps to Cogswell. "Are you hurt, Mr. Cogswell?"

"I'm perfectly all right," Cogswell said irritably. He didn't want her feeling sorry for him.

Prowers again edged in. "You don't understand, Miss Claiborne," he placated.

She whirled on him furiously. "I understand perfectly well that you lied to me, forged my father's name, and that you're an insufferable swindler."

"You've got me wrong, Miss Claiborne." Prowers assumed a voice of hurt surprise. The man was smooth, Cogswell admitted. He was a sleek actor, and almost convincing. "What do you mean?" he went on aggrievedly. "Do you really think that contract wasn't genuine?"

"I'm sure it wasn't," she said.

Prowers spread his palms in a gesture of injured dignity. "But that's perfectly absurd! I can produce two eyewitnesses who saw your father sign that contract."

"Any witnesses produced by you would be as crooked as you are," Elsie said frigidly. "We know you swindled thirty thousand dollars from me and the same amount from Mr. Cogswell."

"Yes," Prowers admitted, "I heard that libelous charge going about town. It's absurd. All I did was foreclose a lien I held against poor Bert Pauly, expecting to bid in the security myself. I had no idea that Cogswell would appear and outbid me. In both your case and his, I acted in good faith."

"I would not believe you on oath, Mr. Prowers."

"Sorry you feel that way, Miss Claiborne. I'd buy back both properties right now if I had the money. But I haven't. I've a certain weakness you know, horses. During the past week I've been playing the ponies by wire. Lost every cent of that sixty thousand dollars. I'm broke flat, Miss Claiborne."

Cogswell stepped in and said brusquely, "Just why did you come here?"

"I told you why I came. To collect a few personals left in my room."

Fifty dollars' worth of shirts and cuff links wasn't a big enough motive, Cogswell thought. "Get them and get out," he said.

Prowers shrugged and then entered the house.

"Let Steve go with him," Elsie said. "I don't trust him."

Steve followed Prowers into the house.

"Maybe the real reason he came here," Cogswell said thoughtfully to Elsie, "is because he knows a bold front will make his case look better in case a suit is filed against him. The courts would look askance on a skulker, so Prowers prefers to play bold and innocent."

"You think he fears a suit?" Elsie asked.

"A little. Because he can't be sure whether Vera Grady told tales out of school. His idea now may be to discourage and forestall a suit by planting a tip that he's broke. No use to sue him if he's broke."

"Do you believe he is?"

"Not for a minute. The chances are he has those sixty thousand dollars in a few big bills, either cached or on his person. Sheriff Yates found out that he was changing the money into vest-pocket size. He might even have the money in his pocket now."

"He'd be afraid of being robbed," the girl objected.

"His fear of that would be less, probably, than his fear of losing it through judgment and attachment. He's a gunman gambler, and that sort very seldom put their stealings in a bank. They either hide it or carry it around in a wallet. I think Prowers ought to be detained and searched right now."

She shook her head. "We've no authority to do that, Mr. Cogswell. In the first place, I can't believe he'd be bold enough to carry that much money with him. In the second place, what if we found the money on his person? We couldn't take it. If we did, in the eyes of the law we'd be robbing him."

Cogswell admitted that she was right. There was nothing to do but let the man ride away, unsearched.

The man now emerged from the house with Steve Lacey. Prowers had a small bundle of his personal belongings. His parting word was, "I was a great admirer of your father, Miss Claiborne. I'd rather lose my right arm than bring pain or loss to his daughter. The brawl on your doorstep was, as you saw, forced on me. For your sake I shall not have the men who assaulted me arrested and jailed. I could, of course. But let it pass. As for the other matter, let me repeat that if I wasn't broke I'd buy the ranch back at the same figures. Good day."

Prowers went through the gate to his horse. He put the bicycle clips on his ankles, mounted, and rode away toward town.

The three watched his retreat, which was defiantly deliberate, at the gait known as the running walk. "Mr. Cogswell thinks he may have our sixty thousand dollars in his purse now," Elsie said to Steve.

"Chances are he'd be afraid to come here with it on him," Steve thought. "Still, those gamblers stick mighty close to their rolls."

"He might have stashed his roll before riding up to the house," Cogswell suggested.

"Wait a minute," Steve said quickly. "I believe I noticed a pair of old range glasses in the house."

He went inside. In a few minutes he came out with a pair of old field glasses such as are kept on most large ranches, used to watch and identify stock at distances on the range. Steve mounted the porch rail and put the glasses to his eyes. He directed his gaze at Prowers, who was now nearly a mile away in the direction of town.

A minute passed. To Cogswell, Prowers was only a speck on the trail, fast fading. But Steve cried out, "Look! He's off his horse. I think you made a pretty close guess, Mr. Cogswell."

Cogswell mounted the rail and took the glasses. With them he saw that Prowers had indeed dismounted.

"He's standing there, looking both ways along the road," Cogswell told the others. "He knows we can't see him from here with the naked eye. And wow! Take a look, Steve! Let's make no mistake about this. If these glasses tell the truth, Prowers is on his knees and feeling under a big rock."

"You're dead right," Steve confirmed after taking the glasses. "He's rolled the rock away and he's copping something that was under it. His wallet, on a bet! Yep, he's slippin' it into his hip pocket. He's climbin' his bronc again. He's off, this time at a lope."

Cogswell took another turn with the field glasses. Prowers had indeed resumed his journey and at a hard gallop. In a moment he topped a slight rise and disappeared from sight.

"Shall we follow him?" Cogswell asked Steve. "It's pretty plain what he did, isn't it?"

"Plain as bear tracks in mud," Steve agreed. "He had the sixty thousand on him, or the bulk of it, just like you thought. He was afraid to bring it to the house, so he stashed it under a rock before he got here. Now he's picked it up, and is burning the trail for town."

"We ought to nab him, the cheap crook!" Cogswell exploded. "Half that money belongs to Els—Miss Claiborne, who's told us it's all she has in the world. Do we let him get away with it, Steve?"

The girl settled the matter emphatically. "If you chased him and took the money from him, I wouldn't touch my half of it. In court we couldn't prove it was our money. It would be just any sixty thousand dollars, obtained by waylaying a man on the public highway."

That blunt phrasing sobered Cogswell.

"And we know he has a pistol," Elsie reminded them. "He'd fight. You'd have to shoot him or be shot. Please, Mr. Cogswell, forget about the money. It's lost. Let's make the best of it. We can't—"

"Listen!" Steve warned suddenly. He had cupped a hand over an ear as though he had heard a distant sound. "Did you hear that, either of you?"

Cogswell thought he had heard a faint sound from far along the road in the direction Prowers had taken.

"A rifle shot!" Steve said with conviction. "A long way off. If the breeze wasn't just right it wouldn't have carried to us. It came from beyond that little rise, from about where Prowers would be now. Looks like someone took a shot at him, saving us the trouble."

"Hardly," Cogswell thought. "No one but us knew he had the money."

"There's one fellah around here, though, who's been gunnin' for Prowers for the last six months."

"Who?"

"Carlos Estabal. He went in yesterday with a load of cheese. He'd be due back about now. And I happen to know he always keeps a rifle on that cheese wagon. He was after Prowers. As for knowing he had the money, maybe he did and maybe he didn't. It's a cinch he did know that Prowers had just sold the ranch for cash, and was likely to be flush."

"Look!" Cogswell was pointing to a speck which had just appeared on the rise. "I think you're right, Steve. It's that same spring wagon we passed yesterday. And coming this way fast."

Using the glasses, Cogswell saw that the distant driver was standing up, whipping his team to a gallop. He made out that the driver was a short brown man in a tall hat.

"It's Carlos, all right," Steve said when the careening spring wagon came nearer. "And he wouldn't be fannin' his broncs like that unless he'd just had a run-in with Prowers. The trail up to the goat colony leads right by this house. Likely Carlos thinks there's no one here. When he passed yesterday, this place was deserted. Gosh, look at him come!"

Hearing the excited comments, the Negress Magnolia came out on the porch. Her eyes rolled when she saw the approach of Estabal. Uncle Jack, the liveryman, came around the corner and joined the group, making the fifth witness to the flight of Estabal.

Because the man's only trail home led directly past the house, this flight was bringing him nearer at the same rate that it was taking him farther from his encounter with Prowers.

"He dry-gulched Prowers, on a bet," Steve said. "Chances are he went through his pockets, too. In that case Carlos now has Prowers's wallet."

"And our sixty thousand dollars!" added Cogswell.

"Which makes it a new deal all round," Lacey said. "Miss Claiborne's argument about highway robbery would apply to Estabal's assault on Prowers, but not to us if we stopped Estabal."

"You're talkin' sense," Uncle Jack chimed in.

"Lo'd a massy, Miss Elsie," Magnolia moaned, her hands flying in distress to her bandanaed head, "if dis ain't a heathen land!"

"You're right, Steve," Cogswell said. "Any bystander witnessing robbery has a right to butt in and lay a hand on the thief. That would tie the money up in the custody of a court, and if we got a judgment against Prowers it'd be right where we want it. Come on, Steve."

By now the careening outfit of Carlos Estabal was directly in front of the gate, the team still at a mad gallop. Estabal was standing up, using his whip on the nags. Thus he held the reins with but one hand. His eyes, fixed on the trail ahead, did not see the group on the porch.

The sudden shoutings as three men came from the gate surprised and alarmed both the Mexican and his horses. Plainly he had supposed these premises to be deserted, as yesterday. When Cogswell yelled, "Stop, you!" Estabal turned about quickly, almost losing his balance.

"Hold on a minute. What's your hurry?" bawled Uncle Jack.

The galloping horses swerved. For a brief moment Estabal lost control of them. One wheel hit a boulder. The rickety old spring wagon bounced up and over this, came near to being a complete wreck on the spot. Estabal was nearly thrown from his driving-platform. To save himself from being spilled he dropped the reins and grabbed with both hands at the seat. Unguided, the frightened horses swerved still farther to the right. The wheels hit another rock, and the wagon almost tipped over.

The horses, feeling no hand on the reins, dashed on at greater speed than ever. It was a mad stampede. The team left the trail and raced at breakneck pace through a gap in the fence which divided the corral grounds from the two-mile race track.

Cogswell, Steve, and Uncle Jack came on in hot pursuit. No saddled horse was available. In fact Steve's, now in a barn stall, was the only saddler on the place. There was no time to get it. So the three pursued afoot. Cogswell yelled again, "Stop, you!"

Steve's command carried more force. He drew his pistol and fired twice over Estabal's head. But Estabal couldn't have stopped even if he wanted to stop. The reins were dragging on the ground. He had lost all control of the panic-stricken horses.

The wagon was now through the fence gap and up on the grade of the old race track. Here was a fine orbit for speed; along it the runaways dashed in an arc for possibly a hundred yards. Then they deserted it, swerving again to the left. Off the track and down into the circular meadow of briars the nags galloped.

As the wagon bumped across a lateral ditch well out into these briars, a rear wheel came off. The wheel rolled free. The axle end, dropping to the ground, immediately acted as a brake. The flight continued, but at lessened speed. The wagon bumped along on three wheels and one dragging axle end, at a pace no faster than a man could run afoot.

The pursuers, Steve in the lead with his forty-five out, lost no more distance. And Carlos Estabal, as his wrecked outfit bumped along over the roughs of the rose patch, jumped to the ground. He was abusing his nags in profane Spanish. Running now at a forewheel he was stooping at every second step, snatching to regain his grasp on the dragging reins.

But without success. Every time he stopped he lost a pace of ground, and the reins just eluded him. The wreck bumped on across the meadow, heading for the grade of the track on the farther side of it. Every hundred yards or so it bounced across another irrigation lateral. Cogswell thought surely it would lose another wheel. But it didn't. Neither did Estabal succeed in recovering the reins. Neither did the bouncing axle end quite succeed in braking the vehicle to a halt. On and across the two-hundred-acre circle went team, wagon, driver, and pursuers, in a formation which would have been ridiculous to a chance observer.

It was a thousand yards across the circle. When the runaways struck the race track again, their flight was checked. The obstacle was the track grade itself, which ascended in a sharp terrace from the lower level of the meadow. The dragging axle butt refused to take this rise and the wreck came finally to a halt.

Steve, Cogswell, and Uncle Jack were two hundred yards back and coming on at full stride. But Estabal stopped them. He snatched something long and shiny from a scabbard on the sideboard of the wreck. He whipped it to his cheek, a rifle. The rifle popped. Bullets began clipping through the wild roses.

"Down," Steve warned, and dropped to his belly in the briars. Cogswell and Uncle Jack likewise dropped flat. Estabal was behind his wreck now, using it as a fort, pumping bullets.

"We're stopped," Steve said. "Him with a rifle and me with a forty-five, at this range, it's all his fight."

"What do we do now?" Cogswell gasped. The run had taken his wind.

"We don't do," Steve said. "If we crawl up any closer, he'll cut us to ribbons. Wonder if he killed Prowers?"

"And I wonder if he copped the sixty thousand dollars?" Cogswell said. "Look, what's he up to now?"

"Can't you see? He's getting ready to move on," squeaked Uncle Jack.

They saw that Estabal had his knife out and was slashing at the traces of the off horse. He crossed to the other side and cut the second horse free from the wreck. Retaining his rifle, the man climbed to the bare back of a horse, sitting astride the slashed harness. He galloped away, straight toward the mountain. The other horse whinnied, then followed. With everything but the wreck of his cheese wagon, Carlos Estabal headed straight for home.

"And nothing we can do about it," Steve admitted. He arose to his feet. "We might as well amble back to the house."

They retraced their steps across the diameter of the meadow, crossed the track, passed through the fence gap, and went on to the gate of the house. As they arrived there, an iron-gray horse came trotting down the road from the direction of town. Its rider had almost fallen off; he was slumped forward and was keeping his seat only by grasping the mount's mane.

The gray horse came on unguided. It was Prowers's horse, and had spent most of its life in the barn it was now heading for. Just as it came opposite the picket gate, Prowers fell to the ground. The horse stopped.

Prowers's vest, Cogswell saw, was bloody. Pain was in his eyes, and his cheeks were pallid. As they stooped over him, he said feebly, "Estabal shot me."

Then the man fainted.

CHAPTER NINE
LANTERN OF MYSTERY

THEY CARRIED MILTON PROWERS into the house and put him on a cot in the south wing. It was the room which Cogswell himself had occupied the night before. Steve took off the wounded man's vest and shirt; they saw that Prowers had been shot cleanly through the body just over the right lung.

Steve expertly stopped the blood flow. He bathed the wound and bound it, using the strips of a sheet for a bandage.

Cogswell, feeling dizzy, went out into the corridor. "Will he live?" Elsie asked him.

"Steve thinks so. But he's in no shape to be moved. We'll have to send for a doctor right away. Also, we need the sheriff to chase Estabal."

"We can send Uncle Jack," Elsie said.

"Right. And you can ride to town with him. I'll stay here with Steve. We'll have to take care of Prowers. Besides, the sheriff will have a lot of questions to ask us."

"Magnolia and I had better stay here, too," Elsie said decisively. "We're witnesses, and the sheriff will want to question us, too. Besides, we haven't settled anything. We haven't decided what to do with this ranch. And if this is going to be a hospital for the next few-days, you'll need help. I can nurse and Magnolia can cook."

Cogswell argued with her. This decrepit ranch house was no place for her, he said. "Steve and I'll get along. You go to town with Uncle Jack."

"No, we'll stay for another day or so, anyway," she insisted. "Besides, if I were in town, I'd die of curiosity to know what's going on out here. I've a feeling something important is going to happen, Mr. Cogswell."

Steve came out and reported that Prowers was conscious, but unable to talk. "He'll pull through, though, if we wrangle a good doctor out here."

Uncle Jack was soon on his way to town, driving one of the two buckboards.

Steve and Cogswell went in again to see Prowers. The man's eyes were open and fixed with a ghastly stare on the ceiling. He was finding it difficult to breathe. Because of a chance that he might die before the doctor and the sheriff could arrive, Cogswell decided to question him now.

"We understood you to say that Estabal robbed you. Is that a fact?"

Prowers nodded listlessly.

"Of what sum?" When the man only stared ceiling-ward without moving his lips, Cogswell repeated the question. Prowers continued to stare, pale and immobile.

Cogswell watched his eyes. Somehow he got the idea that even as he lay at death's door the man was thinking, was scheming some tricky response to the question. The man could not, of course, admit being robbed of any large sum without giving the lie to a previous statement. He had claimed to have lost the money betting on races.

"Of what sum?" Cogswell insisted. Then the man answered faintly. He said, "My billfold; there was three hundred dollars in it."

"Three hundred? Come, Prowers, you can hardly expect us to believe that. You wouldn't have bothered to hide that small amount under a rock. Wasn't it more like sixty thousand?"

Prowers closed his eyes and compressed his lips. Cogswell could induce no further reply.

"Do you suppose Estabal got away with only three hundred dollars?" he asked Steve.

"Not for a minute. I think this fellow had the whole pack of loot. But he's told that yarn about betting on the ponies, so he has to stick to it. I don't believe Carlos would have larruped that team the way he did unless he'd just robbed a man of real money. Which reminds me that the wreck is still standin' over there on the other side of the meadow."

They put water on the bedside table and stationed Magnolia there to attend Prowers. Cogswell and Steve then went to the barn. There Steve harnessed the team they had brought from town.

"We might as well pull that wreck to the house," he said.

They walked across the circular meadow, Steve driving the team ahead of him. They came first to the place where the wheel had come off Estabal's wagon. Cogswell set it on edge and rolled it like a hoop as they proceeded on. Finally they came to the wreck.

Steve hitched the team to it. He asked Cogswell to lift the right rear corner of the wagon so that he, Steve, could slip the wheel on to the axle. Cogswell tried, but couldn't.

The weight was too much for his strength.

"Sorry," Steve said contritely. "I forgot you've been laid up."

Steve himself lifted the wagon with ease. He even released one hand and helped Cogswell guide the wheel in place on the axle. The man was a human jack, Cogswell thought.

"The nut's lost," Steve said. "But if we drive careful, maybe the wheel'll stay on as far as the barn."

They mounted to the wagon seat and drove creakingly around the grade of the race track. They had no more than started when Cogswell felt a moist drop strike his nose.

"It's trying to rain," Steve said. "That big cloud driftin' along the rimrock has the makings of a storm. Well, this range could stand a good soaking."

When the rain came, as it did in a torrent late in the afternoon, neither of them guessed the extent to which it was affecting the fortunes of the Rincon Creek ranch. When the rain stopped, as it did at sundown, and the birds began twittering in the cottonwoods, and the drops dripped from the petals of the wild roses, even then Steve Lacey's only comment was, "Well, it was a good rain, and we needed it."

Steve, Cogswell and Elsie were seated on the porch in the freshness of twilight's rain-sweetened afterglow, when Cogswell inquired, "What's that roaring sound I hear back of the house?"

"Rincon Creek runnin' bank-full of flood water," Steve said. "Always does after a hard, quick rain. But it only runs an hour or two. That's what I meant by goats spoilin' the watershed. They keep the ground hard and the leaves stripped, which makes a quick run-off."

"And what," Elsie asked, "is that brown patch I see out in the rose meadow?"

"It's muddy water overflowing from a lateral," Steve told her. "The main ditch takes out from the creek about a mile above here. During floods, the ditch runs full. The ditch overflows into the laterals. Like all the old Mexican ranchers, Ramon Estabal was a wizard at irrigation. He checkerboarded that meadow and graded it, so that in big floods it gets irrigated without man or shovel. That brown patch you spoke of is spreading now, covers four or five acres. There's another brown patch to the left. Still another to the right."

They watched the brown patches appear here and there in the meadow. Finally it was too dark to see. Gradually the roar from the creek subsided.

"Do you think the sheriff will catch Estabal?" Cogswell asked.

"No," Steve said. "When the posse gets to the goat plaza, up under the rimrock, they'll find everyone there but Carlos. If Carlos has sixty thousand dollars, he'll be on his way to old

Mexico. And that would solve the most serious grief of this ranch."

"Goats?"

"Goats. Let's say Carlos swiped the sixty thousand and is off with it. A big stake like that would be reason enough for him to run with it, but he'll go anyway if Prowers dies. If Prowers dies, it's murder."

"What about the rest of the goat colony?"

"They've depended on Carlos too long to stay there without him," Steve thought. "He's sold their cheese for them, and fought their fights with the gringos. A few months after he disappears, if he does, they'll trail along after him, herdin' the goats by easy stages to wherever he's holding out."

"Suppose, though," Elsie suggested, "that our guess is wrong, that Estabal did not steal any such sum from Prowers! Suppose also that Prowers recovers from his wound. What would Estabal do then?"

Steve rolled a brown paper cigarette thoughtfully. "If Prowers lives," he surmised, "that would bust the murder charge and remove one motive for running away. Then Estabal will read in the news accounts that Prowers claims a loss of only three hundred dollars. Estabal would figure there won't be much hue and cry over a petty crime like that. He'll probably hide close by till it blows over."

"You think Prowers will stick to his story?" asked Cogswell.

"I've a hunch he will. He knows he'll never get the money back, so he might as well save his face. I doubt if he'll prosecute Carlos. Crooks hardly ever fight each other in courts. One's the pot and one's the kettle and they're both black."

Cogswell found himself more and more engrossed with the character and personality of this top hand of the range, Steve Lacey. What sort of man was he? It was plain that he had read a deal more than the market reports on grass cattle. Where did he get it? Cogswell saw the black eyes of Elsie Claiborne fixed meditatively on the cowboy. He had a feeling that her interest was vividly personal.

The roar from the creek back of the house could no longer be heard. Steve said that the stream would be down to its normal trickle by morning.

"It's getting late," Cogswell said. "When do you suppose the sheriff will be showing up?"

Steve thought it would be about midnight. Elsie said she was too excited to go to bed; she wanted to hear what the sheriff and doctor would have to say. She would send Magnolia to bed, though.

She went inside to speak to the Negress. Returning she reported that Prowers was resting well. Magnolia had been sitting up with him.

"I hear someone coming," Steve said. It was just eleven o'clock. Every rain cloud had disappeared, and the sky was bedecked with bright stars. "If it's the sheriff, Uncle Jack made good time to town."

Four horsemen drew up at the gate. Steve and Cogswell went out and met Sheriff Dan Yates, two deputies, and a small, wizened man with a Van Dyke beard who was introduced as Dr. Wade Houts.

Houts went directly in to Prowers. Yates drew from Steve all the known details of the conflict between Estabal and his victim.

"I agree with you, Steve," the sheriff said, "that we won't find Carlos when we ride up to that goat plaza. He may be heading south with sixty thousand *pesos de oro,* or he may be hiding in the timber until he learns whether Prowers goes dead on him. Just the same, we gotta ride up the mountain. Want to come along, Steve? And you, Cogswell?"

Cogswell was eager to go, but lacked a horse. The only saddle mount in the barn was Steve's. Steve suggested that one man ought to stay at the house with Miss Claiborne.

"You're just out of the hospital, Mr. Cogswell. So you stay and I'll go. We won't find Carlos at home, so we'll probably be right back. No use trying to track him after that rain. It'll take an hour to get there and an hour to get back, so look for us at about one-thirty."

Steve went to the barn for his horse.

"While he's doin' that," Yates said, "I'd like to have a confab with Prowers."

Cogswell took the sheriff to the bedside of Prowers. up and wait for them, Mr. Cogswell."

"Very well," he said, but for some unexplainable reason he winced. She seemed to have known "Steve" a long time, while "Mr. Cogswell" was still a stranger.

"Isn't it a glorious night? Think! A few hours ago it was pouring rain and now it's perfectly balmy. I'm getting to love this country, Mr. Cogswell. I'd like to live here forever if—if there just wouldn't be any more shootings or treacheries."

"You would?" His response was eager. "So would I. This old Mexican ranch has taken a strange hold of me. I can imagine that it was once a wonderful place. It gets under a fellow's skin, makes him want to reclaim it and see it bloom."

"You feel that way?" In the midnight starlight her face, vivid and enthused, charmed Cogswell. "Why, I've been thinking the same all day. Let's see, what did Steve say? One must first get rid of the horses, then the goats, then the wild roses. What else, Mr. Cogswell?"

"One must then plant new alfalfa and stock the place with beef. He said by keeping the cattle high on the mountain in summer, and feeding the hay in winter down here in the meadows, one could make the property worth every cent he paid for it."

"It would take heaps of money, wouldn't it?" she sighed.

"Not so much, perhaps. I have a few thousand dollars I could advance. Let's keep the idea in mind. There are two alternatives. One is to force Prowers to take the property back under legal pressure; the other is to list it for sale at whatever sacrifice figure it would bring."

For an hour they talked of these things. The abounding optimism of youth and the magic of the starlit night possessed them.

"One could call it The Ranch of the Roses," she said. Prowers was awake and conscious, with Dr. Houts bending over him.

"Will he live?" Yates asked gruffly.

"Yes, if he's not moved from this cot for a few days," the doctor thought. "A jolting trip to town might open his wound. It's a bad one. He must remain perfectly quiet and under constant attention."

"Let him stay here by all means," Cogswell said quickly. A human life was at stake. No matter if it was the life of the ranch's worst enemy, the issue could not be evaded. "And if you, Doctor Houts, will stay here and look after him, I'll personally guarantee your fee in case Prowers does not pay it himself."

"That's white of you, Cogswell," Yates said. "And now, Houts, can I ask this fellah a few questions?"

"If you're brief," Houts agreed.

Yates sat down beside Prowers. "You say Estabal shot you on the road and took your billfold?"

Prowers nodded.

"Sixty thousand dollars in that billfold, wasn't there?"

The wounded man shook his head. "Only three hundred," he said faintly.

"That agrees with what he told us," Cogswell said.

"No more questions," Houts decreed. "And very well, Mr. Cogswell, I'll stay here until the patient can be moved to town in an ambulance. I'll fix me up a cot right in this room. Leave him to me."

Cogswell and Yates rejoined the deputies at the gate. Steve came up with his horse. Then all the men except Cogswell rode away toward the mountain. Cogswell returned to the porch and Elsie Claiborne.

He explained the verdict and plans of Dr. Houts.

"You did just right," she approved warmly. "We must take the best possible care of Prowers. And now, since Steve said the posse would be back in two hours, let's sit "Isn't that a pretty name, Mr. Cogswell?"

He agreed that it was.

In a little while she exclaimed, "How bright that big yellow star is! The one straight ahead. Do you see it? It's so low that it seems to be lying on the ground."

Cogswell saw it, a star which seemed to be just setting beyond the western horizon. Then he saw that it was moving.

Instantly he was alert. "That's no star. It's jumping around, first to the right, then to the left."

"So it is," she wondered. "Why, it's getting nearer. But it's a long way off. Maybe it's someone with a lantern on the next ranch."

"I didn't notice any ranch over that way. Of course, it's a long way off. Probably two or three miles." In a moment he added, puzzledly, "Odd how it zigzags back and forth that way! Looks like someone's lost. Somebody groping around with a lantern." He looked at his watch. "And it's nearly one o'clock."

"In that case," she said, "Steve and the sheriff should be back soon from the mountain."

They sat silently for ten or more minutes, watching the mysterious lambency off in the western night. It appeared to be somewhere off across the race-track meadow. More and more its antics puzzled Cogswell. First it would move slowly toward the left, then toward the right. But always it came nearer.

Then, for a while, it was still. After that it retreated. Finally it was extinguished altogether.

Five minutes later they heard horses approaching from the direction of the mountain. Four riders drew up at the gate. One of them dismounted. The three others rode on toward town.

Steve came up on the porch and reported. "We guessed right. The whole population of the goat plaza was there except Carlos. They say they don't know where he is. It means he's either hiding in the woods or on his way south. Yates and his men have another case on tomorrow, so they went back to town."

Cogswell told him about the light.

"How far away?"

"Two or three miles, I guess."

"Pretty hard to judge distance to a light by night," Steve said. "A half a mile and three look all the same. There's no ranch over that way. Maybe it was a campfire."

"But it moved in circles," Elsie said.

"Why, there it is again." Cogswell pointed.

The others looked west. The mysterious light had reappeared.

"Somebody with a lantern," Steve said decisively.

Again the light moved uncertainly, as though someone were groping. To the left, to the right, now advancing, now retreating.

"Someone's lost, do you suppose?" Elsie asked.

Steve's face puckered shrewdly. "No, not lost. The light's probably not over half a mile away, which would put it somewhere inside the race-track meadow. At that range the man would be able to see, in the starlight, the dim shapes of these buildings. So he's not lost. Besides, his circles are too short. He's hunting for something."

Cogswell was incredulous. "Who would be out hunting for something in those briars, at one-thirty in the morning?"

"You say the light went out a little while before we got back?" Steve asked thoughtfully.

"Yes."

"Then I'm convinced he's not over half a mile away. At half a mile he could have heard the posse's hoofbeats coming, which is probably why he put out the light. When the hoofbeats passed on, he lit up again."

"You mean he's afraid of being caught?"

"Looks that way. Easy to find out if he is. We can yell at him. If the light goes out, it proves two things—first, that he's no far- ther away than the middle of the racetrack meadow; second, that he's afraid of being caught."

Cogswell went to the picket gate, cupped his hands over his mouth, and shouted, "Hey there, you with the lantern!"

Almost as quickly as sound can carry a thousand yards, the light went out.

"He's afraid of being caught, all right," Steve said when Cogswell rejoined him. "Which brands him, most likely, as Carlos Estabal."

"But why," Cogswell wondered, "would Estabal come prowl- ing back here tonight?"

Steve rolled a cigarette pensively. "Maybe he stole the billfold just like we thought," he offered, "and maybe the sixty thousand was in it. We know the cheese wagon lost a wheel in that patch of briars. Maybe it lost something else. Maybe it lost the sixty thousand dollars!"

"You mean Estabal might have dropped it!" Cogswell exclaimed.

"Why not? Or maybe he'd put the wallet under the cush- ion of his seat, and it was jolted out. He ran all the way across the circle, you remember, stooping and snatching at the reins. I was shooting over his head, too, and he was scared. In any one of a thousand yards he might have dropped the wallet, or it might have been jolted off the seat. Suppose that hap- pened! What would Carlos do? Would he be heading for Old Mexico?"

"No," Cogswell agreed slowly. "He'd be prowling back at night with a lantern, to recover the purse."

"A cinch he would," Steve thought. "He'd be out there tryin' to pick up his own wheel tracks. But he won't find 'em. Not after that rain, when every lateral in the meadow ran bank-full and overflowed silty flood water."

"Come along, Steve," Cogswell cried excitedly. "Let's you and I go out and look for the money."

"No use at night, Mr. Cogswell. A needle in a haystack and a wallet in two hundred acres of briars are not much different. Let's try in the morning. We can pin our memories on just what route the runaways took across the meadow. There'll be no wheel tracks."

"But after all, it's just a theory," Elsie said. "Maybe there's some other explanation for the lantern."

"Maybe there is," Steve admitted.

But Cogswell, when after more futile discussion they had all retired, could admit no other explanation. That one was too pat and logical. Who could the skulker be but Estabal? And why should Estabal, wanted for what he himself must now believe to be a capital charge, risk a return to the meadow unless he had dropped there the wallet of Milton Prowers?

CHAPTER TEN

THE SORREL COLT

C OGSWELL WAS UP an hour after daylight. Steve's cot, in the same room with his own now that one of the south-wing rooms had been given over to Prowers and the doctor, was unoccupied. Cogswell had already learned that Steve was an early riser.

When he stepped out into the corridor, the odors of coffee and bacon indicated that Magnolia was busy preparing breakfast. Just then Houts appeared, fully dressed.

"They'll be calling us to eats in a few minutes, doctor," Cogswell greeted. "How did Prowers make out through the night?"

"Good," Houts said, sniffing at the odors from the kitchen. "Due to his splendid physique, his recovery is certain. He should be able to survive a ride to town in three or four days."

"Have you talked with him?"

"A little. He insists he was shot by Estabal and robbed of three hundred dollars. No more, no less. Why all the suspicion that he might have had sixty thousand?"

"It's based on the fact that he recently bilked that sum from Miss Claiborne and myself. It's all a guess, of course. See you at breakfast, doctor."

Cogswell left the house for a talk with Steve. From the front gate he could see Steve out in the circular meadow. The cowboy was kicking around here and there in the briars.

A thought vaguely disturbed Cogswell. Steve, of course, was out there looking for that lost wallet. It was only natural that he'd want to check last night's theory. Yet suppose that Lacey, out there alone, should find a wallet containing sixty thousand in cash!

Would he bring it to the house? Of course he would. Stanley Cogswell was annoyed with himself for entertaining any other possibility. Yet an imp in his mind persisted in asking what, after all, did he know about Cimarron Steve Lacey? He had known the man but three days. Who was he? A cowboy, a top hand, an expert handler of cows and horses, hired to work for forty dollars a month. What would such a person do if he should suddenly find sixty thousand dollars?

Might he not argue to himself that it was treasure trove, lost booty salvable by the first finder?

Cogswell hurried through the gate and struck out across the meadow to join Steve. When he arrived, Steve was still kicking about in the briars.

"Mornin', Mr. Cogswell. No, I haven't found that billfold yet. I don't think Carlos did, either. I picked up his boot tracks in the mud. The whole field is sticky from the flood yesterday. Estabal's tracks seem to be a good two hundred yards north of where the runaways crossed the meadow. As I recall it, the cheese wagon passed about where we stand now."

Looking at Steve's frank, clean-cut face, Cogswell felt ashamed of himself. Of course Steve would bring the wallet to the house if he found it. Any other idea was ridiculous.

But Cogswell couldn't agree with Steve that the runaway wreck had crossed the meadow at this point. "I think you're way too far north, Steve. My memory says the wreck passed along over there." He pointed.

Steve chuckled. "All three of us remember it differently. Carlos, by his tracks, must think it passed north of my guess, and you think south."

Cogswell could see that it was like hunting for a needle in a haystack. Any spot in an area a thousand yards long and a third as wide might be the place where a wallet had been dropped. It was all a thicket of blooming briars and the flooding laterals had left a film of silt on the ground.

"Anyway, we ought to be able to trail Estabal," Cogswell suggested. "His tracks should lead to his hide out in the woods."

"His boot tracks are plain enough in this muddy meadow," Steve conceded. "But when he got on his horse again he could easily lose his tracks. Remember there's six hundred unshod horses on this ranch. Carlos is smart enough to ride in among those grazing horses; after that he'd ride water to bedrock."

"You wouldn't waste time trying to track him?"

"No. We can put in our time better looking for the money. Besides, Carlos will be coming back, some dark night, for another look himself."

"Unless he found the purse last night."

"Don't think he did. He was too far north. And he was still groping around when you yelled and scared him away."

"In that case, what about breakfast?"

In the ranch-house kitchen they joined Elsie and Dr. Houts. The girl, in spite of having been up most of the night, was as fresh as the rose blossom in her fine, black hair. More roses were in a bowl on the table.

"I was out at dawn for a centerpiece," she greeted Cogswell brightly, "while the dew was still on the petals." Then she extended a small foot whose shoe was stained brown to the ankle. "But Steve got me in a frightful mudhole. Aren't you ashamed of yourself, Steve?"

Steve looked guilty and contrite.

But not so contrite as Cogswell, who knew now that the man hadn't gone out alone to look for the purse. Finding Elsie up and about at dawn, he had taken her with him.

Magnolia had a tray ready for Prowers. Houts offered to take it to the sickroom. When he was gone, Steve said in a low voice, "It might be a good idea not to talk about that lost billfold in front of the doctor."

"But he's probably heard us talking about it already," Cogswell said. "And why not?"

"It's human nature to talk, and the doctor might spread the theory around when he gets back to town. If he does, we'll be having visitors."

"Visitors?"

"Likely. Every loafer in town might want to come prowlin' out to our meadow the first dark night. There'd be more lanterns in that field than roses."

Cogswell thought the point was well taken. Elsie said, "Gracious! We've trouble enough already. Let's keep mum about the lost purse."

After breakfast Cogswell and Elsie arrived at a definite program for the rest of the week. For that period they would stand pat and await developments. Prowers was on their hands, making it necessary that the house be kept in running-order. In the meantime they agreed to list the property with a reputable realtor, for sale on a commission basis. No price would be named; but any offer would be considered.

"If that fails," Cogswell said, "it means we're in the ranch business, whether we like it or not. For my part, I'd like it. I hope the darned realtor doesn't bring us an offer."

"He certainly won't," Elsie said severely, "if his prospects make a tour of this house. It's like a barn. My room, I'm sure, is the only one whose roof doesn't leak. If we only had a few hundred dollars to patch the roof with, and to redecorate the interior!"

"We might raise six hundred," Steve said, "by selling the crowbait mares at a dollar per head. I mean to those traveling horse swappers, the Tolliver brothers. They only live about eight miles from here, over on the San Isidro."

"Let's go have a talk with them," Cogswell said.

They put in the morning looking for the presumably lost wallet, with no success. In the afternoon the two men drove the livery buckboard over to the San Isidro. They found three of the four Tolliver brothers at home. Frank, Bert, and Bill Tolliver were slight, mousy men. But their tongues were silver when they discussed horses. They knew more reasons why horses incoming to their possession were worthless, and why horses outgoing from them were priceless, than Cogswell would have believed possible.

They knew all about the old Rincon Creek mares and insisted that they weren't worth skinning. Steve tried hard for a dollar a head, but the best he could get was seventy-five cents.

"Six bits a throw as they stand," Bill Tolliver said. "I'd as lief go to the poorhouse as pay more."

"You bought 'em," Steve said finally.

A deal was closed whereby the Tollivers were to come to Rincon Creek the next day with sufficient help to round up and drive away the six hundred mares, leaving as payment four hundred and fifty dollars.

"Where's Joe?" Steve inquired after the business was transacted. Cogswell guessed that he referred to the fourth brother.

Frank Tolliver made a wry face. "Ain't seen 'im in a month o' Sundays," he piped. "Joe, he's been arunnin' kinder wild. Hoss-tradin' got too tame for him. You might ast Milt Prowers where Joe is. Joe, he got to herdin' a lot with Pauly and Prowers."

"We'll keep that in mind," Cogswell said as he drove home with Steve. "Some day we may run across Joe Tolliver. If he was thick with Pauly and Prowers, maybe he knows something about the swindle plots."

"Not likely," Steve thought. "It wouldn't be natural for Pauly or Prowers to confide anything as important as that to Joe

Tolliver. Joe's a lightweight, as I recall him, both above and below the ears."

Elsie was waiting for them at the gate.

"We don't have to shoot those crowbaits, after all," Cogswell shouted to her. "Instead, we shingle the roof with 'em, and put matting on the floors, and maybe a few curtains on the windows."

The girl clapped her hands. "*Pink* curtains," she cried. "I've decided on pink curtains, because this is the Ranch of the Roses." Cogswell and Steve could see delicately pink tea roses in her cheeks already.

Nothing had transpired, they learned, except a call from a reporter on the *Trinidad Evening Picketwire*. He had ridden out to interview witnesses about Estabal's assault on Prowers.

"I was careful not to mention our theory about the lost purse. In his write-up, the loss will be put at only three hundred dollars."

"You skipped the mysterious lantern?"

"Yes, I skipped it."

"You can bet," Steve said, "that Estabal will have that copy of the *Picketwire* brought by some kinsman to wherever he's hiding. When he learns he's not wanted for murder, or for stealing any fancy sum, he'll be bolder. He might show up tonight again in the meadow, browsin' around with a lantern."

Estabal, however, did not come that night. At least no light was seen out in the race-track meadow, although Cogswell and Steve took turns sitting up watching for it.

Early next morning the Tolliver brothers arrived with a crew of four wranglers. Frank, the eldest brother, came in for a word with Prowers.

"You know anything about Joe?" he inquired. "He ain't showed up around home since March."

"I haven't seen him since March, either," Prowers asserted. But Cogswell, standing by, saw that his eyes evaded Tolliver. He felt sure the man was lying. Again Cogswell filed a mental note to have a talk with Joe Tolliver at the first opportunity.

Frank Tolliver went out to his crew. Immediately they started a horse roundup. Steve helped, which made eight riders. Because they were all within a few miles of the house, in bunches, the gathering of the mares was accomplished swiftly. Being aged and in poor flesh, they were easy to drive. By midafternoon the corrals were full, and Frank Tolliver came to the house to pay off.

"Our tally is just five hundred and eighty-eight head," he said to Cogswell. "The price bein' six bits a carcass, here's my check for four hundred and forty-one dollars."

Cogswell accepted the check, saying, "But I notice you overlooked one. I see one old sorrel mare standing out there in the race-track circle."

Frank Tolliver gave a deprecatory shrug. "We can't use that one," he said. "She's got a colt born last night. First place, we can't drive her with that twelve-hour colt alongside. Second place, she ain't got enough flesh on her to raise the colt. Either the colt or the mare, or both'll die in a month unless the mare is grained. And I sure don't aim to throw no grain into no six-bit hoss."

"You don't want that one, then?"

"Not for a gift."

The trader returned to his crew. In a few minutes they started toward the San Isidro with the herd of ancient brood mares.

"Let's hope we never see 'em again," Steve grinned. "Still, it's a good deal for the Tollivers. They'll trade each mare for a cripple and five dollars to boot, pretending they don't know they're getting a cripple. The other fellah'll be so heated up to get rid of his cripple, that he'll forget he's payin' boot. The Tollivers'll take the cripple off and shoot it, makin' a clean profit of four dollars, two bits per trade."

"I thought you said those mares were too old to foal," Cogswell said. He pointed to the mare and newborn colt out in the meadow.

"I did," Steve admitted, "but you can figure this case out by algebry. The chances of mares that old and skinny to have colts is about one in six hundred. You had six hundred mares, so you get exactly one colt."

Elsie came out and they told her about the colt.

The news excited her. She wanted to go out and see it right away. So the three strolled out into the race-track circle. As they waded into the rank growth of briars Cogswell tried to follow, as he remembered it, the route of the runaway cheese wagon.

"Maybe we can pick up sixty thousand dollars on the way to the colt," he said.

The mud was dry now. The men kicked about in the weeds as they passed along, but Elsie was more interested in the wild roses than in hunting for a lost purse. By the time they reached the big bony mare, she had accumulated a fine hand of blooms.

The colt arose staggeringly to its legs as the trio approached. The mare whinnied, nosed her foal, and then tried to lead a retreat. The colt took a step in her wake, stumbled to fore-knees, and then stood up with its legs braced wide apart.

"Isn't it cute?" Elsie said. "And pretty. It's the color of goldenrod."

"When he matures he'll be sorrel," Steve said. He cocked a critical eye, adding, "I'll say one thing. If I know horse stock, that's a real colt."

"What are his points?" Cogswell asked.

"Legs and bones. He has 'em. He's a way yonder above the mill run of colts. If his mother was fed, he'd make a real horse. I notice he's got the same color markings as his granddad, or maybe it was his great granddad."

"You mean that fancy stallion of Ramon Estabal's?"

"That's the one. Don Quixote. That stud was a prize running horse in his day. At three years old he won a fancy purse at New Orleans. All the mares we sold today, and this one, are blood kin to Don Quixote. This colt looks like a throwback. See that white cross on the forehead? Every hair on him sorrel except that one white cross. Don Quixote was marked the same way."

Elsie Claiborne was attending with an intelligent interest. Cogswell remembered that she was the daughter of a Kentuckian who had been a lifelong devotee of racing.

"But of course we'll feed his mother, Steve," she said. "Poor thing! Who said we wouldn't? We'll put flesh on her, and maybe this colt will win a big race, some day."

The idea struck Cogswell as ludicrous. He laughed heartily. "It might be," he suggested, "that this represents that mythical purse we were looking for. By all means, Steve, feed the colt—er, I mean the colt's mother."

In spite of his chuckles, Cogswell at heart felt an odd pride in this staggering bit of horseflesh. It was increase, the firstborn of his ranch, and eminently due their homage.

"We must name him," Elsie said.

"Of course," Cogswell agreed. "And since we hope to win a big race with him some day, let's choose a name that'll fool the bookies into giving us nice, long odds."

"*Bueno*," concurred Steve Lacey. "Since he's sorrel, and you paid sixty thousand dollars for him, why not call him Gold Brick?"

The youngling was christened Gold Brick on the spot.

CHAPTER ELEVEN

SHOTS IN THE MEADOW

E ARLY THE NEXT MORNING Cogswell and Elsie drove to town. Steve was left to watch the ranch. He was to employ his time in searching the circular meadow either to find the billfold, or to explode the theory that it had ever been lost.

It was a balmy June morning, scented with sage and piñon. Cogswell, holding the reins beside Elsie, was exuberant. Every figment of depression had been routed from his heart. Elsie, too, was in fine fettle, because she was on her way shopping. She was going to buy two hundred dollars worth of trimmings for a house.

They had agreed to divide the Tolliver check two ways. Cogswell's part was for shingles, nails, and certain important supplies suggested by Steve Lacey. Elsie had *carte blanche* to squander a like sum for curtains, matting, paint, varnish, and for whatever else she thought would interiorly embellish the dwelling built by Don Ramon Estabal.

"A few touches here and there will work wonders," she said as they rolled along.

"Don't make it look too nice," Cogswell argued, "or somebody might buy us out."

He looked slyly from the corner of his eye to see what she thought about that. It was she who had suggested listing the place with a realtor. "Not much danger of that," was all she said now.

Reaching town, they parked at Greenstead's livery barn.

"Look who's here," Uncle Jack greeted them. "You folks are beginnin' to look like honest-to-gosh ranchers. They tell me you already turned a big deal in horses."

"Right now we're going to buy more than we can haul home," Cogswell said. "So we'll order everything delivered here at the barn; tomorrow you can take it to Rincon Creek in a big wagon."

"Leave it to me," Uncle Jack said.

Cogswell took Elsie to the main department store, where he left her to pursue her shopping while he attended his own. Three hours later they met at a restaurant for lunch.

"What did you buy?" she asked eagerly.

He detailed his purchases, neglecting to mention that he had used some of his private funds. Steve had given him a long list of necessities. Nor did he speak of a .38 pistol which was now in his hip pocket. "Fellah ought to have a gun handy, in this country," Steve had told him.

"Also," Cogswell said, "I paid the livery bill to date and made arrangements to keep the buckboard temporarily, also a saddle horse, without charge. I told Green-stead we didn't know whether we'd operate or sell the property. He thinks he sees a chance to sell us the team later."

"You saw a real estate man?"

"Yes. Fellow by the name of Jackson. He'll call tomorrow and appraise the property. Also, I arranged for an ambulance to come out tomorrow and take Prowers to town. Now, what did *you* buy?"

"Pink curtains," she said. "And lots else. Wait and see. Anyway, I haven't a cent left, so we might as well go home."

Taking with them only the less bulky of the purchases, they drove back to Rincon Creek. Tethered to the end gate and trotting along behind was a wiry bay cow pony, loaned by Greenstead with an eye to future business.

Steve was waiting for them. He had just concluded an unsuccessful day searching in the rose meadow.

"Is that all you got for four hundred dollars?" he chided.

"Uncle Jack delivers the big end of it tomorrow," Cogswell said. "Any callers?"

"One. Joe Tolliver."

"The youngest of the four brothers? The one they haven't seen since March?"

Steve nodded. "He rode up and wanted to see Prowers. He asked to be left alone with Prowers, and Houts agreed. When Joe came out he seemed sore about something. He always was a peevish little rat."

"Did you ask him any questions about Pauly and Prowers?"

"Yes, but he wouldn't tip me to a thing. Told me to mind my own business and rode off in a grouch."

That night they sat up late discussing plans. They were on the house porch, but not watching for the reappearance of the mysterious lantern. For two nights they had seen nothing of that light, and Cogswell had reached the conclusion that they would not see it again. He was almost convinced that there was some innocent and natural explanation for it which in no way concerned a sixty-thousand-dollar purse.

But tonight Elsie exclaimed suddenly, "Look! There's the lantern again. Just where we saw it before."

Cogswell and Lacey turned quickly. Off to the west a light was bobbing.

"It's on horseback," Lacey thought. "The lantern's bobbing with each jog of a horse. It's coming this way." In a moment he added, "It's quit bobbing now. It's moving steadily to the left. That means the man's dismounted. He's prowlin' afoot, just like he was the other night."

The light seemed brighter than before, perhaps because this was a darker night. There was a filmy cloud over the moon, and the stars were dim.

Steve went into the house. When he reappeared he was buckling on his gun belt. "A fine, dark night to sneak up on him," he suggested to Cogswell.

Cogswell answered by producing from his pocket the .38 he had purchased today in town. He twirled the cylinder to make sure it was loaded.

Elsie was alarmed. Her hand went restrainingly to Cogswell's arm as he stood up. "Please don't go out there and fight that man."

"It's too dark for a fight," Steve said. "But we can sneak up and look that fellah over."

"We're two to one, and we can grab him without any trouble," Cogswell said. "Come along, Steve."

Cogswell's mind had leaped immediately back to the lost-purse theory. The prowler's return indicated a dogged persistency which could only be inspired by an important stake. That the stake was Prowers's wallet he could no longer doubt. The prowler himself was almost sure to be Estabal.

Steve went with him down the steps and through the picket gate. "Do be careful!" Elsie called anxiously after them.

They crossed the road and groped their way through the gap in the old race-track fence.

On the track grade Steve whispered, "I'll mosey up on him from the north and you from the south. Don't let him hear you. If he does, he'll put out the lantern and it'll be blindman's buff in the dark."

They separated. Cogswell, creeping away to the left, saw no more of Steve. But he could easily see the lantern out in the center of the circular meadow. It was moving to and fro, slowly, as before. The motion was that of a man afoot, searching for some object on the ground.

Cogswell circled to the southwest, closing in gradually on the light. There wasn't much chance, he thought, that the prowler would find the billfold. Steve had searched thoroughly by day without success. A night hunt would naturally be less efficient. At the same time Cogswell was eager to capture the prowler if for no other reason than to make sure of his identity. If he turned out to be Estabal, then certainly he was here looking for an article of value spilled from the runaway cheese wagon.

The light still blinked at him. Cogswell came closer and closer to it. The going was rough. The briars clawed at his feet and once he stumbled prone to his chest as he crossed a lateral ditch. He was afraid the man could hear him. There was no chance of being seen, because he himself could not yet distinguish the silhouette of the lantern bearer.

He could see, though, the outline of the lantern itself. He moved closer, and could make out the hand which held the lantern. Then he saw an arm and a leg. Finally he made out the shape of a man stooping, bent almost double as he examined the ground at his feet.

From beyond came a sharp challenge. "Hoist 'em, mister!" The voice was Steve's. Then a shot came from the same source. Steve was shooting over the man's head. Cogswell took the cue and shouted, "Hands up." He ran forward, firing once into the air.

Instantly the lantern was extinguished. In the pitch-dark Cogswell heard a man running through the briars. Then he heard the hoofbeats of a horse. The man had leaped to his saddle and made off. Cogswell fired twice at the sounds of retreat. Then he tripped. When he got up he bumped into Steve.

"We're chumps," Steve admitted. "We played our cards all wrong."

"How should we have played them?"

"Instead of sneaking up on his light, we should have looked for his horse. Naturally he had to get off his horse to look for the purse. But he was closer to it than I thought. That's how he got away."

"Could you see whether he was Estabal?"

Steve shook his head. "He was somebody with a lantern; that's all I know.

Elsie, who had heard the shots, was in considerable suspense when they returned to the house.

"Nobody hurt," Cogswell assured her. "He was too quick for us."

"Next time we'll grab his bronc," Steve said.

"Next time? Do you suppose we must go through with this every night?" Elsie inquired anxiously.

"He might show up once or twice more," Steve thought. "But it won't take him long to get discouraged. As for finding that purse, if he can find it at night when I can't find it by daylight, he deserves it."

On his way to bed Cogswell stepped in to see Dr. Houts. "I ordered that ambulance for your patient. It'll be here in the morning."

"Prowers can ride it by then," the doctor said. "I'll go with him and put him in a real hospital."

"Has he loosened up yet about how much was in the billfold?"

"Three hundred dollars is his story, and he sticks to it," Houts said.

"Knowing what a liar he is, that only serves to convince me there was a lot more."

Cogswell went to bed.

After breakfast the next morning, he went out with Steve into the meadow to see if they could read any sign from last night's encounter. They found boot tracks, as before.

"He was closer, this time," Steve said, "to my idea of the route of the runaway wagon."

"Personally, I think the runaways passed more over that way. About where that mare and colt stand." Cogswell pointed.

"That little he-horse looks right frisky this morning," Steve said. They went over for a look at Gold Brick, the colt.

"Four sacks of grain'll be out on Uncle Jack's wagon today," Cogswell said.

"So I might as well get the mare corralled, ready to feed," Lacey said. "Right now she looks more like a rail fence than anything else. Grain her good, though, and she'll have milk for the colt."

He tramped back through the briars toward the barn. Cogswell returned to the scene of last night's encounter with the prowler. Carlos Estabal, he knew, had been raised on this ranch. He had worked all through his youth for old Don Ramon, and many times must have helped to mow and irrigate this meadow. Knowing the ground so well, the man's memory of the route of the runaway wagon might be more accurate than Steve's. Estabal might recall some particular bump which had spilled the billfold.

It was even possible that Estabal might have stooped quickly to hide the wallet under some root or in some gopher hole. Men were chasing him, shooting at him. Having himself just shot Prowers, the fellow wouldn't want to be caught with blood money in hand. So Cogswell now searched the environs of last night's encounter thoroughly.

Steve, mounted now, came out to drive mare and colt to the barn. "That'll be Uncle Jack coming," he said, pointing.

Cogswell could see a heavy wagon approaching from the direction of town. A second vehicle was not far behind it.

"Probably the ambulance I ordered for Prowers," he said.

"*Bueno*," Steve said. "We've already got rid of six hundred crowbait mares and now we get rid of Prowers. A little more luck and we'll be shed of Estabal and the goats."

Cogswell lingered for further search in the briars. Steve passed him, driving mare and colt slowly toward the corrals. The old mare moved reluctantly, head turned back, while the colt did its awkward best to keep alongside. The little fellow was now sixty hours old, Cogswell calculated. He saw Steve reach the corrals with it just as Uncle Jack's heavy freight wagon pulled up in front of the house. The second vehicle, an ambulance, arrived a minute later.

Just then Cogswell saw something which had been almost hidden among the wild roses. He picked it up. It was a felt hat, high and peaked, and encircled with a two-inch buckskin band. Through the tip of the peak was a bullet hole.

It was the hat of Carlos Estabal! The hat must have been shot from the man's head last night. It proved the prowler's identity beyond any reasonable doubt.

Elated, Cogswell hurried with it to the ranch house. As he came face to face with Elsie Claiborne in the corridor, he waved the hat.

"We were right—the lantern prowler was Carlos Estabal," he said exuberantly. "Either Steve or I shot a hole through it last night. That makes it a pretty fair bet that sixty thousand dollars is out there lying loose in the rose patch."

He saw Elsie's finger go to her lips. She was looking beyond Cogswell. Cogswell turned. He saw an audience discomfortingly large. In the parlor doorway stood two men. One was the realtor, Jackson, who had promised to come out and appraise the ranch. The other was a moonfaced youth who, no doubt, was the ambulance driver. Jackson had evidently ridden from town either on the ambulance or on Uncle Jack's freight wagon. Back of the pair, in the parlor, was Uncle Jack himself. The teamster had just carried in a bundle of house furnishings.

On the other side of the hall, in the doorway of the room used as a ward for Prowers, stood Dr. Wade Houts. Beyond Houts, on a cot, lay Prowers himself. Prowers was supporting himself on an elbow and was giving alert attention.

To make it worse, Jackson remarked jokingly, "That gives me a great talking-point, Mr. Cogswell. It ought to be a cinch to sell a ranch for say thirty-five thousand, if sixty thousand cash goes with it. Ha !"

Cogswell now saw that Steve had appeared at the main entrance. Magnolia was peering from the kitchen. They were all there. Cogswell, holding Estabal's bullet-rived hat in hand, realized with dismay that he had given a maximum of publicity to the lost-purse theory. He had even established it with evidence, the hat. Steve Lacey's level gaze seemed to rebuke him.

All he could do was to laugh it off. "We're offering no bargains like that, Jackson," he said lightly. "Whatever's lost out there we'll scoop up before we turn loose the property. Have you seen the barns and corrals yet? Let's take a walk around."

With this ruse he escaped with Jackson.

"Please don't mention that lost-purse story in town," he said outside. "It's only a fine-spun theory, and yet it might make mischief for us."

Jackson promised.

Cogswell pointed out the lay of the ranch and they discussed values. "Cow ranches are a drug on the market just now," Jackson said. "And this one looks all shot to pieces. There's a slim chance, though, I might get an offer of around thirty-five thousand. That way you and the young lady would get back a little better than four bits on the dollar."

"We'd consider an offer like that," was all Cogswell would promise.

When they returned to the house, Houts and his patient had departed in the ambulance. Uncle Jack had unloaded his freight and was ready to go. The realtor rode back with Uncle Jack.

"He promised to keep mum about the lost wallet," Cogswell said.

Steve had secured the same promise from Houts and the ambulance driver. "But that's too many people to keep a secret. One tongue is almost sure to wag. Pesos to doughnuts there'll be a front-page yarn about it in tonight's *Picketwire*."

Cogswell agreed gloomily. "Cash Fortune Lost in Rose Patch!" was the headline he foresaw.

"Will it give us any trouble?" Elsie asked.

Steve thought it might. "Most folks won't believe it," he said. "Still and again, it might stampede a lot of crooks and near crooks out this way. But no help for it. I guess I'll get busy and shingle the roof."

A dozen bundles of shingles, unloaded by Uncle Jack, lay in the yard. Cogswell worked with Steve all day on the roof.

When they went inside they found Elsie covered from neck to ankle with a becoming gray apron. A paintbrush was in her hand. There was a speck of paint on her nose.

"Don't touch anything," she warned. "I'm painting the woodwork. Go around to the back door."

The next day was even busier. Uncle Jack had brought out many rolls of bright new matting. There were pink curtains. The men were excluded from the front part of the house, where Magnolia and her mistress began what promised to be a magic transformation.

All day Steve and Cogswell worked on the roof, patching wind-blown gaps with new shingles. Each time Cogswell came down for another supply, he could see Elsie standing on a chair, at a window, her arms bare to the elbows. He could hear the Negress rapping tacks into the matting.

By night they were all weary. Yet Stanley Cogswell felt a triumph and a thrill. He was in sympathy with all things about him. This, after all, was a good old house. This was a good old ranch. All it needed was work. And work was a good thing. Magnolia, he thought, was the best cook in the world. Steve was a great old scout. And Elsie, still with bare arms and in a paint-spotted apron, was beyond question the most appealing vision he had ever seen.

Supper in the kitchen was a gay banquet.

In the cool of night the three sat together on the porch and looked out across the starlit circle of meadow. A strange company, like a settled family. Strange, because the girl had come here only for an hour's inspection. By a marvel of chance she was still here. It amazed Cogswell that he himself should still be here. But something was here that needed saving, and they were working together to save it. Work, service, had brought them close together.

There were still no plans. They were simply taking things as they came. What other things would come, Cogswell wondered.

"Reserved seats for the big lantern show," Steve said. He rolled a cigarette, then passed the makings across Elsie to Cogswell.

"You expect Estabal tonight?" she asked.

"Him and maybe some competition. Wouldn't be surprised if we had a two-or three-ring circus."

"How thrilling! But you and Mr. Cogswell must keep out of it tonight, Steve. Tonight we'll simply look on."

"All right, Miss Elsie," Steve promised. "I'll sit here and be good. But you'll have to hold Mr. Cogswell. He's the fellah burned most of the powder the other night. He went on the prod and shot a hole clean through Estabal's hat."

Cogswell elevated his feet comfortably to the railing and pondered on the peculiar relation which the top hand had adopted toward his employers. In every way the slender, blond cowboy was conducting himself as one of three partners. It had been so from the first. There was nothing officious about it—it was all natural, easy, graceful. He was simply one of three humans facing a common problem. The girl, Cogswell was sure, had forgotten that Steve was a hired man. Then he realized that she had just called him "Steve," and that Steve had addressed her as "Miss Elsie."

"Isn't it funny, Mr. Cogswell?" she was saying now. "Steve says that Gold Brick's mother doesn't know how to eat corn."

"But she'll learn in a day or two," Steve said. "I mixed some grain with some cured grass stems and put 'em in the trough. After old Bess swallows a few grains by accident, she'll know what's good."

"You mean to say that a horse that old doesn't know how to eat grain?" Cogswell found it hard to believe.

"No horse does, till it's taught. But look! The show's startin' early tonight. Isn't that a lantern out there?"

Cogswell's feet came to the floor with a pop. He looked out across the meadow and for an instant saw a light. Then it disappeared.

"Carlos is careful tonight," Steve suggested. "Chances are he's got a black rag on the house side of his lantern."

Steve was on his feet, hitching at his gun belt.

"Sit down." Elsie tugged at his arm. "You promised to be good."

Steve sat down. For an hour they kept an alert watch on the meadow. Occasionally they caught a faint glimmer, which would immediately disappear. Suddenly another light appeared in quite another part of the meadow.

"What? *Two* prowlers!" cried Cogswell.

"Exactly that many," Steve said. "And they're a good quarter of a mile apart. See, that other fellah hasn't any black shade over his lantern. You can see it all the time."

"They're getting closer together," Elsie said. "This is perfectly thrilling."

"The first prowler must be Estabal," Cogswell thought. "Estabal's had experience, so he's cautious about showing his light."

"That light off to the north is movin' south," Steve said. "It's about at the center of the circle now. If Estabal sees it, he probably thinks it's us creepin' up on him."

For some minutes they had seen no glimmer of the first light. Presumably Estabal had put his lantern entirely out, so that the stalkers would not be able to find him.

"The other fellow can't be very far away from him, though," Cogswell offered.

Suddenly the second light went out. The entire vista was quite dark. Then it was stabbed by a dozen lights. Flashes, followed by reports of gunfire. Flash for flash, the prowlers were giving battle in the meadow. At a range of about sixty yards, each combatant fired six times. After the twelfth shot those on the ranch-house porch heard a faint scream.

Then everything became dark and still. The fight was over. One man, Cogswell guessed, was hit. They must have been shooting at each other's flashes. Steve and Cogswell were already running toward the gate. Elsie tried to stop them in vain. They hurried across the road, through the fence gap and over the race-track grade. Down into the dark meadow they rushed blindly, with drawn pistols. Cogswell stumbled in the briars, scrambled up, and followed Steve toward where they had heard a man scream.

A groan guided them. They came to a victim who lay prone in a tangle of briars. The man's darkened lantern lay beside him. Steve struck a match and lighted its wick. He held it to the face of the man who lay moaning on the ground.

"I know this fellah," Steve said after a close inspection. "He's Joe Tolliver."

Cogswell was surprised. He had expected the victim to be Carlos Estabal. "What would Joe Tolliver be doing here?" he wondered. "But see how badly he's hurt."

"He's more scared than hurt," Steve said. He had already examined the wound. "It's just a crease on the scalp, not deep. Joe, what's the idea of your prowlin' around here with a lantern?"

Tolliver whimpered unintelligibly. Finally, when he found he wasn't badly hurt, he sat up and became sullen.

"Come, Joe," Steve coaxed. "What did you come here for?"

It took a good deal more baiting and coaxing before Joe would answer. At last he blurted out, "Milt Prowers owed me money. I nailed him for it, and he said he was broke. Said every cent he had was layin' out here in this rose patch."

"What did Prowers owe you money for?"

Joe Tolliver's mouth, shaped like a rat's, closed stubbornly. He would not say on what account Prowers owed him money.

"I think he's hurt worse than you think, Steve," Cogswell said. "There's blood on his cheek." He took his handkerchief and wiped at a red splotch on the man's left cheek.

But the red did not come off. The dim lantern light had deceived Cogswell. Now he recalled a description wired to him by Luther Hayes, the details of which he had never repeated to Steve Lacey.

"It's not blood," he told Steve now. "It's natural, an oval birthmark on the left cheek. Now I know why Milton Prowers owed him money. This is the fellow a bellboy at a New York hotel saw come out of a phone booth at the same hour a fake telegram was telephoned to Western Union. Joe Tolliver was the pawn Prowers and Pauly used to frame this horse ranch on me, Steve."

When he gave Steve the details of the description wired by Hayes, Steve was convinced. "Funny how it all comes out in the wash, like this," he said.

CHAPTER TWELVE
PROOF

THEY TOOK JOE TOLLIVER to the house. Though uncommunicative, he was easy to handle. Cogswell and Steve kept him in their south-wing room all night, taking turns watching against his escape.

"Not that he's likely to do us any good," Cogswell admitted. "He'll probably prove as tight-lipped as that other witness, Vera Grady. By the way, what ever became of her?"

"From what Sheriff Yates said the other day, I reckon they've turned her loose," Steve told him.

"Yates tried to make her talk, but couldn't. Maybe he'll have better luck with Joe Tolliver," Cogswell said. "We'll hustle Tolliver to town tomorrow and let Yates work on him."

Morning found Tolliver docile but silent. Elsie said that she and Magnolia wouldn't mind being left alone all day, so Steve and Cogswell hitched up the buckboard and drove Tolliver to town. In the jail office they arraigned him before Yates.

"Were you in New York on the fourth of this month?" Yates asked.

Surprisingly, the little rat-faced man admitted having been in New York on the date named.

"But what of it?" he challenged. "Any crime if I went to New York?"

"Did you telephone, on that date, from a booth in the lobby of the Ambassador Hotel?"

"Sure I did. I called up a friend, but no one answered the phone."

"You didn't phone a telegram, using the name of Luther Hayes?"

"Naw. What's it all about? I never heard of Hayes."

He stood pat. Yates, though he used everything but third-degree pressure, failed to get any further admissions. In the same way the man stood pat as to his motive for last night's prowl. Prowers, he insisted, owed him a hundred dollars.

"Your fee for phoning the fake message?"

"Naw, an old poker debt. I hit him for it the other day, and he claimed he was broke. Said his wallet was lost in the race-track meadow. Said Carlos Estabal swiped it off him and then lost it in a runaway."

"Did he say how much was in the wallet?"

"Yeh. Three hundred dollars."

"Was it Estabal you had the shooting-match with last night?"

"How would I know? It was dark as hell."

That ended the testimony of Joe Tolliver.

Yates, conferring aside with Cogswell, was forced to admit that it was a blind lead. He pointed out that even if the New York bellboy were imported West as a witness, and positively identified Tolliver as the man seen emerging from the booth, it would be no more than Tolliver had already admitted. It would in no way definitely prove that Tolliver had telephoned a fake message.

"As for last night," Yates concluded, "there's nothing to charge him with except trespass. He didn't hit Estabal, if it was Estabal. And Estabal will, of course, make no complaint against him. Nothing to do but turn him loose."

"What about the Grady girl?"

"We turned her loose yesterday. There was no one to complain against her, either. On his own, the DA. didn't feel like prosecuting her. All she did was shoot at a deserting lover and miss him a mile. No jury would break down and cry over that."

"Steve Lacey," Cogswell said, "thinks it was Estabal who shot Pauly."

"Prove it and I'll be after him with every gun in the courthouse," Yates promised. "As it is we got a case against him, all right, but not a very hot one. The man he robbed is getting well, and hasn't filed a complaint. The evidence is that Estabal stole three hundred dollars and then promptly lost it. If I didn't have three or four capital cases on my hands in other parts of the county, I'd be after Carlos even for that. As it is I'm lettin' it slide for a while, while I hunt bigger game."

Cogswell, as he went out, was gloomily pessimistic as to his ability to pin fraud on Prowers. He said so to Steve when the two entered the Toltec Hotel dining-room for lunch.

"What we might be able to prove, though," Steve said, "is that Estabal killed Pauly."

"All very fine for law and order," Cogswell objected, "but it would pin no swindle on Prowers. It wouldn't help to get back Miss Claiborne's thirty thousand dollars. Forget about mine; I'd just as soon keep the ranch and run it. But, Steve, we've got to consider what's best for the girl. She's game, all right, but ranch life'd be too hard for her."

Steve nodded soberly. "We ought to get her money back," he agreed, "and then she could go home to Kentucky."

"Right, Steve. The best way to get it is to prove to the satisfaction of a court that Prowers is a swindler. The court would give us a judgment. Prowers couldn't hide his assets, either, because they're already hidden in our rose patch."

"Why not find the cash there and simply hand it to her?"

Cogswell frowned. "I've hashed that over with Miss Claiborne and it won't go. She's got a fine, straight-laced sense of honor that won't let her do it. She insists that legally the money belongs to Prowers. That even if we find it we must turn it over to a court and recover it therefrom through a court order. That means we've got to prove, even if we find the money."

"And if you fail on both counts, you figure you're stuck with the ranch?"

"Yes. The conviction of Estabal for murdering Pauly wouldn't help the issue a bit."

"That's where you're wrong," Steve disagreed. "Because you wouldn't be stuck with the ranch if it was a good ranch. It would be a good ranch if you were rid of the goats. You would be rid of the goats if you were rid of Estabal. You would be rid of Estabal if you could prove he murdered Pauly."

"But that," Cogswell said thoughtfully, "raises another ethical point. Suppose that we did turn up positive proof that Estabal shot Pauly. We couldn't warn Estabal, giving him an opportunity to leave the country. We would have to tip the sheriff, who would eventually arrest him and Estabal would be hanged. That would leave the goats still in the Rincon. Granted that his kinsmen would follow him to Old Mexico, they'd hardly follow him to the gallows."

Steve grinned. "I getcha. If you got proof and didn't slip it to the sheriff, it would be like blackmailing Carlos out of the country for our own gain. No, I don't reckon Miss Elsie would stand for that. But look! Either way it turns out would help our case. If he leaves the country, all right. If he's caught, we're still to the good. That goat colony without Carlos wouldn't hurt us much. It was his dry-gulching gun that always backed up their trespassings. Without him they'd soon scatter."

"How would you go about getting evidence against Estabal?"

"Why not go up to the room the killer stood in when he shot Pauly? Maybe we can stumble on a lead."

"If Yates couldn't, how can we?" But Cogswell was willing to try.

After lunch the two men went to the desk and asked permission to look in at room 204.

"It's been empty since that gunplay couple of weeks ago," the clerk said. "Dull season. I had plenty rooms without using that one."

They took the key and went up. To Cogswell the room seemed to be exactly as he had left it on the day of Pauly's murder.

"Where was the forty-five layin'?" Steve asked.

"Right on the floor under that window."

"Was the window closed?"

"Yes, just like it is now."

The window was directly opposite the curb where Pauly's cab had been parked. Steve raised it. When he removed his hand it fell shut with a bang.

"Humph! No counterweight in this sash. It looks like the sniper had to hold it up with his left hand while he used his right to shoot with. And that," he added doubtfully, "would be an unhandy way to shoot."

"Perhaps he put a stick under the window," Cogswell suggested, "to hold it open while he performed the sniping. Then he could remove the stick, letting the window down to keep smoke from drifting out, or so that an open window wouldn't draw attention from the street."

"That sounds reasonable," Steve agreed. "No man could shoot very straight with his right hand if he was holdin' up a heavy weight with his left. So let's say the sniper put a stick under the window. What would he use for a stick? A hairbrush, maybe?"

"There wasn't any hairbrush on the dresser," Cogswell said. "Prowers had checked out and taken everything with him."

They looked about the room. Neither of them could see a stick or other article usable for the propping open of a window.

"If he didn't hold it open with his left hand," Steve thought, "he must have taken something from his pocket to use for a prop."

"He'd be in a hurry, too," Cogswell said. "He didn't have much time. Pauly was only in the cab over there a minute or so. And the killing of Pauly, we think, wasn't premeditated. Estabal came here to kill Prowers, only taking a shot at Pauly on the spur of a suddenly presented opportunity. Here he stood at the window.

He saw Pauly over there. With a gun in his right hand, he opened the window with his left. He found the window wouldn't stay open, so—"

"I got it," Steve interrupted. "He was packing two guns. When the window wouldn't stay open, he pulled the other gun and stood it end up on the sill for a prop. Then he shot Pauly with his right-hand gun, snatched the prop out, dropped the hot gun on the floor, and beat it with the cold one."

"Sounds good," Cogswell agreed. "In that case the gun he used as a prop is the only one he has left, the one he nicked Joe Tolliver with."

"Let's See if that prop left a muzzle mark on the sill," Steve suggested. He opened the window wide. Cogswell held it open while Steve examined very carefully the sill and the lower bearing surface of the window itself.

"Look at the extreme left, next to the frame," Cogswell said. "He wouldn't put the prop in the middle because that would interfere with his shooting, as well as be conspicuous from the street."

Steve was kneeling. He examined the sill at the extreme left and found nothing. Then he looked up at the bearing surface of the sash. Suddenly he produced his pocketknife and began prying at the wood.

"We were wrong," he said as he gouged something out. "Carlos didn't use a gun to prop the window."

"Did he use anything?"

"Yes. This." Steve exhibited a tiny triangle of steel, less than a half-inch in equilateral dimension, which Cogswell at first mistook for one of those triangular zincs often used to reinforce the putty about panes.

"It's the tip of a knife blade," Lacey said. "If Carlos had a second gun, he didn't use it for a prop. The only other thing he could have carried in his pocket long enough to use for a prop would be his knife. He'd naturally carry a skinning-knife, him being a goatman, one that would be maybe a foot long with the blade open. He opened the blade and propped the window. When he snatched the knife out, its tip broke, remaining in the sash, and here it is."

It was, Cogswell conceded, important evidence. "That knife, with the tip of a blade broken off, may be in the man's pocket right now," he said. "If this chip of steel fits it, then—"

"Then," Steve cut in, "it would be enough either to hang Carlos or scare him out of the country."

"Good. Our cue's to catch him and have a look at his knife. Let's go home, Steve."

They got their team from the livery stable and drove home.

"We had two callers today," Elsie greeted them. "Each offered to lease the ranch for cash."

"Lease it?" objected Cogswell. "But we want to sell. Were these fellows sent out here by Jackson?"

"Yes. They came separately and had nothing to do with each other, but each said he had been sent out by Mr. Jackson, the realtor. Mr. Jackson had priced the place at thirty-five thousand. Neither was prepared to buy, but each offered to pay cash rent."

"How much cash rent?"

"One," Elsie said, "offered fifteen hundred a year, payable semiannually in advance. The other offered two thousand a year, payable quarterly in advance. Perhaps we should accept that last offer, don't you think, Mr. Cogswell? It would solve everything, wouldn't it? We would get about three-per-cent interest on our investment."

"Y-es," Cogswell admitted uncomfortably. Suddenly his heart became very heavy. He knew he didn't want to separate himself from this ranch and from Elsie Claiborne. "It would solve everything," he admitted. "Three per cent is a mighty good return on a gold brick."

"Who were these fellahs?" Steve wanted to know.

"One came in the morning from the east and introduced himself as Ike Zachary. The other came in the afternoon from the west, and was a Mr. Kincaid."

"Those fellahs!" Steve exclaimed. "Why, I know 'em both well. Ike Zachary's a fine, upstanding calf thief from Johnson Mesa. He's flat broke. You'd never collect a nickel rent outa him, makes no difference what he promises. Kincaid has money, all right, he's a big Frijoli sheepman. He'd probably come across with the first quarter's rent. But he's tricky. No good would come of any deal you made with him. What they both want, of course, is an excuse to rake over the race-track meadow for the lost wallet."

"Oh, do you think so?" Elsie's eyes were round.

"Dead sure of it. They've both got plenty of range and don't need ours. They're hot after that lost money. Maybe Jackson, anxious to pull down a commission, has spread the story around."

"Sounds plausible," Cogswell thought. "Probably Jackson tried to line them up as prospective buyers. But these fellows figured it was cheaper to lease than to buy. Any excuse to get us off and them on. Three months raking around in the briars, with or without success, and they'd turn the ranch back to us."

"Zachary would," Steve agreed. "But Kincaid would simply default on the second quarter's rent and stick on the place, sheepin' it to the grass roots, and you'd have to sue to regain possession. I advise turning them both down."

"Steve," Cogswell cried enthusedly, "you're the best consulting cowboy in seven states. My idea exactly."

Here was a strange paradox, Cogswell thought as he helped Steve unhitch at the barn. Supposedly he was trying to get the property off their hands, yet at the first passing of a chance he felt an immense relief. Either a sale or a lease would end his association with Elsie Claiborne. He didn't want that ended, he knew, on any terms whatever. It had become a thing vital and precious to Stanley Cogswell.

He strolled out into the corral while Steve was feeding the team. The sorrel colt was skipping friskily about, while its bony mother was nibbling at hay in a trough. Steve had scattered kernels of whole com through this roughage.

Steve joined him. "She'll be chewin' grain in a day or two," he said, "and then she'll get some tallow on her. Say, look at the legs on that colt! And his back! There's the makings of a real horse. He's the dead image of his granddaddy."

"You say that Don Quixote was a winner?"

"A champion of champions. Won the Old Planters' Sweepstakes in New Orleans, at three years. Next ten years he was a famous breeding stud. Which means that five dollars' worth of com planted in the belly of this old mare might pay a few dividends."

A pleasing transformation confronted them when they entered the house. The corridor and adjacent rooms were laid with bright new matting. At the front windows were crisp rose curtains, raffle-edged and looped back at mid-height in Colonial style. On the wall of the parlor Cogswell saw an attractive stage-coach print in a neat black frame. Prim little cushions sat at upright attention on the couch. There was a braided rug and a round tea table.

"Do you like it?" Elsie stood charmingly eager at his elbow.

"Everything about it," Cogswell said.

Magnolia came in, with a snowy bibbed apron over her starched dress and her sleek, ebony face wreathed in smiles.

She rolled her eyes. "It sho' looks diff'rent, ain't it de troof, Mistuh Cogswell? Miss Elsie, she plumb wore herself out afixin'."

"Stop fibbing, Magnolia. I don't look 'wore out,' do I, Mr. Cogswell?"

He wanted to say that she looked fresh and beautiful. Her cheeks were rosy. At his lingering regard they grew rosier still. Her black hair was in delightful disorder, and the pride of homemaking was aglow in her eyes. The pink housedress with white collar and cuffs, he thought, was ravishing. To Steve he said, "Whenever I rent this place to a Johnson Mesa calf thief or a Frijoli sheepman, take me down to the creek and shoot me, Steve."

"You'd sure deserve it," Steve said soberly.

"But you *have* been working too hard," Cogswell said to the girl. "You should have let Steve and me in on it."

"Don't worry, I've loads of work laid out for you and Steve. Tomorrow I want to water the hollyhocks along the picket fence. There's hundreds of them, but they're dying."

"Easy," Steve said. "There's an old lateral through the yard. It's busted somewhere, but I'll patch it up. Then with a few loads of brush and rock I can turn the creek right through it."

"Perfect," Elsie exulted.

At supper in the kitchen she said, "We've cleaned up the house pretty well, except the cellar. We don't need the cellar, though."

"Is there a cellar?" Cogswell was surprised.

"Right under this kitchen." She pointed to a ring on the kitchen floor. Cogswell saw that it was the handle of a floor door which no doubt gave to descending steps. They could forget about the cellar until there was need to use it, he agreed.

Elsie, tired, went to bed early.

"Did you tell her about the broken knife blade?" Steve asked.

"No. Let's not worry her any more about Carlos. Of course, if that fellow comes prowling around again with his lantern—"

"There he is now," Steve cut in. He pointed westward across the dark meadow. "Persistent devil, he is."

"I didn't see any light."

"It's gone, now. But I got a flash of it. He must have it shaded again tonight."

Cogswell arose briskly from his seat on the porch. "This time we sneak up on his horse, eh?"

"You took the words right out of my mouth," Steve said.

Armed with revolvers, they walked briskly out across the race track and into the circle of briars. The night was again cloudy and black. They couldn't see the light. Steve knew, though, that it was there.

Separating, Steve went to the north and Cogswell to the south. Each was to grope about without giving forth any challenge whatever until one of them stumbled on Estabal's horse.

Cogswell came upon the animal sooner than he expected. Almost at the same time he saw the lantern. He was far out in the meadow now, and the lantern bearer had only shaded the house side of his light. Cogswell was farther from the house than the light, and so could see its unshaded side.

Nearer him was a saddled horse. Cogswell slipped up and grasped a trailing bridle rein. The horse started, jerked, snorted. Cogswell held fast to the rein.

The light was about fifty yards away. At the snort of the horse, it went out. Everything was dark again. But Cogswell could hear a man running toward him. Putting the horse between himself and the runner, he waited. The runner arrived at the horse and climbed to the saddle. As his boot came over it, Cogswell seized the man by the leg. He yanked mightily. Carlos Estabal came down atop of him. The two fell in a clinch on the ground. The horse snorted again and ran free.

Cogswell was on his back, holding on. Estabal was clawing him like a catamount. Cogswell managed to hug him, pinioning his arms. There was a gun in the man's right arm. As he jerked to free himself, it roared like the crack of doom. The flame of the shot burned Cogswell's cheek. He could smell the powder. Estabal was writhing furiously, cursing in Spanish at whoever was hugging him like grim death.

In a minute Cogswell, still on his back, let go one hand and biffed desperately at the man's face. The gun roared again; but the impact of the blow caused a miss. An instant later there were three in the tangle. Steve had come on the run. He dived in and jerked Estabal away with a snap.

When Cogswell stood up, panting, Steve had the man's gun.

"Nice work, Mr. Cogswell. Now suppose we get his bronc and mosey along to the house."

Cogswell limped to the horse which, with trailing reins, hadn't gone far. Then, Steve prodding Estabal and Cogswell leading the mount, they proceeded across the meadow toward the barn. Steve stopped at the first of the adobe huts in the old peon quarter.

"Let's take him in here," he said, "and work him over."

"We'll need a light."

"I've got his lantern," Steve said.

They pushed the prisoner ahead of them into the old mud hut. It was fouled with cobwebs, with a dirt floor, a roof partly caved in, and a paneless window. The only furnishing was an old grain box. After lighting the lantern, Steve set it on the box.

"You watch the door, Mr. Cogswell, and I'll watch the window." Steve was holding two guns, his own and Estabal's. In the dull, lambent glow Cogswell watched Estabal. The man stood with his teeth bared, venomous, his flat face savagely defiant.

"Court's called," Steve said cheerfully. "Anything to say, Carlos?"

Carlos spat at him.

"You went up to Milt Prowers's room at the Toltec, didn't you, on the afternoon of the third? You was after him but he wasn't there. Right?"

Estabal dived toward the door. Cogswell caught him, tossed him back with a bang against the rear wall.

"You saw Pauly in a cab across the street," Steve resumed steadily. "You potted him. But first you propped a window open with a knife. Let's take a look at that knife, Carlos." Steve put two gun muzzles at his stomach and said, "Reach your hands up, if it's not too much trouble."

Carlos raised his hands. His eyes darted first to the window and then to the door. Steve passed one of the guns to Cogswell. Then with his free hand he began patting the prisoner's pockets. He produced from those pockets a soiled page from the *Evening Picketwire* of recent date, a sack of tobacco, and a pocketknife.

Cogswell took the knife and examined it. It was an ordinary clasp knife. When he opened its three blades he found that not one of them was broken. Every tip was intact. This knife, then, could not be the one used to prop open the hotel window.

"He probably used a skinning-knife for that," Steve said. "Maybe it's in a sheaf on his saddle. Watch him, while I go for a look."

Steve went outside to the horse. Cogswell remained there, covering Estabal. The only light came from the besmoked lantern. In the dimness, Cogswell failed to see one of the prisoner's feet move a little. Suddenly Estabal kicked at the grain box. It tipped over, the lantern with it. The lantern went out.

As Estabal dived at him, Cogswell fired in pitch-darkness. Pain shot through his own shoulder. He went down, felt Estabal's boot on his face. "Steve!" he yelled.

Steve was already in there, groping for Estabal in the dark. Then Cogswell got to his feet and fumbled for a match. He struck it. He saw Steve just within the door, in a position to make sure the prisoner couldn't escape that way. But the man *had* escaped. He was gone. Cogswell felt pain and blood at his shoulder. A long knife was impinged there.

Steve, at the first flicker of the match, ran outside. He yelled, "Stop!" Cogswell heard him shoot. He heard a horse gallop off. He knew that Estabal had dived through the paneless window and reached his horse.

When Cogswell staggered outside, both the man and his horse were gone. Cogswell could see nothing but the dim shape of Steve Lacey.

"Looks like you got his knife, after all." Steve plucked out the knife impinged in Cogswell's shoulder. It had passed through a double fold of the coat and taken only a pinch of skin.

It was a long hunting-knife. Estabal evidently had carried it in some concealed sheaf in his boot, on his back, or under his coat.

The blade was sharp, but half an inch of its tip was missing. Steve produced a handkerchief which, when unfolded, disclosed the clue found yesterday at the hotel window. A triangular bit of steel.

When he placed it in contact with the end of Estabal's blade, the steels matched. It was an exact fit.

CHAPTER THIRTEEN
BIRTH OF A COW RANCH

FOR THREE DAYS Sheriff Yates, on information lodged by Cogswell, combed the Rincon and all the other mesa slopes from Fisher's Peak to the Trinchera, in an effort to apprehend Estabal. Steve Lacey rode with the posse. Cogswell remained at home and completed the patching of the roof.

Estabal was not caught. The belief was that by now he had read certain facts published in the *Evening Picket-wire.* A zealous reporter had nosed these facts out. They were to the effect that the Pauly murder mystery was definitely solved by the broken tip of a knife blade.

"Carlos is below the border by now," Steve thought when he came back from the hunt. "And it probably won't be long until his cousins begin trailing along after him. They'll take the goatstuff with 'em."

"Leaving Prowers's wallet in our meadow," added Cogswell. "It looks like we're beginning to get some breaks."

"Any more purse hunters show up?" Steve asked. He was shaving in the south-wing apartment which he occupied jointly with Cogswell,

"Half a dozen of them." Cogswell laughed. "They all wanted to lease the ranch. That fellow Kincaid, the Frijoli sheepman, was the most persistent. A plausible chap, at that. Claimed he'd never heard of any lost billfold and offered me a quarter's rent in advance. I turned him down just the same. Then I put up a few 'No Trespass' signs around the race track. Today everything's been quiet."

"You and Miss Elsie about decided to operate this layout permanent?" Steve asked, as he wiped lather from his cheek.

"We've told Jackson to quit sending us lease prospects. It's sell for cash or we simply wait until we do. In the meantime we might as well let the place pay its way. So we've arranged a temporary copartnership. I'm advancing what little money I have, and we want your advice how to spend it, Steve."

That evening, on the starlit veranda, Steve delivered the advice.

"Stock the works," he told Cogswell and Elsie, "with as many cows as you can and as few horses. No money in horses; profits come from cows. Buy nothing but young stuff. Pay real money for young stuff and refuse old stuff as a gift."

"What do you mean by stuff?" Elsie asked.

"Stuff is any kind of livestock. Now there's different ways that the Rincon range might be stocked. You might stock it with steerstuff. That means you'd buy steer calves, just weaned, run 'em two and a half years and then sell 'em as three-year-old grass beef. Another way is to buy two-coming-three-year-old cows and never sell 'em, except at old age for canners. Your crop would be calves every season. Those Rincon benches are great bone builders for calves. I recommend the Cow-and-calf game."

"Fine," Cogswell agreed cheerfully. "Let's say we buy cows and sell calf crops. How much does a cow cost?"

"There's three kinds of cows," Steve explained. "Dogies, grades, and purebreds. Right now a dogie costs about ten dollars. A grade'll set you back about twenty; whereas a purebred heifer will run about sixty dollars."

Cogswell laughed. "That's easy. Inasmuch as I only have about four thousand dollars, we'll have to buy dogies."

"Don't do it," Steve warned. "Dogies would bust you. They're southern cattle, runnin' mostly to bellies and horns. Liable to be any color, and they never make real meat. Buy either grades or purebreds."

"Which would you get, grades or purebreds?"

"Grades now, ultimately purebreds if you stay here long enough. I'd advise purebreds now if you had the money and experience. The registered heifer costs three times as much, but her calf brings fancy prices. Registered calves aren't beefed, as a rule, you understand. Farmers and stockers all over the country buy 'em for breeders. As long as you run this ranch, keep your sails set toward winding up with a fancy, purebred outfit. Here are some of the reasons. You need fewer of them, which means you need fewer riders and horses—cowhands and broncos are what make stockmen die poor; you have less stock and your grass grows higher; and you play safe against the day when the open range is gone. Right now, assuming the goats leave, you have a forty-thousand-acre range. But you won't always have it. This country is migrating West, and some day all government land will be homesteaded. That will leave you with only six thousand deeded acres, and cut you to a small herd, anyway. When that happens you'll want few and fancy cattle."

Cogswell and Elsie exchanged glances. Each of them was amazed at Steve's farsightedness.

"But for a start," Steve said, "buy grades. Grades are native, or northern, cattle. They're color-marked like the standard native breeds, such as Hereford, Durham, Angus, but with no papers to prove it."

"How many of these grades should we buy?" Cogswell asked.

"Start easy. The Rincon will run three thousand head, but start with only three hundred. That way we'll need no hired help outside you and me. They'll cost you around six thousand dollars. Borrow it from the bank if you can, giving a chattel mortgage back as security. Save your own four thousand to buy teams, saddle horses, hay wagons, mowin'-equipment, saddles, fence wires, seed, grub, payroll, and such stuff. This fall we ought to plow up the race-track meadow and sow it to alfalfa."

"Can't we plow somewhere else?" Elsie objected, with a frown. "I don't want to spoil those pretty roses."

"It ought to be done, Miss Elsie," Steve argued. "It's the best meadow on the ranch. Old Don Ramon Estabal picked and graded it for his own hay stand, and he knew land. We could, though, use that level stretch of bottom across the creek. Meantime we'll need a little feed for this coming winter. Maybe we can find a few good spots of vega in the foothills, too low down to have been tramped out by goats. We might mow enough to fill the barn loft. Then we oughta lay in a few ton of cake."

He meant cottonseed-oil cake. He continued to expound the cow business until the brains of his auditors buzzed. But he made his thesis enticingly convincing. What pleased Cogswell most was to note that Elsie Claiborne's enthusiasm matched his own. Mention of this year and the next seemed not to daunt her in the least.

"Everything I have is invested here," Elsie said. "I have no place else to go. The house being divided into two private apartments, I can't see why I shouldn't stay here and run the place until we can sell it for at least half what it cost us."

That inaugurated the reclamation of the Rincon Ranch. Not many days later Stanley Cogswell borrowed six thousand dollars from the Picketwire National Bank, with which he purchased three hundred two-coming-three-year-old white-face heifers. Ballies, Steve called them.

"What about bulls?" he asked.

"We better get about seven, registereds, from a different outfit," Steve said. "If we got 'em from the same outfit, we'd maybe get inbred increase."

"Don't we have to brand these heifers?"

"Later, but not necessarily now. They've got a Diamond Six on 'em, and your bill of sale from the Diamond Six protects 'em. Any increase we get we'll slap on the CC." Cogswell had already taken out a brand, CC, from the State Brand Inspector's office in Denver.

"And we're due a small sprinkling of increase this fall," Steve added. "I notice some of those heifers are calvy right now."

They drove the heifers high into the Rincon, to quaking-asp timber a mile below the rimrock. They were left near a water hole about four miles east of the goat colony.

Cogswell rode back to the ranch. Steve rode over to find out what was going on at the goat colony.

At breakfast next morning he reported. "It won't be long now. They're getting ready to pull out. They've already sold most of the goats, saving only a small picked herd of the best milkers. In a week or two they'll be migratin' south over the mesa, drivin' those goats ahead of them by easy stages. In time they'll join Carlos south of the border."

Elsie Claiborne astonished them by bursting into tears.

"It makes me feel mean and guilty," she said later. "It's the only home those poor people have, and I feel like we're driving them away."

"But Steve explained that," Cogswell said gently. "They're just squatters, illegally trespassing. We can't help—"

"We *ought* to help them," she said. An intense sympathy was in her voice. "Why can't we let them stay there?"

"Because Steve says goats and cows don't mix."

"But they haven't so many goats now," she pleaded. "They've always been there. It would spoil everything, I mean it would make me feel cheap and miserable if we had anything to do with driving them away."

"But we're not driving them away," Cogswell argued.

Suddenly she turned to Steve Lacey. "It's our highest water hole they water at, isn't it?"

"Yes'm," Steve said. "Their shacks are just above it. There's about a thousand acres of government land, brushy and dry, between them and the rimrock."

"I wish we could help those poor people," she said. "Why not give them the use of our highest water hole? We could ask them to fence it off with the thousand acres between it and the rimrock. We could tell them they can stay inside that fence with their goats as long as they want to, couldn't we? Don't you think that would be right and fair, Mr. Cogswell?"

Cogswell saw her as he had never seen her before. Until now she had been just a pretty girl. Now she was a good deal more than that. Cogswell felt a warm glow himself. It made him know that he was in love with Elsie Claiborne. He said simply, "You are right. Steve, will you ride up there and tell them that?"

Elsie's hand impulsively found his own. "Thank you," she said. Then she took Steve's arm and went to the barn with him, stood by talking earnestly while he saddled his horse.

It was after dark when Steve came back. He found Cogswell and the girl in the prim little parlor.

"I told 'em," he reported. "A few of the orneriest of 'em are pullin' out, anyway. They'll head south to join Carlos. The best of 'em 'll stay right there, and they appreciate it a lot, Miss Elsie. They promise to build the fence and stay on the top thousand acres."

Elsie was radiant. "It makes me feel heaps better, Steve."

"One of them, his name's Pancho Estabal, came back with me. He's out at the gate now. He wants to thank you."

"Show him right in," she said promptly.

Steve brought in a small brown man, timid and dressed in ragged denims. Elsie shook hands with him. Cogswell gravely followed her example. The man stood servilely and embarrassed for a minute. Then he unleashed a chatter of Spanish.

Steve translated. "He says you are a kind lady. He says you are a gift to his people from the Holy Mother. He says they will always keep their goats above the fence, and never give you any trouble."

"Tell him we also shall be good neighbors," Elsie said.

Steve told him.

"Ask him if there are any children of school age in the colony."

Steve learned that there were three. Pancho had two between six and ten years. His brother, Arturo, had a thirteen-year-old boy.

"We must try to do something for them," she said. Again she shook hands with Pancho Estabal. She asked him to come back and see her again in a few days.

The man left, calling upon her head benedictions.

"I may be wrong," Steve said aside to Cogswell, "but I've an idea he'd fight his weight in wildcats for her, any time, any place."

The next morning Elsie asked Steve to drive her to town. They went in the buckboard. It was late evening when they returned.

"What did you do in town?" Cogswell asked.

"We didn't go to town," Steve said, grinning. "We stopped at a big Holstein dairy just this side, and Miss Elsie went in for a talk with the boss. She came out disappointed. Then she made me take her around to a dozen other dairies at the edge of town. Finally she landed a milking job for Pancho Estabal."

Cogswell stared at him.

"Sure she did," Steve said. "She figured if he can milk goats, he can milk Holstein cows. She finally talked a dairyman into takin' him on. Pancho will live in a shed there at the dairy, with his wife and two kids. The kids can go to school in town."

Cogswell felt a lump in his throat. "She's made us look pretty cheap, Steve."

"I reckon she has. I reckon we're learnin' a few things about how to win a grass war," Steve thought.

"Looking at the other fellow's side of it goes a long way."

"I guess it does. On the last showdown, I guess it beats all the bullets in the world."

For a few days Cogswell rode the mountain, getting acquainted with his cattle. Then he went to town with Steve and bought additional equipment. Most important was a haying-outfit.

Later, they harvested a few loads of vega, found in swales of the foothills where flood water had spread from the canyons. This was stored in the barn loft. There were dozens of things to do every day. Never in his life had Stanley Cogswell worked like this. He became as brown as Steve.

Night came like a cool benediction. Magnolia set out ample Southern suppers which the men ate ravenously. Then they would sit on the porch with Elsie and talk it all over. It was a strangely intimate partnership, more and more delightful to Stanley Cogswell. He gained weight. Cheer and vigor came to him on the Ranch of the Roses.

By mid-July the blooms of the race-track circle were gone, however, and the great meadow became a tangle of weeds and briars. Burdock, milkweed, thistle, all the parasites of mature season took possession of the field. When it could no longer lay claim to loveliness, Elsie was consoled by the tall, rank growth of hollyhocks along the picket fence. The yard lateral was now repaired, and a constant streamlet of clear water flowed through it. Cogswell whitewashed the pickets of the fence.

Gold Brick, suckled by a grain-fed mother, grew sturdily. Being raised in a corral, the colt became gentle. Elsie made a pet of him. She took over the chore of putting grain in the old mare's trough each day, a convenient duty because she had to go out anyway with a grain pail to feed chickens and ducks. Cogswell had stocked the barnyard, to the delight of Magnolia.

"This heah's beginnin' to look like a real plantation." The Negress chuckled. Twice a week, with gusto, she decapitated a fat cockerel.

No more lanterns were seen out in the meadow. They heard nothing more about Milton Prowers.

"Why do you keep lugging around that great pistol, Steve?" Elsie asked one evening. They were seated on the front steps, just as twilight was beginning to fail.

"Sort of a habit, I guess." Steve's blue eyes smiled. "But if you'd rather I'd—"

At that instant fate came conveniently to Steve's rescue. Squawks and quacks came from beyond one of the old dilapidated outbuildings. Then a gaunt coyote dashed into view. In its jaws was a large white duck. A forty-five appeared with eye-baffling suddenness in Steve's right hand. He was holding it with a grip braced rigidly against his hip.

He shot twice. No part of him moved except his trigger finger. His first shot missed. But the bullet plowed dirt ahead of the coyote, causing it to drop the duck. The duck waddled frantically away. At the second shot the marauder stopped, howled, turned to bite at a sting at his flank.

Then Steve fired a third time, and the beast crumpled, midway between the old church and the barn.

A week later Cogswell was riding through a copse of quaking asp high in the Rincon. Suddenly he rode outright into a brood of quarter-grown wild turkeys. The turkey hen ran past him, whistling a call to her *polios.* One of the *pollos,* panic-stricken, flew flapping its young wings with such small experience that it banged squarely into Cogswell's face. Only surprise kept the rider from snatching it with his hand.

Magnolia, when Cogswell reported the incident, was indignant.

"Just let one of them tukkeys go floppin' in my black face!" With her hands on her broad hips she rebuked Cogswell. "If it'd a been Mistuh Steve, I bet he'd a fetched one of them bi'ds home for suppah."

The next day Cogswell resumed the practice of pocketing his own pistol.

Occasionally Elsie rode up the mountain with him. But more often she rode with Steve. On that score Cogswell began to fret a little. He watched Steve. He decided that Steve was himself in love with the mistress of the ranch. For that Cogswell couldn't blame him. Nevertheless he began to be nettled whenever the two rode out together.

The twinge of jealousy grew sharper as the summer waned. Stanley Cogswell began to magnify small things, looks, words, inflections, began to translate them as evidence of a budding romance between his partner and his top hand.

He realized that as men about a cow ranch, Steve outpointed him in every act and judgment. Steve could ride, shoot; he could do anything, he knew everything. Cogswell was a novice. Small wonder, he fretted, if Elsie Claiborne should rate them as they stood, two men with boots on, in the roles of daily life! All the while Steve was comporting himself like a partner and a comrade. Cogswell was Mr. Cogswell; he handed out a check for forty dollars on the first of each month. Beyond that there was no social distinction.

Yet the blond top hand was never officious. He never gave advice unless it was asked for. Then his replies were definite, confident, thorough. He was man-to-man with Cogswell and man-to-woman with the girl. Cogswell himself was always ready to lean on Steve's advice and yet, as the season waned, he became annoyed because Elsie was even readier. To her Steve was an oracle, a wise man of the West. "Steve says we mustn't," or "Steve says we ought to," she would say.

By night the green imp harassed Cogswell, danced on his brain, robbed him of sleep. He became morose, irritable. "She thinks he's the only man around here," he kept fretting.

One morning he arose early for a turn outside before breakfast. Steve's cot was empty. When he emerged on the porch he saw his top hand in the distance. Steve, he saw, was out in the center of the race-track circle kicking about in the briars. Cogswell stared at him unkindly. The imp in his brain began whispering. This was the fourth time he had found Steve out there in the meadow in the first light of summer dawn.

Why was he so persistently there?

Later in the day the proposition came up again about plowing for an alfalfa stand. Time and again Steve had said that a ranch wasn't a real ranch until it had a perennial hay stand for winter feed, and that alfalfa was the roughage most suitable for this particular soil and climate.

"The race-track circle is the place for it," he advised again. "It's graded and rigged up with lateral ditches. Ramon Estabal picked it and he knew his business."

"I'll hire a plow hand for that job," Cogswell said, "so you. can look after the cows."

"Better let me do it myself," Steve said. "Bring in an outsider and he might not get under the roots of those briars. That meadow's got to be plowed deep."

"Why," the imp whispered to Cogswell, "is he so anxious to plow it himself?"

"Please, Steve," Elsie begged, "let's leave the circle as it is. We have other waste land, and those roses look so pretty in June." On that one point she was stubborn. "Let's sow alfalfa across the creek."

"Why, of course, Miss Elsie," Steve agreed. He went to the barn to rig an evener for a four-horse plow team.

When he was gone Cogswell blurted out petulantly, "Why do we have to say please to Steve? It's for us to choose our meadow and for him to plow it. You'd think he was boss around here."

Elsie stared at him. Her black eyes had never been so wide and round. "Why, Mr. Cogswell!"

"This 'Please, Steve' is getting under my skin," he said crossly.

"But what on earth would we do without Steve's advice?" she argued. "He always knows best, doesn't he? He's right this time. It's just my sentimental stubbornness that makes me want to save those roses."

That was too much. The imp goaded Cogswell, and words rushed from his lips. "He wants to plow that circle himself, you notice. He doesn't want me to hire a plowhand. Why? And why does he always get up at daylight and kick around in the briars?"

Her eyes were even rounder. "Well, why?"

"He's thinking about that billfold of Prowers. It's on his mind all the time. Suppose he finds it! Our money, our sixty thousand dollars! Do you think he'd say anything about it? Do you think he'd bring it to the house?"

Her face flushed. Her chin went up. Her voice was like ice. "Yes, I think he would. I *know* he would, Mr. Cogswell."

She turned her back severely and went to her room.

CHAPTER FOURTEEN
HOT IRONS

THE RESTRAINT ENGENDERED by that tiff lasted several weeks. Cogswell was miserably penitent. Sober reflection told him that he'd been unfair to Steve. He abused himself for a jealous, blundering fool.

Elsie was right, he reasoned. Of course Steve, if he should happen to find that wallet, would deliver it to the owners of the ranch. Anything else was unthinkable. The more so because Steve was himself enamored with Elsie Claiborne. Of that Cogswell was sure. Steve wasn't a man to wear his heart on his sleeve, yet there was always a quick, eager movement of his head at her footstep, always a light on his face when she called his name.

As autumn advanced, Elsie formed the habit of riding out every afternoon. The daughter of a Kentucky horse fancier, she rode well. She rode with skirt and sidesaddle, according to the traditions she had known.

More often she rode with Steve, but Cogswell happened to be her companion when they found the calf first born to the CC brand. It was on a chineried bench, just short of the first coniferous timber up the Rincon slope.

"That cow's all by herself, Mr. Cogswell." She pointed to an animal which grazed alone in the center of the bench and without any other bovine in sight.

If Steve had been there, he could have told them why the cow was alone.

Cogswell said, "That's funny; they always herd in bunches. But she's our stuff, all right. I can see the Diamond Six from here." He was getting proficient with terms like "stuff."

They rode on, dipping across a brushy ravine and up onto another bench where there were no cattle. Clumps of scrub oak dotted the bench. They were half a mile from where they had encountered the lone cow when the girl's hat, a wide-brimmed leghorn, blew from her head.

"I'll get it," Cogswell called. But Elsie had already dismounted. She was reaching into the chinery bush where the hat had lodged. Suddenly she drew back quickly. "Oh, how perfectly darling!"

Cogswell came up to see what she had found. Lying on the ground within the screen of the bush, he saw a ball of red-and-white flesh, as immobile as a hair cushion. It was curled up, its soft white nose stretched back on its flank. It regarded the invaders, but the pink eyelids did not blink.

They stood watching it with a degree of awe. It struck them as pitiful—this tiny calf forsaken here by all creatures of its kind.

Yet it was an exciting find. It brought a fine thrill to them. True there was Gold Brick, the colt, the first increase of chattel, yet this infant calf brought a fine and awful thrill. Here was life, accrued to their own support and care, born high up on this lonely mountain.

In a minute Elsie was distressed. "Poor thing! Its mother's gone away and left it. Or maybe it got lost!"

"That must have been her we saw half a mile back, over on that other bench," Coswell said. It seemed to him that he had noticed that the cow's bag had been full, almost swollen.

"Why on earth do you suppose she deserted the calf?"

"It beats me." Cogswell was hardly less concerned. "First thing you know some timber wolf will happen along and have veal for supper."

All this while the calf hadn't moved. Elsie reached into the bush and stroked the silky, white-lined back of it. The calf twitched one velvet ear, moving no other muscle.

They couldn't bring themselves to leave the calf. Not while there were wolves loose in the woods. "We'll hang around until its mother shows up," Cogswell said.

They took seats on the ground and waited an hour. No cow appeared.

"I don't like it," Cogswell said. "It'd be bad luck to lose our first calf."

"Maybe the poor little thing's hungry," Elsie worried. "Maybe we ought to take it to the house."

Cogswell thought that was impractical. "Tell you what we'll do. We'll ride over and drive that cow to her calf. Let's go."

Mounting, they rode across the ravine to the other bench. The cow was still there, grazing alone. The two riders got behind it, and Cogswell yelled, "Hiah, hiah!"

The cow drove docilely for a hundred yards or so; then she became exasperatingly stubborn.

She balked. Finally she became wild-eyed and excited, lifted her tail high and cut back in a gallop between the drivers. Cogswell rode hard to head her off. But when they got her back to the ravine between the two benches she eluded them again. This time she cut straight upslope to the coniferous timber.

Cogswell and Elsie followed. Just inside the timber they found the cow at a standstill. With difficulty they got her out and again headed toward the calf. For a third time she dodged back. She would go any direction except that one.

"I'll bet she's loco," Cogswell complained. He had heard Steve speak of a poison weed which grew sparsely in the Rincon, the consumption of which was likely to make either a horse or a cow almost undrivable.

"Anyway, she seems determined to desert that poor calf," Elsie worried. "I think we'd better go tell Steve about it."

That was it. In all emergencies they had to fall back on Steve.

Riding home, they found Steve at the barn. He had just come from work and was unhitching his four-horse plow team. The job of plowing the level strip of bottom land across the creek was now almost completed.

"We've got a dear little calf, Steve," Elsie announced. "But its mother won't claim it."

"The little dickens is sure lost and a long way from home," Cogswell supplemented. He told about their efforts at forcing the cow to join her calf.

Tiny crowfeet of amusement formed at the corners of Steve's eyes. His cheeks creased. Then quickly he passed a hand over his bronzed face. In a moment he was gravely sympathetic.

"Cow deserted her calf, did she? Well, maybe you folks made her ashamed of herself. Maybe she's behavin' better now. Let's see."

It was near sunset, and the level light was shining squarely on the Rincon benches. Steve went into the barn and came out with a pair of range glasses. He trained them on a particular bench a mile and a half above them and to the southeast. At last, with a grin, he handed the glasses to Elsie.

Elsie, still seated on her horse, looked intently in the direction indicated. When her eyes turned they were smiling sheepishly. "You're making fun of us, Steve. Go ahead and laugh all you want to. I don't care."

She passed the glasses to Cogswell. With them Cogswell made out two dots of life, high on the distant bench. The larger dot was walking slowly across the bench, its head turned back all the while encouragingly. The smaller dot was wobbling along about two lengths behind.

"Yeh," Steve said, "that cow sure got repentant after you folks left. Went right over there and claimed that calf. Bet she hides it this time where you couldn't find it in a week."

He was right. A week passed before human eyes saw that calf again.

That fall and in the early winter a dozen more calves were born on the Rincon Rranch. Cogswell, riding forth daily, took note of the increase with a growing pride.

Steve was too busy to ride. He finished plowing fifty acres across the creek, harrowed them, dragged them with an old barn door heaped with stones. For a sparse nurse crop he used wheat. Snow flew at last, but it wasn't necessary to round up the cattle and bring them down from the benches. Winter itself accomplished the roundup, causing the herd to seek lower and warmer levels. Bunch by bunch they drifted down to the cottonwood bottom.

On Steve's advice Cogswell bought and stored five tons of oil cake.

"We won't need it with an open winter," Steve said. "But we got to be prepared, seein' as there's no hay stacked."

Luckily it was an open winter. Deep snow fell on the higher levels, but the fall on the flats never exceeded three inches. Intervals of warmth swiftly melted these light snows. Not a pound of cake was fed.

"Save it for next winter," Lacey said. "We'll have a few haystacks by then, too. That means we could take on another three hundred head of cowstuff."

The first casualty was old Bess, mother of Gold Brick. The ancient mare lay down beside her grain trough in the corral one evening; in the morning she was dead. Grain-fed though she was, the husky stallion colt had drained her strength by seven months of vigorous nursing.

But the colt was now weanable. Reared at a feed trough he had learned that the world offered other nourishment than milk. He was an outstanding colt, weighing nearly five hundred pounds at the time of his enforced weaning.

"The spit image of his granddaddy, Don Quixote!" Steve admired more than once. He continued the practice of leaving the corral gate open, so that Gold Brick could roam at will from feed trough to the creek. The routine kept him gentle and easily approached.

The next casualty came near to being Cogswell himself.

"That east drift fence ought to be tacked where the wire's loose," Steve said one April morning. "It ought to be done before we haze the cowstuff uphill for summer, too. We ought to brand what few calves we got, next week or so."

"Leave that drift-fence chore to me," Cogswell offered.

Early one morning he rode east. The Rincon range was not fenced as a whole. Its south limit being the rimrock, no fence was needed there. From the projecting hubs of this U-shaped rimrock, drift fences led downslope through the timber and out a few miles on the flats below, forming a trap rather than an enclosure. The two drift fences were old, having been built originally by Don Ramon Estabal.

Cogswell, equipped with hammer, staples, and a few pieces of baling-wire for patching, rode until he struck the east drift fence. There was no snow on the ground. It was a balmy spring morning.

He found the fence in better shape than he expected. In the first mile of his ride along it he had to dismount only occasionally to tack fallen wire. Then he topped a rise and came upon a three-year-old cow. The cow was standing on the west side of the fence, with her white neck stretched over it; she was bawling plaintively toward the east. Cogswell recognized the cow by the fact that she was line-backed—the white of her neck extending on down the ridge of her back.

She was the very same cow which Cogswell, six months ago, had attempted to force back to her newborn calf. Cogswell hadn't seen the calf for several weeks. The cow was branded Diamond Six and held by bill of sale.

Why was the cow bawling? She was not only bawling but she was pawing at the fence. Cogswell now saw that the fence between these two posts was patched with baling-wire. The baling-wire was bright and new. Recently someone had repaired a gap here.

But repaired none too well, for the cow, even as Cogswell watched, broke through. An old fence post snapped at its rotten root, and two wires severed. The cow jumped over the remaining two wires and started east at a trot. Cogswell got his horse through and followed.

The cow trotted ahead of him, bawling lustily. Her course was as straight as the flight of a crow. She topped a rise, Cogswell following. This rise was the backbone of the sloping divide between the watersheds of Rincon Creek and the San Isidro. Cogswell could now see the San Isidro's cottonwood canyon, with the bald tableland of Johnson Mesa rising beyond. He saw something else, nearer. The smoke of a fire.

Then he made out a man squatting by the fire. Lying on its side near by, one hind foot bound to two fore feet, was a six-months-old calf. The calf was bawling. The man was applying a hot iron to its flank.

The line-backed cow, Cogswell ahorse at her heels, made straight toward the bawling calf. The man saw them. He dropped his branding iron and stood up. His face flushed. A gun appeared in his right hand.

The man had fired twice before Cogswell even thought about the gun on his own hip. A third bullet sang by. A fourth burned through Cogswell's leg and his horse reared. He got his gun out. Before he could aim it, a fifth bullet creased the mane of his mount; the animal squealed, plunging frantically.

The plunging unbalanced Cogswell. He fell heavily to the ground. His ankle snapped like a brittle stick. The pain of it goaded him to fury. He writhed to one knee, saw the smoke of the branding-fire, saw a thickset man with a warty face and a red mustache standing by it. The man was cramming five new shells into his gun.

With an unsteady wrist Cogswell covered him. The earth was spinning, and the range was thirty yards. He had no idea he could hit the man. He had never shot at anything but rocks and rabbits. "Hands up, you!" he yelled in a strange voice.

Instead, the man fired again. Cogswell began pulling his own trigger. Bullets came at him. He gave bullets in return. All this while he was on the dizzy edge of a faint. It all seemed fantastic, unreal. It was like a nightmare. Even with a powder stench choking him and with warm blood on his thigh, even then he could hardly believe he was here, shot and shooting, taking or giving death.

He fired his last shell. Through a mist he saw the warty man look surprised, stagger a pace to one side, and fall in a sprawl. Cogswell stared at him crazily, then tried to get up. Pain pulled him down. He grew dizzier. He thought he heard the hoofbeats of his horse as the animal retreated toward the fence gap. The earth spun faster; he heard the bawlings of a calf and a cow. Then the pain and the nausea whipped him, and he fainted dead away.

A creaking brought him to his senses. He opened his eyes. Steve Lacey, on the seat of a buckboard, was pulling up beside him. A few blocks of sulphuretted salt were in the bed of the vehicle.

Then Steve was kneeling by him, supporting his head, holding a canteen to his lips. A look of complete understanding and sympathy was on the cowboy's face. "Knew you'd had grief," he said, "when your bronc came loping by with a bloody mane. I was haulin' salt around to the water holes."

Steve looked over toward where a man lay on the ground, thirty yards away. The hog-tied calf was still there, and a smoking fire. A cow stood by, bawling.

"You don't need to tell me a thing," Steve said gently. "Can't I see a fresh-scorched UBAR9 on the calf? That's Ike Zachary's iron." He had once described Zachary as a "fine, upstanding calf thief from Johnson Mesa."

Now he went over and released the calf. The calf ran to the Diamond Six cow, who claimed it maternally. "That alone's enough evidence to close the matter up, with only a question or two," Steve said. "There's plenty more, though; we'll leave it right here for Yates to see himself." He motioned toward the fire, the UBAR9 branding iron in it, and brass shells scattered on the ground about Zachary's gun. Zachary himself was shot through the brain and was dead.

Then Steve got Cogswell to the seat of the buckboard. He loaded the dead man into the bed of the wagon and drove off toward home.

Again it all seemed hideously unreal to Cogswell. Had he really shot it out with a cattle thief? Had he really killed the man? It seemed outrageously impossible. It seemed to put him absurdly out of character. Cimarron Steve Lacey might have done a thing like that, but not he himself, Stanley Cogswell.

They made the house by noon. Steve stopped at the barn first, got a tarp, and used it to cover the corpse of Zachary. Then he drove on to the picket gate.

He carried Cogswell in and laid him on a bed. Elsie and Magnolia came in. The Negress rolled her eyes. Elsie dropped to her knees beside Cogswell. Cogswell felt her hands touch his face tenderly.

"A run-in with a rustler named Zachary," Steve explained. He added no details. They could see for themselves that Cogswell was shot through the thigh. The same leg was broken at the ankle. Silently Steve bathed and bandaged both the wound and the break.

Cogswell slipped into another faint.

"I'll drive to town now," Steve said, "and bring a doctor."

"And you bettah fetch de sheriff out, Mastih Steve," Magnolia said indignantly, "fer to put he hand on dat no-count white trash, Zackarias!"

Steve averted his eyes. He preferred not to explain, just now, that that part of it wouldn't be necessary.

But when he went out to the buckboard, Elsie followed him. She wanted to know more about it.

"You go in the house, Miss Elsie," Steve evaded. "I better be joggin' in to town. Get up, Brownie, Nellie."

But she stood holding to the side of the wagon bed, staring. A tarpaulin was spread there. She saw a long, rounded bulge. Whatever was obscured lay quite motionless.

The girl sensed what was there. Her eyes widened in horror. Her cheeks went white. She shrank back from the wagon bed. Steve jumped down from his seat. His arm went around her to keep her from falling.

"You killed him, Steve?"

"The only reason I didn't," he said gently, "was because I wasn't there. This fellow began shooting first. Six inches higher and he'd have killed the whitest boss I ever had."

She knew then that Cogswell had killed Zachary. She hid her face. "This is ghastly!" she cried. "Killing men like this! The ranch, the cattle—nothing is worth it."

He said gently, "I know it isn't your way, Miss Elsie. You showed us your way, and it's the best way. It beats bullets. But this time there wasn't anything else to do." His arm was still around her. His voice was tender. He was like a mother with a child. "Please go in and take care of him, Miss Elsie."

She steadied herself and went into the house.

Steve drove to town with the body of Ike Zachary.

CHAPTER FIFTEEN
THE FROLIC AT FRIJOLI

H E WAS BACK FOR SUPPER, bringing Dr. Wade Houts with him. The next day the sheriff, the coroner, and the district attorney came out. They asked a few questions. Only a few, for they knew the reputation of Ike Zachary. Steve took them over to see the ashes of a fire, with empty brass shells and a UBAR9 iron beside it. He showed them a Diamond Six cow suckling a calf freshly branded UBAR9.

"A plain case of catching a thief in the act," the district attorney admitted.

"A self-defense homicide," the coroner added.

Yates growled, "We ought to pin a medal on Cogswell." Yates had been a cowman before he was sheriff.

The matter was dropped. The only other reference Cogswell ever heard to it came on his trip to town after recovering from the encounter. He was at the counter of a cigar store buying tobacco. In a far corner two loafers were discussing him in whispers.

"They tell me that fellah's plain poison for rustlers," one whispered.

"Bet they leave his calfstuff alone after this," the other said.

Cogswell left the store with a flush on his lean cheeks. Talk like that mortified him. He knew it put him in a false light.

Down the street he found Steve, who had driven him in, talking to a big, hearty stranger. "Your bunk at the Bar 37's waiting for you, Steve, any time you want it."

"Thanks," Steve said. "But I like the job I got now."

"Well, if you ever change your mind, drop around."

The man passed on.

"Who was that?" Cogswell asked.

"Big cowman I used to work for, in Texas," Steve explained.

They drove home. On the way, a sticky, wet snow began falling.

"Just what we need," Steve said. "Not only for spring grass but to give that new alfalfa a real start. Next job's to brand what few calves we got and push the bunch uphill."

At supper he said to Elsie, "I stepped in at Hogan's dairy to see how that milkhand you wished on 'em, Pancho Estabal, is makin' out. He and his family are doin' fine. Gettin' civilized. Their two kids are in school."

"I wonder if we could do something for his brother Arturo's thirteen-year-old boy," Elsie puzzled. "That goat colony is no place for children."

They decided to offer the boy a job as chore boy here at the Rincon Creek ranch. The increase of work justified it.

"The boy's name is Eusebio," Steve said. "He'd be tickled to death with twenty a month and found. And he could earn it. First we brand, which needs a three-man crew. Then we ought to get three hundred more cows, now that the goat smell is leaving the benches. We'll have hay enough to feed six hundred head through the winter. We'll need the boy to help harvest that hay. In the fall we ought to plow again and double the hay stand."

The next day they sent for Eusebio Estabal. They found him slim-chested, timid, with sharp, hatchetlike features the color of a copper kettle. The ranch awed him, but he was willing to work.

Steve rigged up a branding-chute. There were only forty-one calves, merely the increase with which the heifers had been heavy at time of purchase. These were run through the chute in short order, Eusebio hazing the calves into the chute, Cogswell working the squeeze lever, while Steve applied the big C iron twice to the left ribs.

The calves were returned to their mothers, and the men went to the house.

At the wash bench outside the kitchen door, Steve said, "Wash up and come right in to dinner, Eusebio."

It raised a point Cogswell hadn't thought of. Just how was the boy going to fit in, domestically, in a household already diversified with a Kentucky girl of Bourbon blood, an ex-professional man from New York, and a western cowboy?

Elsie was already seated when they entered the kitchen. "Where do you want Eusebio?" Steve asked.

"Sit right next to me, Eusebio." She was a thoroughbred in the truest sense, Cogswell saw.

The boy bowed timidly. "Very thanks, señora."

"But I am not a señora," Elsie protested, and the boy was all pardons. He had assumed her to be the wife of either Cogswell or Steve.

That afternoon they pushed the cattle up onto one of the lower benches of the Rincon. Steve said they'd drift higher as the season advanced, following the retreat of the snow line.

"Won't stuff from neighboring ranches come in?" Cogswell asked.

"A few," Steve said. "Not many on account of the drift fences, and the lay of this range. Folks around here know we own all the water in the Rincon. Most cowmen'll grab all the grass they can, but they won't mooch water. To get what few drift in here they'll send straymen, every so often."

A week later Cogswell called at the Picketwire National Bank. He asked Cashier Clarke to accept interest to date on his note, to extend his note for six months, and to lend an additional six thousand dollars for the purchase of three hundred more cows.

"How's your feed?" Clarke asked.

"We've only got in fifty acres of alfalfa," Cogswell admitted, "but we'll double it this fall. Stored five tons of cake last winter and got by without using any of it."

"What's your overhead?"

"I do the work with the help of two men, Steve Lacey at forty dollars and a chore boy at twenty."

The cashier slapped his customer on the back. "I'm going to take a chance on you, Cogswell. I like that Rincon layout because it's isolated. No mixed roundups. It's these cowmen who run stuff all over hell's creation, which takes a big outfit of riders and a big cavvy of mounts, who're the tough risks. Overhead eats 'em up. There are two more reasons. You're one. We haven't forgot the time you stood pat on that Prowers's check, protecting this bank. I mean the time you could have left us holding the bag by wiring a stop order to New York. The other reason is Steve Lacey. I like that fellow, and I understand you're operating on his advice."

The loan made Cogswell's total indebtedness to the bank twelve thousand at eight per cent. The copartnership of Cogswell-Claiborne also owed about three thousand, at four per cent, to Cogswell personally. He had been writing personal checks for equipment and payroll right along.

Three hundred more heifers, coming-threes, and eight more young bulls were purchased and pushed up the Rincon. The CC was coming into its own as a stock ranch. Cogswell rode the benches almost daily, keeping an accurate tally on all bunches. Occasionally he found strays. He let them stray until he chanced to meet the owners on the road or in town, when he would make mention of them. Usually an owner would send a stray-man around within a week. Thus trespassing cattle were kept to an inconsiderable figure.

"Not that we can't spare the grass," Steve said. "It's the habit. We don't want to let the habit get started. Some day we'll have enough stuff to graze the whole Rincon. Meantime, what grass we don't graze is resting. Grass needs rest. That's why it grew higher on the plains in the old buffalo days than it does now. There were no cows, and the range was understocked with buffalo. Grass got a chance to rest."

June came, and the big circular meadow bloomed again in a riot of pink and white blossoms. Elsie enthused over them. Her cheeks were as pink as the roses. The black dress in which Cogswell had first seen her was laid aside. Now she wore pretty, colorful ginghams and prints.

Cogswell himself presented an aspect quite unlike that of his first appearance at the ranch. He had gained twenty pounds, and his face was wind-burned. He went about in a flannel shirt and with pants legs tucked into spurred half boots. On days which took him high into the timber he wore *chaparejos.*

Cogswell had given up all thought or effort toward finding the billfold in the race-track circle. That it was there now seemed almost as improbable as a myth. He was inclined to ridicule the theory whenever it was mentioned. Steve, on the other hand, took the idea as seriously as ever.

"How else can we explain those nightly prowls with a lantern?" he would always say. "What else could Estabal have been looking for except that wallet of Prowers's? The question is—how much was in it? Did Prowers have the whole stake? Or just part of it?"

Often, especially of mornings, Lacey would take a walk around the meadow, kicking here and there in the briars in search of the purse.

"Best way to find it's to plow the circle for alfalfa." Steve was obsessed with that point. "We ought to get rid of those ornery briars, anyway."

"You'll have to get rid of me first," Elsie would always object.

In July they had a strange caller. When the man drove up in a livery rig, Cogswell chanced to be at the gate.

"I'm lookin' for a Miss Claibo'ne of Lexington, Kaintucky," the man said.

Cogswell was at a loss to classify him. In some ways he looked like a prosperous stockman, yet in other details he appeared foreign to the range. He was a midget, barely over five feet, gray-whiskered and about sixty years old. He wore loose-fitting corduroys and a creased Panama hat.

Bud LeFever was the name he gave Cogswell.

"Why, Uncle Bud! Where on earth did *you* come from?" Elsie Claiborne ran down the steps, rushed to the gate, and kissed the stranger with warm affection.

LeFever held her at arm's length. "Bless my soul, if she ain't purtier 'n ever!"

Cogswell was introduced. He learned that LeFever was no relation to the girl, but had been a valued retainer of her father's in Colonel Claiborne's palmier days. LeFever had, in fact, been the trusted and efficient trainer of the colonel's racing-stable back in Kentucky, in the days when Claiborne was an important character around bluegrass tracks.

"Got a few colts of my own, now," LeFever told Elsie. "Nothin' fancy, y'understand. But I'm buildin' up all the time. Might win a race yet befo' they measure me for a coffin. Right now I'm on my way home from Califo'nia where I went to look at a young stud."

"Did you take him on?" Cogswell asked.

"No, suh. Didn't like the legs of 'im, suh."

LeFever was installed as an honored guest. Magnolia donned her best bib and apron, put out for his delectation enormous servings of fried chicken. No effort was spared to make the old trainer feel at home.

Cogswell offered to take him riding up the mountain for a look at the cows. But LeFever wasn't interested in cows. He was one-hundred-per-cent horseman. Horses were the one passion of his life. On the second day of his visit he noticed a yearling colt out in the corral, a big, rangy sorrel with no white marking except a cross on the forehead.

Cogswell saw him walk around this yearling about ten times. He backed off, pulling at his gray mustache, cocking a critical eye. Then LeFever perched on the corral fence and studied the colt for an hour. At supper time he inquired, "Where did you get hold of that track stud?"

"Didn't know we had one," Cogswell answered. He had forgotten that Gold Brick was a descendant of racing-stock.

"I mean that big sorrel yearlin'," LeFever said. "There's track blood somewhe'e in them long laigs o' his. Why, suh, if I'd seen him anywhe'e 'cept on a cow ranch, I'd a put him down for a regular paddock show hawse."

"Ever hear of a stallion named Don Quixote?" Steve asked.

"Which Don Quixote?" Suddenly the trainer bristled with interest. "You don't mean *the* Don Quixote, do you, suh? That big, white-starred sorrel that—" LeFever stopped suddenly; his deep-brown eyes became intensely reminiscent. He went on as though talking to himself. "Yes, he was a sorrel with nary a white sock, only with a white cross in his forehead. Won the Planters' Sweepstakes at New Awl'ns eighteen, no, it was nineteen years ago!"

"That's the horse," Steve prompted. "He belonged to a sport named Ramon Estabal."

"Right you are, suh. And do I remembah that race? I reckon I do. Yo' father, Elsie, had a three-yeah-old in the same start. But he placed second. It was Don Quixote that romped home by five lengths."

Steve explained that this ranch had once belonged to Ramon Estabal. "That yearling out in the corral is Don Quixote's grandson," he said.

LeFever became too excited to eat. "What are you all plannin' to do with that colt?" he demanded.

There were no plans.

The next day Bud LeFever inaugurated a plan. He was out in the corral admiring Gold Brick when Elsie joined him. Cogswell, Steve, and Eusebio were across the creek stacking alfalfa.

"Look heah, Elsie, there's real possibilities in this yea'lin'. Why not try him out?"

"You mean on our track, Uncle Bud?"

"No. He's got to be trained first, Elsie. He's got to get mo' age and size and he needs a real track jockey. Him sproutin' from Don Quixote has set me thinkin'. Why not let me ship him to my stable, back in Kaintuck, and train him fo' you?"

"That, I'm afraid," Elsie objected, "would be a bigger gamble than we can afford. It would cost a lot of money, and we need all we have to pay interest at the bank." She went on to explain how Cogswell had advanced all his personal funds to operate the ranch, and that they had no surplus at all.

LeFever stood staring at the yearling for a while, tugging at his mustaches. Then he said, "I know how to take the gamble out of it, as far as you're concerned. Suppose I ship the colt at my expense, and train him fo' two yeahs. Then suppose, for my trouble and expense, I take just what I can earn off him in one three-year-old start. That is, I run him once for what there is in it, then he's yours, a trained race hawse."

"That wouldn't be fair to you," she objected.

"Yes, it would," LeFever insisted. "Not such a big gamble for me, 'cause I'm runnin' a track stable, anyway. One mo' hawse won't crowd me any. And I got a hunch. Got a hunch I could play this colt for a clean-up on long money. Who knows him? Nobody. He'll be a rank outsider and pull long odds. Anyway, I'll gamble. Give 'im to me for two years, then he's yours for keeps, a trained hawse."

They argued at length, but finally Elsie capitulated. From the ranch's standpoint there was nothing to lose and everything to gain. It was agreed that LeFever should take the yearling and train it for two years at his expense, in return for any profit which might accrue during that period.

When he heard of it, the deal rather amused Cogswell. He offered no objection. A week later the colt went to Kentucky with

Bud LeFever, who was to be its legal guardian for the next two years.

At the Rincon Ranch, Gold Brick was soon forgotten in a rush of work. There was mowing, raking, shocking, and stacking of hay. This was no sooner accomplished with one crop before it became necessary to clean laterals and irrigate for the next. Then there were stack pens to be built. Twice during the summer, cloudburst floods carried away the rock and brush diversion dam which fed the main ditches, and the dam had to be rebuilt. Then there was the occasional riding of the drift fences and keeping check on the cattle. Whenever he had a day to spare from those duties, Steve put it in plowing across the creek. The alfalfa acreage must be doubled by next year.

"Ranch life is just one chore and then another," Steve said.

It was. The risings and the settings of suns were the only limits of work. Hard work. But Stanley Cogswell thrived under it. And the results were well worth the effort. By mid-October, when the third hay crop was finally harvested, there were nine stacks, three each in three stack pens. The last three were pea-green. The look and the smell of them was good.

The night after the last stacking, Cogswell, Steve, and Elsie sat on the porch and watched a fine, round harvest moon float on the rimrock. Eusebio Estabal sat on the steps, sharpening a knife on the sole of his shoe. Somewhere within the house they could hear Magnolia singing an old plantation song. Out in the corral they could see a dark mass of life, work horses crowding around a rick of new-mown hay. They were tired, all of them, work horses and working men. But—

"Ranch life is just one chore and then another," Steve reminded. He bent his blond head over a lighted match. In the glow his face shone like polished copper. "Tomorrow we got to round up and brand. I look for a purty good calf crop; maybe two hundred sixty-seventy calves."

So the work horses got a rest, but the men and saddle stock didn't. The next day they began bringing cattle down from the mountain. By November first the CC was stamped on two hundred and forty-four calves. Casualties of the summer season were but three—and they found all three carcasses. One cow and two calves. The cow from lightning. One calf had tried to ascend a niche of the rimrock and had broken its neck. Steve's guess on the third casualty was rattlesnake poison.

"Less than a normal loss for our size herd," he said. "We're lucky, because we took a big chance on blackleg. Next year we'd better breed dewlaps."

It was decided to sell the steer calves and keep the heifers for stockers. A Sunflower Valley feeder bid twelve dollars per head, which made the steer calves bring seventeen hundred dollars. After paying interest and a small amount on principal at the bank, Cogswell had six hundred dollars left. He handed half of this to Elsie Claiborne.

He didn't tell her that he was putting his own slim dividend back into the ranch. He had no choice, for the wheels of operation had to turn. The cost of equipping the property had drained his original resources to the last cent.

To save Elsie worry he did not tell her that. She accepted her three-hundred-dollar dividend and went blithely to town for a day's shopping. It was the first money she had handled for more than a year, and her wardrobe, naturally, had become almost shabby.

Cogswell drove her to town. There he left her to her own devices until midafternoon. When he rejoined her at an appointed corner, he found her talking to a tall, barrel-chested man whom Cogswell had met several times and knew to be Buck Kincaid, the Frijoli Creek sheepman. Kincaid was in his middle thirties, smooth-shaven and well dressed. His nose was a trifle too red, Cogswell thought. Beyond that his only prejudice lay in the fact that this man had been one of the would-be opportunists who had tried to lease the Rincon Ranch just after the published notice about the lost billfold. Steve, Cogswell recalled, had said that Kincaid's proposition was in all likelihood insincere, that his real motive for leasing centered on the lost money.

Here now, on a street corner, was Buck Kincaid, in attentive conversation with Elsie. He withdrew at Cogswell's approach. The blow fell as they were driving home.

"You and Steve have been working too hard," the girl said. "Both of you should relax; you must go to the big dance they're having next Friday night at the Frijoli schoolhouse."

Cogswell knew there was a schoolhouse at Frijoli Creek, because the road to the ranch passed right by it. He had heard nothing, however, of a dance. Immediately he enthused over the prospect.

"Great! We'll all drop in there and have a hot time. Where did you find out about it?"

"From Mr. Kincaid. He's going to take me."

Cogswell stared at her. "He's going to take *you!*"

"Of course. Why not?"

Cogswell was so stunned by the news that he could hardly say a word all the rest of the way home. The idea of Kincaid horning in like that! Although at times he had nursed brief twinges of jealousy in regard to Steve Lacey, Cogswell had completely omitted outsiders from his calculations. He was in love with Elsie and was reasonably sure that Steve was, too. All his fears had been of Steve. Now it suddenly appeared that there were other men in the world eligible to be charmed by Elsie Claiborne.

And what could he do about it? Nothing. On the other hand he was forced to concede that both he and Steve were inexcusably at fault. Elsie was young. She needed fun. He and Steve had been busy pitching hay and chasing calves by day, basking by evenings in the girl's companionship, entirely overlooking the possibility that she might not be deriving a commensurate enjoyment from theirs. Now the sheepman, Kincaid, had stolen a march on both of them.

He was taking her to the Frijoli frolic. The nerve of him!

That evening Cogswell and his top hand were blood brothers. Down at the barn they conferred at length in whispers. The phrase they employed most earnestly was "That damned Frijoli sheepman."

Friday evening brought Buck Kincaid. He drove up in a smart top buggy pulled by a team of spanking bays. Kincaid himself was rigged up like Solomon in his glory, or at least like a wealthy sheepman at a wedding. He wore an imported velour hat, a belted overcoat with a fur collar, patent leather shoes, and bright-yellow kid gloves. His suit of clothes was a blue serge bought especially for the occasion.

Elsie greeted him prettily at the door. She had bought a becoming blue frock the other day in town. Cogswell and Steve, keeping well out of the way, were sharply reminded of the comparatively drab feathers in which they themselves must attend the frolic.

Cogswell would have preferred staying at home. But Elsie had insisted that they both attend. So they trailed along on riding-horses about half a mile in the rear of Kincaid's top buggy.

A gala crowd was at the schoolhouse. There was an assortment of ranch wives and daughters, a few young couples from the county seat, cowboys, sheepherders, and Mexican bean growers. The orchestra was two-piece, a fiddle and an accordion.

Festivities began with a square set, although thereafter the dances were round. For the square set Steve Lacey was promptly drafted as caller. It developed that Steve knew all about square sets. He was a champion caller.

"Where you been these last four or five shakedowns?" a Picketwire cowboy yelled at Steve. Everyone knew Steve. "We been missin' you, Steve," more than one buxom lady said as she swung past the caller.

Soon it became clear to Cogswell that his top hand was the most popular man on the floor. Somewhere in his dark past the fellow must have been a favorite beau. Where, everybody wanted to know, had Steve been hiding out?

Cogswell had the feeling that he himself wasn't fitting in. He stood morosely by, not too well pleased at the sight of Elsie in this heterogeneous throng. Here were guests of every estate, the high and the low, the washed and the unwashed. Yet in that whirling mass Elsie seemed to have forgotten every fact but one, that a dance was going on. Her head was high, her black eyes were sparkling. She was taking her fun where she found it.

Cogswell would not attempt the square set. But when a waltz was called he elbowed his way to Elsie. But Kincaid was there, claiming the right of an escort. It was given him. At the next dance, Steve was there first. Cogswell became embroiled with the horse-trading Tollivers, who were gossiping near the door, and so Kincaid beat him again to Elsie.

"Seen that no-count kid brother of ourn lately?" Bert Tolliver asked.

Cogswell, his eyes fixed moodily upon Elsie, shook his head.

"We ain't neither," Bert said. "He ain't been home since that time he got shotten up by Estabal. Ain't seen nothin' o' Milt Prowers, have you?"

"No."

"Well, we ain't heard nothin' definite, either. But they's a rumor Prowers is flyin' high. Some folks claim he went back to his old racket, bookmakin' at the tracks. They say he's cleaned up a pot o' money."

"That so?" For the first time Cogswell was really interested. "Well, I'd like to get something on that fellow. If that kid brother of yours would talk, or the nurse Vera Grady, we'd have Prowers where we want him."

"I seen the Grady girl the other day," spoke up Bill Tolliver, "when I was out on a swappin'-trip."

"Where did you run across her?"

"She's waitin' table at a Harvey House," Bill said, "down at Las Vegas, New Mex."

The dance ended just then, and Cogswell made straight for Elsie. "This is mine, or I start a range war," he said.

He waltzed away with Elsie. After a turn or two he asked, "How do you like Kincaid?"

"He'd be nice," she said a trifle uncertainly, "only—"

"Only what?"

"Oh, never mind. He's all right." Yet he saw that she was reserving something.

Later he noted that Buck Kincaid was making trips frequently to his top buggy. That, and the growing hilarity of the man, told Cogswell that Elsie's escort was imbibing a bit too freely of hard liquor. So were a few of the other men.

By midnight Kincaid was drunk. Not rowdily drunk. He was simply overly hearty and reeled a little. Cogswell began to worry. He didn't like the idea of Elsie driving eleven miles home with an inebriated escort.

Kincaid continued to take between-dance trips out to the buggy. He became redder, louder, unsteadier all the while. Yet he insisted on dancing every third dance with Elsie.

At one a.m. Cogswell conferred with Steve. "He's in no shape to take her home, Steve."

Steve agreed with him.

"I'm going to have a talk with him," Cogswell said.

"He won't listen to you," Steve warned. "If you insist, you'll only start a fight."

The idea of a brawl on the dance floor was repugnant to Cogswell. "But what else can we do?"

"Leave him to me," Steve said. "Maybe I can get him to fade out of the picture peaceably."

Steve then went over to a group of men who were wisecracking near the door. He knew and trusted them all. With these men he went into a huddle. What he said caused the others to chortle uproariously. The group then scattered to various parts of the room.

In a little while Buck Kincaid came in from outside. In mid-floor he became aware that a man was staring fixedly at the seat of his, Kincaid's, pants. He saw that man nudge another one. The two men whispered behind cupped palms.

Before Kincaid could find his next partner, it happened again. And again. Four times he saw a man observe his rear view with a gaping interest. He saw nudgings and whisperings. One man, passing directly behind Kincaid, broke into a fit of uncontrollable mirth.

Then Steve appeared and laid a comradely hand on Kincaid's arm. He whispered, "Follow me outside, Buck. There's something you ought to know."

Steve walked out into the night. Kincaid stood blinking for a moment, indecisively. Then he followed unsteadily in Steve's wake.

"Who did it, Buck?" Steve asked concernedly, outside.

"Who did what?" Kincaid was getting sensitive about all this mystery.

"It was a lousy trick," Steve said. "I guess somebody took white paint and painted that picture on the chair you been sittin' in. So when you sat down next time, it got drawn there right on your pants."

"Whashat? Pisher of what, Steve?" Kincaid hiccuped and tried in vain to look at the seat of his own pants.

"Anyway," Steve said, "there's a sheep painted right where you sit down, Buck."

"Zha hell you say!" Kincaid was indignant. He went into contortions trying to look, but his neck was too short. He thought he knew now the reason for all those whisperings and nudgings inside. And Kincaid, a sheepman, was sensitive about appearing before cowfolks with a sheep pictured on the seat of his pants. It was an insufferable humiliation. His present state of intoxication only increased the man's anguished shame.

Steve Lacey's arm lay sympathetically around his shoulders. "We got to get that damned sheep off o' there, Buck. If the girls see it, they'll laugh their heads off. Look out, you'll smear it."

He stopped the man's frantic and blind effort to erase the stain with his bare hands.

"Let's go in the woodshed," Steve said, "and see if we can get it off with benzine, or horse liniment, or something."

He guided the unsteady Kincaid to the schoolhouse woodshed. It was dark in there. "Take off your pants, Buck. I'll see if I can't rub that sheep off o' them."

Kincaid took off his pants. Steve took them and said, "Wait here, Buck. Soon as I get that sheep rubbed off, I'll be back."

He went out. There was no sheep or any other figure, or stain whatsoever, on the garment. Steve Lacey stuffed it into a badger hole and returned to the ballroom.

He went straight to Elsie. "Kincaid," he said, "is in no shape to take you home. What about me?"

"Why, of course, Steve."

"That's just fine, Miss Elsie. We can use Kincaid's buggy outfit. He won't mind a bit."

When the party broke up at three a.m., Buck Kincaid was still shivering in the woodshed. Steve Lacey embarked in the top buggy with Elsie, cracked the whip over the team of bays, and drove smartly toward home. His own saddle horse, tied to the rear of the buggy, trotted along behind.

Far back of them rode Stanley Cogswell. He rode drearily. A light snow, the first fall of the winter, began descending in fat, wet flakes. He could hear the wheels of the buggy creaking on the road ahead. The vehicle which had been Kincaid's and which was now Lacey's. Cogswell didn't know just how Steve Lacey had managed that. He did know, though, that Lacey had made a huge success of his night out. Contemplation put bitterness in Cogswell. He thought bitter thoughts.

Who was this man Lacey, anyway? Just a forty-dollar cow-hand. Why should a fellow like that win out with Elsie Claiborne? Heartsore and lonely, the rider listened to the creaking of those wheels. In the bleak darkness, with cold crystals falling about him, the little imp again ran amok through Cogswell and sowed iron in his soul.

CHAPTER SIXTEEN
HARD TIMES

EVERY DAY FOR THE REST of that winter, Cogswell felt that he was losing ground with Elsie Claiborne. He dipped into the doldrums of despair. He brooded jealously. There were days when he hated Steve Lacey. To Steve she was always bubbling over with confidences. It was Steve this and Steve that. She was always calling on Steve, and Steve was always making good. Cogswell came to suspect that a sentimental understanding already existed between the two. His top hand, he thought, was simply waiting until he could save a small stake of money.

Money! The idea brought a sour amusement to Cogswell. He was destitute himself. The ranch had drained his purse dry. On February first that second winter he couldn't even rake up enough money to pay the sixty dollars wages due Lacey and Eusebio.

He hadn't told Elsie just how hard they were pressed. No use to worry her. Steve, though, guessed the trouble.

"Let my pay slide, Mr. Cogswell, until we get a break," Steve said.

There was nothing else to do. Cogswell paid Eusebio, but simply credited Steve with forty dollars in a little memo book where he kept his accounts. He decided to sell a few cows, even though the market was weak. Because the cows were mortgaged chattel, he had to get permission from the bank. The bank consented to the selling of fifty cows, provided that half the money was applied on the notes.

The fifty cows brought a thousand dollars, of which the bank took five hundred. Cogswell planned to save the rest for payrolls. But bitter weather defeated him. Mid-February brought a foot of snow, the third big storm of the winter. Seven of the nine stacks and all of the oil cake were gone. The bank called Cogswell in, asked about his feed, then insisted that he protect the liens by storing ten tons of cake at the Rincon Ranch. That purchase again stripped Cogswell's purse.

Another big snow in March took the last of the hay, except stall feed stored in the barn loft. They finished the winter on cake.

"Let my pay slide till we get a break," Steve kept insisting.

Thus for five straight months Steve's wage was defaulted. By June first his pay was two hundred dollars in arrears. Cogswell didn't like it. He resolved not to put himself under further obligations to Steve, and to his relief there came during June a small personal check from New York. It was an overdue engineering fee, long forgotten. Out of this he paid Steve forty dollars on July first, the wage for June, but the two hundred dollars deficiency still stood on the books.

A week later Elsie learned about it. Emerging suddenly on the porch she heard Cogswell say, "I'll dig up that five months' back pay as soon as I can, Steve."

"Let it slide. I'm not losing any sleep over that," Steve said.

"What do you mean?" Elsie queried anxiously. "Do we owe Steve for five months?"

Cogswell was forced to tell her about it. And it hurt the girl's pride that Steve should go unpaid.

"We've simply got to sell something and pay Steve," she worried.

"What can we sell?" Cogswell countered. "If we sell cattle, we have to give the money to the bank. Clarke's left them. The new cashier is hard-boiled. They used to allow me a fifty-per-cent hold-out, but now I've been notified that all cattle sales must be applied in full on the notes."

"Horses?" she suggested doubtfully.

"Our horse stock wouldn't bring much. And how could we put up the hay?"

"Forget it," Steve insisted. The discussion embarrassed him. "You're not broke. You just think you are. All ranches have these flurries to weather, and it's just your turn. With a fat calf crop and a good market in the fall, you can pay off the bank and have a nice bunch of clear stuff on the hill."

"But I don't like Steve going unpaid until fall," Elsie objected. "Two hundred dollars, did you say? Why, we have just that sum. I mean, we can get it. A letter came yesterday from Uncle Bud.

"Uncle Bud says that the colt, Gold Brick, is coming along fine. He says the colt's worth two hundred dollars as he stands, and offers that in cash. He advises, however, that we let the deal ride on the present arrangement—that he uses the colt until it runs one race for him at three years, and then turns it back to us. I'd rather settle with Steve, though. Let's assign Gold Brick to Steve for his back pay. Steve can cash him in for two hundred dollars or take the gamble himself."

Steve protested. They argued. Cogswell didn't care one way or the other. He had forgotten all about Gold Brick, who would now, he calculated, be coming-two years old. Finally Steve accepted the proposition, plainly for no other reason than to end an embarrassing discussion.

"I'll write Uncle Bud and tell him to send you two hundred dollars," Elsie said.

"No," Steve said, "if you insist I take the colt I'd rather let the present arrangement ride. First time I ever had a chance to own a race horse."

He went to attend some errand at the barn. Cogswell changed the subject, and the matter was not referred to during the remainder of the summer.

That year they put up twelve stacks of hay. The only casualties of the season came when six cows wandered down from the Rincon during a September rain. Breaking into wet alfalfa, they were quickly bloated. Steve found three of them dead, puffed like balloons. The other three were grotesquely inflated but still on their feet. Steve chased them in circles at a gallop until they opened their mouths to pant, and the gas escaped.

They had been too occupied either to breed dewlaps or vaccinate, but by good luck there was no blackleg on the range that year. There was hail, though. It came in October, just as Steve was oiling his mower for the third cutting. A black cloud came suddenly over the rimrock and unleashed a downpour of ice. It lasted only ten minutes. Yet when it was over, so was haying for that year. What should have been a third alfalfa crop was ripped to shreds.

On November first the copartnership sold two hundred and ten steer calves on the Denver market. They brought thirteen dollars per head. Cogswell took the check into the Picketwire National to see what kind of a hold-out he could get.

"We must have all interest to date and a one-thousand-dollar bite on the principal," the new cashier decreed. On this he stood pat. Cogswell wasn't as well entrenched with this official as he had been with his predecessor, Clarke. Clarke had been willing to gamble a little on the characters of Cogswell and Lacey. The present cashier knew nothing of the incident when, two and a half years ago, Cogswell had taken a loss of thirty thousand rather than penalize the bank.

"Crimped again," Cogswell admitted later to Steve. "What I have left will buy a few ton of cake and pay you and Eusebio through the winter. Seems like we can't get anywhere."

"Things'll be pickin' up before long," Steve thought. "But now you can see what I meant when I advised purebred stock. Suppose we had purebreds! We'd have cashed in at forty a round for our bull crop, 'stead of thirteen for steers. The purebreds wouldn't have eaten any more grass, cake, or hay than the grades. Same overhead, and three times the take back."

"Three times the original investment, too," Cogswell complained. "Three times the interest."

"Sure. An outfit's got to ease into registereds little by little. The day'll come, maybe, when the Rincon will be dotted with registereds, and not a dime lien on 'em."

Just where he got this optimism Cogswell couldn't see. Results thus far were definitely discouraging. Cogswell reflected ruefully that he himself hadn't owned a decent suit of clothes for two years.

They stored ten tons of cake, and then the weather turned graciously perverse. Prepared for a closed winter, they had an open one. Until the middle of March there wasn't as much as two inches of snow at any one time.

They used none of the cake and only a little hay.

No necessity for feeding gave them the first leisure in many weary months.

"I think I'll take the sulky and rake the weeds in the big circle up into windrows," Steve said in March. "The way I figure it, that sixty-thousand-dollar wallet of Milt Prowers has laid out there long enough."

He spoke lightly, but Cogswell knew that his top hand had never entirely abandoned the theory of the lost purse. For the chances of finding it, Cogswell himself wouldn't have given a penny. He had reverted to the belief that some other motive must have inspired those nocturnal prowls of Carlos Estabal. Or maybe Carlos himself had found the wallet. Or maybe Prowers had told the truth, and the pocketbook had contained only three hundred dollars. The idea that a huge fortune had lain all this time out in the race-track circle seemed too absurd and forlorn to be taken seriously.

Elsie agreed with him. But she raised no objection to Steve's program of raking the winter-cured weeds and briars with a sulky rake.

"Just as long as you don't spoil the wild roses, Steve," she said.

"It won't hurt the roots any, Miss Elsie. It'll do 'em good."

He hitched to the sulky and went to work, just as though he were raking the swaths of a new-mown crop. When he had raked up about thirty acres of the two hundred in the circle, he put his team away and began sifting through his windrows with a pitchfork.

When he came in from work Cogswell chided him.

"Didn't harvest any ten-thousand-dollar bills, did you, Steve?"

"Nary a one," Steve grinned.

The next day there was no laughing, because the cashier of the bank rode out with an ice-cold ultimatum. It seemed to spell doom to the Rincon Ranch.

"Two big cattle outfits and a string of coal mines went broke on us," the caller said. "That means we've got to call every overdue note. You'll have to ship the CC herd, Cogswell, and pay off."

Though Cogswell argued desperately, the man was as hard as nails. "Ship this week," he decreed, "and pay off. Otherwise we foreclose the brand."

Gloom bathed Cogswell when the man was gone.

"But we can save out every cow with a newborn calf," Steve consoled, "and every springer. The rest ought to pay the notes, and leave us a few clear stuff."

Cogswell, Steve, and Eusebio made an out-of-season roundup. Everything was corralled, and Steve sorted out a hundred cows which either had newborn calves or were due for calves in a short time.

"Those stuff wouldn't do any good on a beef market, anyway," Steve said. "So we might as well keep 'em. As near as I can figure, the rest'll clear the notes. That will leave us with a hundred head with calves by side or comin'."

"And not a peso owed to the damned bank," Cogswell agreed. "Well, that's something. It means we can sleep at night, anyway. We'll have two hundred head of livestock to show as a net profit for three years of operation."

It turned out that Steve's estimate was accurate. The shipped cattle wiped out the bank debt, with a few hundred dollars to spare. With this money Cogswell paid all back bills. They were ready for a fresh start.

When it was all done, Cogswell felt better. Now he knew where he stood. When he and Steve came back from Denver, where the cattle were sold, the old ranch looked more like home than ever before. The array of ancient adobe buildings lay peaceful and solidly comforting under the March sun. They found Elsie on the porch, waiting with a cheerful welcome.

Steve, after changing to ranch clothes, went out into the big circle to spend the rest of the afternoon sifting through his windrows. "I feel lucky," he called to the others.

A grim expression settled on Cogswell's face as he remained on the porch with Elsie. All the way down from Denver he had been summoning his courage.

Why not? Steve said he felt lucky. Maybe he, Cogswell, might be lucky. Here she sat, the girl his heart was aching for, near him, her black-curled head bent over sewing. When would he ever have a better chance?

Brusquely he said, "We've been partners for quite some time, Elsie." She looked up, startled by the unnatural tone of his voice.

"From the start I've been loving you," he plunged on. "Every minute. Will you marry me, Elsie?"

He knew it was absurdly sudden, and he felt like a fool. The surprise had shocked her, he saw; her hand had moved quickly from her work. The needle pricked her finger tip, and he saw a tiny dot of red there. A thimble fell from her lap and rolled with a tinkle across the floor.

"Will you, Elsie?" he pleaded.

She sat staring, rubbing the bleeding finger tip against the other palm. "I've been loving you three years," he said earnestly. "All along I've known what I want. You. We could go to town tomorrow and be married at the courthouse."

Her silence hurt him. He could read no gladness in her eyes. A fear chilled him, a fear that she would say no.

"Say yes," he pleaded.

"I can't," she said. Her voice seemed uncertain. She was still nursing that pricked finger against her other palm.

Then he saw that she wasn't looking at him at all, but beyond him. Her look was fixed upon faraway space. It impelled Cogswell to turn around. Far out in the big circle he saw Steve Lacey, tossing cured weeds into the air as he sifted a windrow.

Steve looked up, saw them, and waved.

Elsie raised a hand, mechanically, to wave back. Then Magnolia appeared at the door with a bell. She was calling supper. Steve heard the bell. He stuck his pitchfork upright in a windrow and came briskly toward the house.

The Negress withdrew to the kitchen.

Cogswell wanted to press the issue. But he couldn't now, not with Steve coming toward them. And what was the use? She had already answered. The blow had already fallen. And he could see that she was wretchedly confused.

He sensed that it was to cover up the situation that she went to meet Steve at the gate. "Harvest any purses, Steve?" she asked in a voice of forced gaiety.

"Not a one, Miss Elsie."

She took Steve's arm as they came up the steps. That intimate touch, at this moment, hurt Cogswell. But then she slipped her other arm through Cogswell's. In such formation the three went to supper. It had happened often before. It had long been a gay boast of Elsie's that she always had two dinner partners and positively couldn't get along with fewer.

Through supper, Cogswell tried valiantly to keep from looking dour. He must be a sport about this. He mustn't be a poor loser. Elsie was chattering about that infernal purse. He knew that she was merely trying to cover up a confusion.

"But what earthly good would it do us, Steve, if we *did* find that horrid old purse? You know I've always insisted we couldn't keep it. It's loot. Legally it belongs to Prowers."

"Yes, Miss Elsie, I remember you always said that. You said we must give him a chance to claim it, and it'd be his till we could beat him in court on a judgment. But there's another side to it."

The girl debated the issue with him. To Cogswell it was plainer all the while that she was talking to fill a void. Steve took her seriously. He turned the point of ethics inside out. In the end he capitulated. "All right, Miss Elsie," he conceded with a laugh, "if I find the purse I'll take it to Milt Prowers with your compliments. Last I heard he was in New Orleans, flyin' high."

As usual, they went to sit on the porch after supper. The men smoked. Elsie sat by, sewing, thinking, watching them. She *was* confused. Her mind was a jumble of uncertainties. Stanley Cogswell's brusque declaration, crashing upon her complacency out of a clear sky, had been like a bombshell. She was taken utterly by surprise. There was a time, during the first year here, when she had expected something like that. Nothing had happened. She had become used to thinking it never would.

But it had. It left her in a maze of conflicting doubts and emotions. With startling force it brought back a similar incident which had transpired more than a year ago. It recalled a certain three-o'clock-in-the-morning ride with Steve Lacey, through falling snow, in a top buggy. Steve had run truer to form. He hadn't waited two and a half years, as had Stanley Cogswell. He had asked her that very night, while they rode snugly under the buggy top, driving home from the Frijoli frolic in the wee hours of morning.

She hadn't known her heart and mind then. Nor had she known them tonight, at the sudden declaration of Stanley Cogswell.

They were totally different, she thought now, as she looked from one to the other of them. So utterly unlike that it was hard to compare them. She watched them covertly in the twilight. Steve was a boy, she thought, and Stanley a mature man. Yet the two were of an age—and they were always leaning on Steve.

Steve was saying now, "The Bar 37, down in Texas, 's been tryin' to get me back. Used to work there. But I reckon I'll stick around here."

"You and I both, Steve," Cogswell returned listlessly. "Which reminds me I must go to town tomorrow and send a wire to New York. An old client's been asking me to take charge of a job for him. The answer, of course, is no."

Elsie Claiborne felt a new tension. It frightened her. She saw startling possibilities which hadn't occurred to her before. These two men were young, life lay ahead of them, and there were other corners of the world than this ranch. One corner of it had just called to Lacey, another to Cogswell.

Neither was going, this time. But some day one of them would. It was inevitable. Some day one of these dear, fine friends would go. It might be Steve Lacey. It might be Stanley Cogswell.

Then she knew. It was as sudden as a summer dawn, yet definitely final. She knew which going would break her heart—unless she, Elsie Claiborne, went with him. With a blazing certainty the truth flashed, bringing a flood of crimson to her face. She bowed her head lower over the workbasket, while a breathlessness, as still and as precious as the twilight, filled her. She knew now which was a tried and true friend, and which was the eternal husband of her heart.

CHAPTER SEVENTEEN
FALSE WITNESS

"There's a half hour more of light," Steve said. "Guess I'll go fork over a few more windrows."

"I'll go feed the barn stock," Cogswell said. He arose and went to the barn. Steve went into the race-track meadow, leaving Elsie alone on the porch.

She wasn't alone long. A suitor came. He was the last man in the world she wanted to see, especially tonight. But there he was, tethering his horse at the gate and with a box of sweets under his arm. At first Elsie felt like laughing, then she wanted to cry at the irony of his calling tonight. There was nothing to do, though, but make the best of it. She greeted him with all the graciousness she could muster, then led him into the prim little parlor.

He took off his fur-collared overcoat and sat down with a red-faced seriousness. "I'm shippin' seven thousand pounds o' wool this shearin'-season," he said for a starter.

When Cogswell looked in, an hour later, Buck Kincaid was still expounding his personal resources. Cogswell was not so indelicate as to intrude. Nor was Steve Lacey, when he passed the parlor door a few minutes later.

Toward midnight Kincaid reached his peroration. His proposition of matrimony was politely declined. Kincaid then mopped the perspiration from his rubicund nose and said, "Well, I kinder figgered it was a long shot. But no harm in askin', was there?"

"None at all," she said. "I have been greatly honored."

"I figgered it was a long shot," he droned on. "The chances are, I figgered, that she's aimin' to hook up with that fellah Cogswell. Guess I figgered it out about right, didn't I?"

Elsie's face was like a poppy. "I can't discuss that, Mr. Kincaid."

"Or maybe you aim to hook up with Steve Lacey," he amended brightly. "Well, you might do worse. Steve done me dirt once, but still, you might look further and do worse."

Elsie stood up. "I'm sorry. I've a headache, though, and I'll have to ask you to go."

"Or maybe it's nip and tuck between 'em!" Kincaid offered shrewdly.

"Please, Mr. Kincaid!"

He put on his overcoat. She went to the door with him. There he turned with a final inquiry.

"You're dead sure I'm plumb out o' the runnin', are you?"

"I'm quite certain of it," she said.

Kincaid went to his horse. Mounting, he rode not home but to town for the purpose of drowning his sorrow.

The next morning Cogswell and Lacey were also riding to town. Cogswell wanted to pay the county taxes, settle a few outstanding bills, and send a telegram to New York.

Steve's errand had to do with a jury summons which had been served on him. He was merely going in to beg off. He was sure to be let off, he said, because the case to be tried was against a man who had been a boyhood friend of Steve's on the Cimarron.

Both Steve and Cogswell were preoccupied as they jogged toward town. Cogswell's shoulders were noticeably stooped. He had a tired and discouraged look this morning. He had tossed fretfully all night, unable to sleep.

Steve rode erect, but no less preoccupied. Suddenly he asked, "Do you remember the date on the sale contract Prowers claimed to have made with Colonel Claiborne?"

"Which?" Cogswell asked in surprise.

"The one Prowers used to fleece Miss Elsie. That time he flashed a phony contract on her, in Denver."

"What about it?"

"I want to know if you remember the date on the contract."

Cogswell failed to see what difference it made. However, he happened to remember the date. "It was May 30th, three years ago this spring," he said.

"Check," Steve agreed. "That's the way I recollect it, too. Just wanted to make sure."

He fell into another brown study. Ordinarily Cogswell would have been curious, but now his own troubles quite filled his mind. They rode silently on.

After putting their mounts in Greenstead's livery barn, they separated. A man who was emerging from the Palace barroom, directly across the street, saw them separate. The man was Buck Kincaid. For ten hours Kincaid had been drowning his sorrow, and had made a good job of it.

Kincaid was drunk. When he was drunk, he was sensitive. Sight of Cogswell and Lacey reminded him that those men must know about his unsuccessful courtship. They had looked in on him in the midst of it. He held no doubt but that the girl and her two companions had had a good laugh at his own expense, this morning at breakfast.

Kincaid went back into the Palace barroom and had another drink. His only comeback, he decided, was to get a laugh out of it himself. Which of those fellows was she going to take, he wondered? Most likely his third guess was right, that it was nip and tuck between them.

Kincaid swayed at the bar. He drank again. He grinned at his own flushed image in the bar mirror, a grin sheepish, yet in a degree mischievous and mildly malicious. Steve Lacey, he remembered, had once stolen his pants, his buggy team, and his girl.

And it was nip and tuck between them! Steve and Cogswell. Could he, Kincaid, get a consoling laugh out of that? He could, he decided after another drink, if he could start a jealous fight between them. Today. Here in town.

Cogswell went about his errands. He paid the taxes and the minor bills. Then, as he was passing a saloon, he became aware of an arm thrown around his shoulder. A whisky breath was on his cheek.

"Lesh have a drink, Coshwell," Kincaid pleaded with a maudlin familiarity. "We bosh need it. We're bosh in zha shame boat."

Cogswell jerked free.

"What do you mean?" he asked.

"Lesh drown our shorrow, Coshwell. But lesh not get sore about it. If she likes Steve besher'n us, it's her business, ain't it, Coshwell?"

"What the devil are you talking about?" Cogswell was angry.

Bleary tears stood in Kincaid's eyes. "She turned me down, she did, and she told me why. It's her and Steve. Zere's geshin' married in June, Coshwell."

Cogswell tore loose and hurried down the street. He was a fool, he thought, for not knowing it before. That damned sheepman, of course, was telling the truth. A man that's drunk, he thought, wouldn't have any capacity for guile.

Elsie, he reasoned, hated to tell him. She hated to hurt him. He was her friend and partner. But she was going to marry Steve. He, Cogswell, had been standing blindly in the way. Well, he would get out of the way. He would make it easy for them. He could go build that bridge in the East; then he could come back and lease his part of the ranch to Steve, on Steve's own terms.

Cogswell came to a grim resolution. It was the only way out. He entered the telegraph office. Instead of wiring a negative to the old client in New York, his answer was yes.

That, he thought as he returned to Greenstead's barn, would relieve the situation. He would quit clogging up the triangle. As for taking a trip East, the time for that was peculiarly opportune. Bills were paid and the cow herd cut down to a small number. All notes were paid at the bank.

At the livery barn, he wrote a note addressed to Elsie and gave it to Uncle Jack.

> *Have decided to build that bridge. When I come back, I shall offer to lease or sell the ranch to Steve on his own terms.*
>
> *Stanley Cogswell.*

An hour later Cogswell was riding toward Kansas on a Santa Fe train.

And Buck Kincaid, watching for Steve Lacey's return to Greenstead's, had pulled Steve into the Palace barroom. In almost identical phrasing the sheepman broke big news to Steve Lacey.

The only difference was that Cogswell was now the hero of a June wedding.

"I jush sheen him in Tom Moore's shoolry shore buyin' a gold ring," was the only touch Kincaid added.

Once again his own state of intoxication made the man seem guileless. Steve Lacey believed him.

He believed all the more because he had almost arrived at the same conclusion himself.

"I reckon she sort o' hates to tell me about it," he said to himself as he went out. "Naturally she don't want to make me break down and cry."

He stood on the walk and thought it out. He had been employed as a consulting expert three years ago when Cogswell was green about ranching. Well, Cogswell knew the game now. He could get along. A ranch with only a hundred cows didn't call for a top hand, anyway. They were probably keeping him just out of sentiment. They could get along without him. The

Bar 37, in Texas, wanted him. Why not make it easy for all hands?

The note which Steve handed to Uncle Jack read:

Am taking a little pasear through Texas. Send my wedding invite care of the Bar 37, at El Paso.

Steve.

An hour later he was riding a train over Raton Pass. His supper stop was Las Vegas, New Mexico. There, at the Harvey House counter, a girl with a strangely familiar face took his order.

When she brought his supper, Steve recognized Vera Grady.

"You're lookin' fine," he greeted. "What do you know about Milt Prowers?"

The ex-nurse was plumper than she had been three years ago, with less hardness in her face. Standing behind the counter in her starched uniform, as Steve saw her, she appeared wholesomely attractive.

"Don't know anything about Prowers," she said. "Honest, Steve, I didn't have anything to do with that frame-up, if there was a frame-up. Bert Pauly crossed me, that was all. I never knew Prowers."

"Know where he is now?"

"I've heard he's rich. After he left this country, so I hear, he cleaned up keeping books at races. They say he's got a stable of his own now, and lives at New Orleans."

"That's what one of the Tolliver boys told me," Steve acknowledged.

The conductor was calling, "All aboard." Steve returned to his train and rode on to El Paso.

CHAPTER EIGHTEEN
THE PEDIGREE

WHEN THE SUN DIPPED below the rimrock of Rincon Mesa that evening, a chill wind came up from the northeast; darkish clouds drifting before it gave promise that winter was not yet over. Elsie told Magnolia to hold supper for Cogswell and Steve.

Night came without them. The girl decided that Steve had been held for jury service and that Cogswell had simply failed to conclude his business in town. It was not, of course, the first time that she had been left overnight without their protection. That had happened on occasions of shipping cattle to market, and on scouting expeditions for the purchase of new stock.

During the night the wind came up hard. Elsie arose in the morning expecting to see snow. There was no snow, but the weather had turned bitterly cold. Eusebio made roaring fires in every stove.

"Do you think the cattle will be all right?" Elsie asked anxiously.

"Ver' few cattle now," the boy said.

"Mr. Cogswell and Steve didn't get home. We must decide whether or not to feed."

Eusebio advised feeding. He said the cows didn't need feeding, but if they were fed they'd be in better shape in case a snow came, a snow too deep for the hay wagon.

"You think there might be a deep snow, Eusebio?"

"*Quién sabe?* Many time I know deep snow in March. *También* in April, May. Many time these winter fool you. Plenty open in March; then come April, May, snow like hell."

"Feed the cattle, Eusebio," Elsie directed.

In midmorning, when she was out putting a few ambitious hens in a coop to break them of a premature inclination to sit, she saw Eusebio feeding. The small herd of a hundred cows and fifty odd very young calves were across the creek on the alfalfa bottom. They were crowding up to a stack pen and mooing while Eusebio, inside the pen, forked hay onto his rick. Later she saw the boy drive out with a full, shaggy load. He drove at random across the field, pitching off hay, making a long, green line of it on the ground. The cattle formed in a pretty feeding row of red backs and white necks.

Her own chores completed, Elsie returned to the house and wandered about restlessly all day. Every minute she expected the return of her men. They did not come. Night fell, colder than ever, with the northeast wind still blowing. The sound of it made the girl lonely. It put her nerves on edge. On the wings of it came the howlings of coyotes. She lighted the parlor lamp, then went to the door and looked out. An icy breath poured in. She shivered.

What could be keeping Steve and Stanley? Jury service, of course, might hold Steve for a week, but what about Stanley? She could think of no excuse which would account for his absence over a second night.

The second night passed, though, without the return of either man. Elsie was genuinely alarmed by the third morning. There was still no snow, though the wind held in the northeast. She told Eusebio to throw out another load of hay.

Then, about noon, Uncle Jack rode up leading two saddled horses. He put the horses in the barn and came to the house.

"I'm headin' for the Cross H on the San Isidro," he said, "and gotta fan along. Steve Lacey, he left a note for you. So did Stan Cogswell."

The old wrangler handed Elsie two sealed notes. Then he mounted and rode away.

Elsie Claiborne read those messages with wide eyes. She read them many times. Each time she read them, she changed moods. They piqued her; they angered her; they made her laugh; they made her cry. She took them to her room and read them again. She stared dully at first one, then the other.

In the end she was gripped by a pity of infinite tenderness toward two foolish men.

Each thought she was betrothed to the other one. Each had made a wrong guess. Each had stepped aside to avoid embarrassing a fortunate rival.

Where had they gone? She saw that Steve mentioned an address in Texas, but Cogswell gave none at all. Nevertheless Elsie had an idea where he could be reached, indirectly. She knew that Stanley Cogswell had kept his dues paid up at the Engineers' Club of New York. A communication sent there should ultimately reach him.

Should she write these erring lovers, and set them straight? She decided she would. Then she decided she wouldn't. She couldn't, with proper feminine restraint. When she read the notes again, her mood of pique returned.

She'd write them no line whatever. If they loved her, they'd come back of their own accords.

A week went by. It was a week of bitter loneliness. The weather kept close to zero, and the wind high. Eusebio fed a load of hay every day.

"If big snow she come," he said, "cows in plenty fine shape."

At the end of a week Elsie could stand the suspense no longer. She sent Eusebio, in spite of bitter weather, on a hurried ride to town for the mail. She thought surely she would hear from both of the missing men.

But the single missive which the boy brought back was from neither of them. It was postmarked New Orleans. Elsie opened it, saw that it was from Bud LeFever, the horse trainer.

The important news in the letter would, at any other time, have excited Elsie. Now she read it only with a dull interest. It informed that LeFever had entered Gold Brick, the Rincon Creek colt, in the Old Planters' Sweepstakes soon to be held at the New Orleans track. This race was a feature limited to three-year-olds. LeFever admitted that Gold Brick was a rank outsider, a long shot. In conclusion the trainer reminded Elsie that after this one race the colt reverted to its original owners. LeFever's fee for trouble and training must come out of this one race, or not at all.

Elsie tossed the letter aside. Just now she wasn't interested in Gold Brick, or even in Bud LeFever. A growing irritation edged every other consideration from her mind. Why should Steve and Stanley desert and ignore her, leaving her alone on this bleak, windswept ranch? What if they had made a foolish mistake! They could write her letters, couldn't they? Elsie went to a window and looked miserably through the pane. The squat, mud outbuildings built by Ramon Estabal today looked drearier than ever before.

Another week went by. A week of cold and wind, though without the ever threatening snow. No word came from either Cogswell or Lacey. Eusebio fed the cattle every day. He had now fed out two stacks and was slicing into a third. At meal times Elsie and the Mexican boy sat across the kitchen table from each other, served by Magnolia. It was a weird domestic triangle—with two empty chairs. Steve Lacey's and Stanley Cogswell's. Sight of those empty chairs would bring pique and then pity and then tears to her eyes.

Would either of those two men ever come?

One of them *must* come. A certain one of them must come. The one she loved with all her heart must come back.

Yet neither came. During the third week Elsie again sent Eusebio to town for mail. She thought surely there would be letters from Stanley and Steve. But again Eusebio returned with a single letter addressed in the hand of neither Cogswell nor Lacey. Also there was a telegram.

Her fingers trembled as Elsie stripped the cover from the telegram. From which would it be, Stanley or Steve? Pain came to her eyes when she saw it was from neither. It was from Bud LeFever, and read:

> *Training your colt was best speculation I ever made. Gold Brick romped home, leading the favorite, Son-of-War, by four lengths. Letter follows.*
>
> *Bud LeFever.*

Stupendous news! Elsie knew she should be thrilled to the bottom of her heart. All that was spoiled, though, by her depression and disappointment. The man she wanted to hear from hadn't written at all.

What good was this news, when she had no one with whom to share it? If Steve and Stanley were only here! They would all three be joining hands now, dancing in a circle, shouting and cheering like children.

She opened the letter, which was the one predicted by the telegram.

> *Dear Elsie,*
>
> *I suppose you got my wire. Yes, Gold Brick romped home for the big money. Made a monkey out of Son-of-War, touted by experts to lead the field. It was the classiest bunch of three-year-olds ever assembled on a southern track. Every entry was a headliner except mine, and mine knocked the dope book seven ways from Sunday.*
>
> *I made plenty. By agreement the colt's earnings are mine for this one start. But he's now yours, and worth a fortune.*
>
> *I've already picked up a sweet bid on him, and advise you to take it. After the race, four or five big stable sports came around and wanted a price on Gold Brick. They*

wanted to look at his pedigree, too. I just looked down my nose and kept a poker face. I said the colt had real track blood in his legs, because his granddaddy won this same race years ago. That got 'em excited; they wanted to know who the granddaddy was. I wouldn't say. But three of them made cash bids, anyway. The colt's usable, you understand, for both a race horse and a stud.

I listed the bids and said I'd write the owner for a decision. Who is the owner, they asked. I wouldn't say.

The fattest bid is from a new-rich sport named Milton Prowers. He offers thirty thousand dollars. He insists, though, that he gets a pedigree when he buys.

Accept the offer, Elsie. Dope up the best pedigree you can and send it along.

Bud LeFever.

When she read that, Elsie really cried. Not in elation, but in bitter sorrow that Stanley and Steve weren't here to share the triumph with her. After three years of struggle, how they would all celebrate! To sell Gold Brick to Milton Prowers for thirty thousand dollars!

It was the very amount he had swindled from her. A like amount he had tricked from Stanley Cogswell. Swindled and tricked them with six hundred crowbait mares—and now the progeny of a single mare was bringing back to them that same fateful sum!

But suddenly a fact of truth flashed to her mind. Not herself, not Cogswell, but Steve Lacey owned Gold Brick. She recalled the time two years ago this spring when Steve's pay was five months in arrears. To liquidate that debt, they had made Steve the legal owner of the colt. Steve, though reluctantly, had accepted Gold Brick in lieu of two hundred dollars pay.

That made Steve the owner now. It was he who had taken over the gamble. Therefore it was Steve who must profit by this miracle of fate; he must inherit the stake accruing to Gold Brick's fame and prowess.

Elsie thought of this, and it came to her not as a blow, not as a loss, far less as a calamity of ill fortune. She exulted for Steve Lacey. Steve had done everything for them. The windfall was Steve's, and he deserved it. Not for an instant did she think of evading the clear-cut fact that Steve Lacey owned the colt.

How better could it be, she thought. Steve had risked his life many times to serve this ranch, he had worked and fought hard for its mistress, its master, and its chattel. For forty dollars a month, often in arrears. How better than this could it be?

But, oh, if they were only here! If Steve and Stanley were only here, so they could cheer about it together!

She reread LeFever's letter. *He insists, though, on getting a pedigree when he buys. Dope up the best pedigree you can and send it along.*

But, she remembered, the colt had no pedigree. How could she "dope up" one? The Claibornes never doped anything, either a race horse or a pedigree. So how dare she say in black and white that Gold Brick was a grandson of the great stallion, Don Quixote? That was probable, but, of course, not positive. He was merely a colt born on the old Estabal ranch, a colt with the same color markings of Don Quixote. The very fact that Gold Brick had it in him to win this big race was indicative of his blood.

But there was no proof of it. It was a pure guess. Therefore Elsie knew that she couldn't, with honor, mention Don Quixote in a pedigree. She was impelled to rigid rectitude. A traditional sense of honor, the same which would not allow her to quibble at Steve's ownership, deterred her from faking anything into the pedigree of this colt.

Finally she took up pen and paper to answer Bud LeFever.

First she wrote out an honest pedigree for Gold Brick. As per instructions, it was the best pedigree she could devise.

In the body of her letter she said:

Prowers must take Gold Brick as he stands and looks, on the record of his performance. Do not give him the pedigree until you get his certified check. Then endorse the check to Stephen Lacey and mail it to him care of the Bar 37, El Paso, Texas. Mr. Lacey owns Gold Brick by recent transfer from Mr. Cogswell and myself.

To the letter she attached a pedigree, which read:

GOLD BRICK.
Born about three years ago on an unrecorded date, in a circle of wild roses by Rincon Creek, Las Animas County, Colorado.
Sex: Stallion.
Dam: An old buckskin mare culled from six hundred similar crow-baits, a decrepit herd sold for seventy-five cents the head. This dam was left behind as not worth the price.
Sire: Unknown.

CHAPTER NINETEEN
THE WHITE WILDERNESS

ANOTHER WEEK and still the wind blew. High above the Rincon and to the south and west fleecy clouds billowed from the rimrock, an ever ominous threat of snow which failed to come. Instead, there was only cold and wind and desolation.

"Surely it won't snow now, Eusebio," Elsie worried. "This late in the spring!"

"No can savvy," the boy said. "One time I know big snow in May, *muy hondo,* high like a barn door. Next month before come plenty wind, just like these."

"That would be awful. If the snow came three feet deep, how would you get out with the hay wagon?"

"Leave hay wagon in the corral," Eusebio said. "Three feet snow, then I go out and tear down stack-pen fence. The cows, she crowd in and eat plenty hay."

Elsie knew that that would be a wasteful way to feed, but she admitted that it would be better than letting the cattle starve.

The windstorm came to a climax on the last day of April. It increased in fury that morning, blowing such a gale that Eusebio did not need the hay wagon to feed. He merely stood on a stack and tossed forkfuls of hay into the air. Freed from his fork the roughage blew many yards to leeward, alighting without the stack-pen fence and being pounced on immediately by the cattle.

By noon Eusebio couldn't even have done that. He could not have stood on the stack. The walls of two old adobe buildings collapsed under sheer wind pressure. One of these was the ancient church of Ramon Estabal. Elsie, looking drearily from a window, saw it fall. The blown dust from the old adobe bricks spanked the pane before her face. When it cleared she saw a heap of old earthen cubes, with the cupola bell lying grotesquely atop of them. The sight seemed a portent of disaster, a weird and harsh prediction of doom impending over the hopes of her heart.

Why, oh, why had Stanley and Steve left her here at this desolate place?

She left the window and walked restlessly through the house. Finally she went to the south wing, the separate apartment which had been occupied solely by the men. She came to Cogswell's room. Her eyes softened as she saw articles of his effects strewn about. It was plain that he hadn't meant to leave for more than a day.

She sat down at a little desk where Cogswell had been in the habit of keeping accounts. Her restless fingers touched objects here and there on it. In a little while they touched a small red memo book. She opened it. Her eyes strayed through its penciled pages.

She saw a story written there. A hundred notations brought back incidents of the last three years. Here were the accounts of operation. So much received for this, so much paid out for that. Here was an item about the brooder which Cogswell had bought for her chick crop last year. Then her eyes saw the name of Steve Lacey.

The memorandum read: *To Steve Lacey $200 cash, five months' back pay last January to May inclusive.*

The item stirred a troubled current of thought in Elsie's mind. Two hundred dollars. Five months' back pay. Something about that seemed all wrong. Why should Steve have been paid two hundred dollars in cash?

Then she remembered. A year ago they had defaulted Steve's pay for five months. Or was it two years ago? But that defaulting, of course, had been settled. They had canceled the account by assigning Steve the colt, Gold Brick. Steve had accepted. Therefore, the two hundred dollars was no longer a debt.

What was the answer? The answer, she decided, was that Cogswell in the worries of succeeding months must have forgotten that transaction. Or perhaps he had never taken it seriously. Or perhaps Steve Lacey, who had always been reluctant in the matter, had persuaded him to cancel the arrangement. Elsie was aware that, until the sensational telegram from LeFever had recalled it to her mind, she had almost forgotten it herself.

Now she could foresee complications. According to his memorandum, Steve had been paid the two hundred dollars in cash. By accepting, he had in effect relinquished title to the colt. Which meant that the windfall of fortune did not properly accrue to Steve, but to the partnership of Cogswell-Claiborne.

It was badly mixed. She had instructed LeFever to send Steve a properly endorsed certified check for thirty thousand dollars, the tremendous price offered for the colt. No doubt LeFever, by now, had complied with this instruction.

Then what about Steve? Steve would know, of course, that he had already received the arrears pay in cash. Therefore he would also know that he was not due this larger sum sent him by LeFever. He couldn't be paid twice for the same debt.

Having accepted and used the first payment, he must renounce the second. What else in honor could he do? And Steve was honest, Elsie knew, as honest as daylight. He was foursquare. His wasn't the type of mind that would attempt to raise some technicality which would excuse his keeping the big stake. He'd bring it back. Why, if he failed to do so, Elsie thought, he'd be little better than a thief.

Steve a thief! Absurd! On a point like this she'd trust him as unequivocally as she would Stanley Cogswell himself. In that one way they were alike, Cogswell and Lacey—two honest, true-blue men.

A disturbing memory, though, pricked her. She recalled a tiff she'd once had with Cogswell. Of course, Cogswell, that day, had been jealous and bitter. She remembered her hurt at his suggestion that Steve might not be as foursquare as they'd thought him. The thing had resulted from Steve's insistent suggestion that he personally be allowed to plow the race-track circle. The implication of the outburst was that Steve only wanted to get his hands on a sixty-thousand-dollar purse.

Later the girl knew that Cogswell had been contrite and ashamed. He had come to accept her own estimate of Steve Lacey.

Of course Steve was honest. And here now would come a clean-cut proof of it. In error he had been sent thirty thousand dollars. A dishonest man would keep it; an honest man would bring it home.

Which meant that she was sure to see Steve, and soon. Her faith clung to that as a certainty. After getting the thing straight in her mind, Elsie found herself not at all sorry that she had erred in her instruction to LeFever. The mistake merely insured the return of Steve.

Which would likewise insure the return of Stanley Cogswell. Cogswell would need to come back to attend to the division and disbursement of the money.

Suddenly the girl became aware of a quiet out of doors. The wind had stopped. She looked from a window and saw that the tops of the cottonwood trees were no longer swaying. Instead, from a gray sky, fat white flakes were falling. With the dying of the wind the long threatened snow had begun.

They were the biggest, fluffiest flakes Elsie had ever seen. They were coming straight down, so thick that she could barely see the barn. The ground was already covered. She could see Eusebio tramping toward the house.

She opened the kitchen door for him. "I theenk maybe she snow long time," he opined cheerfully. "My old padre used to say, 'Long March blow make big May snow.'"

Eusebio remained in the kitchen. Elsie went to a front window and gazed wistfully up the trail toward town. The snow kept falling steadily down, relentlessly. She judged it was already three inches deep on the ground.

By dusk it was twice that. It was then that she saw a distant dot townward along the trail. Immediately she was excited; she knew it was an approaching horseman.

Stanley? Steve? Her heart beat swiftly. Who else but one of those two would be riding to the ranch on a day like this? The dot took shape. It was indeed a horseman; the drifts were shank-deep to his mount as he rode slowly toward the house.

As he came nearer, she saw that he wore an ankle-length bearskin overcoat and a fur cap pulled well over his ears. It wasn't Steve, then; at least she couldn't imagine Steve in a fur coat and cap. It would be more like Cogswell, city-bred, to rig himself out like that.

When she saw that the rider was extremely tall, she was surer that he was Cogswell. But he seemed even taller than Cogswell, and much broader. But perhaps the ankle-length bearskin coat would account for that. On no appraisal could he be Steve Lacey. Elsie awaited his approach tremulously.

His features were all but concealed by the pulled-down cap and the turned-up collar of the coat. He wore bearskin gloves. With one of these he was constantly rubbing his nose, as though that exposed feature might be frozen. He took his hand away when he was within fifty yards of the house. Dismally the girl discerned that he was neither Cogswell nor Lacey.

The man gave scarcely a glance at the house as he rode by, proceeding directly to the barn. There he dismounted stiffly. The barn door was in two halves, the upper half open and the lower half closed. Elsie saw the visitor reach a hand over the half door and deftly slide back a wooden latch. She knew then that he was no total stranger. He had unlatched that slide without even looking over the half door to locate it. A stranger would have fumbled.

She saw him slap his horse on the flank. The animal ran into the barn, saddle and all. The man closed the half door and strode toward the house. He was even bigger than she had thought, big in every way, from the shoulders down. The coat made him a hairy giant. He was walking stiffly, after a long, cold ride from town.

He came to the porch and knocked. Elsie opened the door. He entered like a great shaggy bear, shaking the snow from his coat. He had a fat face and small darting eyes. The girl's heart sank when he removed the cap. Recognition frightened her. Hoping for the best, Cogswell or Lacey, the worst had arrived. Milton Prowers!

"Rough weather we're having, Miss Claiborne," he greeted. She knew that booming voice, though she hadn't heard it for three years. When he took off the big coat he exposed a suiting of wide brown stripes and an enormous diamond glittering in an Ascot tie. He was still a showman, more like the owner of a circus now than a mere ringmaster. A pampered life had made him fat; sagging jowls spoiled his one-time claim to good looks.

He stood pinching at his frost-nipped nose.

"Cogswell around?" he inquired.

He was looking past Elsie toward the kitchen. The ebony face of Magnolia was peering from there. By the Negress stood the thin, slim boy, Eusebio. The girl wondered just how much protection those companions would afford her against a man like Prowers. The small eyes of Prowers, though, seemed sly rather than hostile. Why was he here?

"I'm expecting both Mr. Cogswell and Mr. Lacey at any moment," she said.

The caller threw back his head and laughed. "You wouldn't fool me, would you?" Then he added, "I'm about frozen. Where's the hottest stove in the house?"

"In the kitchen." She led him to the kitchen. As he was entering, he turned and went back to the hall rack where he had hung the bearskin coat. Elsie saw him take something flat and shiny from it. He transferred it to the pocket of his striped suit. Then he came and stood warming his hands at the kitchen stove.

His next abrupt query surprised Elsie. "Is Vera Grady around?"

"No. Why should she be here?"

"Just wanted to know." He seemed relieved.

"Why are *you* here, Mr. Prowers?"

"I wished I wasn't," he boomed, and rubbed his nose again. "Wouldn't have started if I'd a thought it would storm like this. Not used to it. I feel a cold in the chest coming on. Got any whisky?"

She shook her head. "You wanted to see Mr. Cogswell or Mr. Lacey?"

His booming laugh dropped all semblance of courtesy. "If I did, I wouldn't look for them here. They won't be here. Anyway, Steve Lacey won't be here. He's skipped the coop, and you know it."

"What do you mean?"

"Just that, Miss Claiborne. He's skipped the coop, and you know why. Gosh! I'm numb. Sure you haven't got anything that'll thaw me out?"

"Nothing but a hot stove," she said. And was glad of it. Liquor, she thought, might make this caller harder to handle.

Prowers grimaced. "Dickens of a note!" he complained. "I ride twenty mile through a snowstorm, get my nose frozen and a cold in the chest, and then can't get a—" He checked his speech suddenly and turned to Magnolia. "What about that case of red-eye Bert Pauly and I left here? Is it still down in the cellar?"

The Negress had stood scowlingly belligerent ever since the man had invaded her kitchen. Now she glared at Prowers, without answering.

"Well, here's hoping!" he said. "With your permission, Miss Claiborne."

He pushed back the table from the center of the room. Stooping, his fingers grasped a metal ring and pulled. A cellar door opened upward, ushering in a damp smell from below. Elsie knew about the cellar; but it was so dark and gloomy, being without entrance except this trap in the floor, that they had not used it.

"Got a candle?" His tone and manner were getting more overbearing all the while.

She gave him a candle. He lighted it and descended steep steps out of sight. They heard him stumbling around down there.

The Negress whispered, "Look heah, Miss Elsie. Want me to lock dat fool man in? He ain't gwine do us no good. Lemme slam down dat doo' and ram a bolt through de ring."

Elsie was tempted. There was genius in the suggestion. But she decided against it. She couldn't risk smothering Prowers. Or starving him. If they locked him in the cellar they'd have to take him food. Then he would overpower the food bearer and escape. Once escaped after such an indignity he would be more likely to give serious trouble.

She shook her head. In a few minutes Prowers reappeared with a quart of whisky. "This is something like it," he boomed.

After closing the trap door he put the table back in place. He brushed cobwebs from the bottle. Then he took two glasses from the cabinet and filled them. "Join me, Miss Claiborne?"

"No, thank you."

When the glass was halfway to his lips Prowers paused, asking, "You don't happen to know where that Grady girl is, do you?"

"You mean Vera Grady, the nurse? No, I never saw her in my life."

Again Prowers seemed relieved. He drank deeply. Then he turned with a sly, fat grin.

"Fine. I thought Steve Lacey was lying, and he was. He fed me a cock-and-bull story about something he claimed the Grady girl told you folks. Thought he was bluffing. Either bluffing or blackmailing. Now I know it. Here's looking at you, Miss Claiborne."

He drained the glass in a series of swift gulps. Elsie watched him with a growing dread. What was he here for, anyway?

"You've seen Steve?" she asked. "What do you mean by saying that he's skipped out, and that I know why?"

"You *do* know why, don't you?" Genuine surprise was evident in his voice.

"I have no idea what you're talking about," she said.

"You don't know that Lacey found a billfold of money out in your race-track meadow, and skipped high and wide with it?" He wiped his lips with the back of his hand. The small eyes now seemed both sly and malicious.

"I know nothing of the kind," she said stiffly. "And most certainly I wouldn't believe it on *your* testimony."

The laugh boomed again. "I see. You've gone soft on that cow-herder! You think if he'd found that money he'd have brought it to you like a nice little boy. Well, he didn't. He found it. He kept it. You'll never see a nickel of that money, or Steve Lacey."

CHAPTER TWENTY

SNOWBOUND

"LIGHT THE LAMPS, Magnolia," Elsie directed, although she was barely aware that the kitchen was now almost dark. She was trying to think of words stem enough to rebuke Prowers. She was incensed. Not for an instant did she accept his absurd arraignment of Steve Lacey.

Of one thing, though, she was fairly certain. Steve and Prowers had met, somewhere, and Steve had been matching wits with the man. Steve had frightened Prowers. Presumably he had mentioned the name of Vera Grady, hinting that the ex-nurse had betrayed the secrets of the swindle three years ago. Prowers was now rich. He was too wealthy to be judgment-proof. And naturally he didn't want his playhouse pulled down. So he had come here to learn the worst, to find out just what the Rincon Creek crowd knew about him.

More than likely he wanted to find Vera Grady, hoping to bribe her silence.

"Yes, that cowherder turned crook on you," Prowers chided.

"Not in a thousand years," she said.

Then she sparred with him. She tried to find out just where he had met Steve, but without success. Prowers was evidently here to acquire information without giving any in exchange.

In the end he said, "I know all I need to know. You admit you've had no communication with the Grady girl, so Lacey was bluffing. Or maybe he was trying to blackmail some coin out of me. I'm ready to pull out, except for this storm."

"The longer you wait, the worse it'll be," Elsie said.

He went to a window and looked out.

"The drifts are getting deep," he said. "Riding to town in the dark through deep drifts don't suit me. So I'll stay all night, and pull out first thing in the morning."

She could not, even if she had the physical power, put him out in this storm at night. There was nothing to do but endure his presence here until morning.

"Serve supper to Mr. Prowers and Eusebio, Magnolia. Bring mine to my room."

Elsie went to her room in the north wing and locked the door. Magnolia could stay with her through the night. The parlor adjoined. She decided to have Eusebio sleep on the parlor lounge. That would give this unwelcome guest the other wing of the house, and the kitchen, all to himself.

Putting that plan into effect, Elsie saw no more of her guest that night. Magnolia, coming in at bedtime, reported that he had never left the kitchen table. He was playing solitaire there, and drinking. He had brought more liquor up from the cellar.

"If he goes down theah again, an' I ketch 'im," the Negress vowed, "I'se gwine slam down dat doo' and lock 'im in."

In the morning when Elsie went to the kitchen for breakfast, Prowers was not there. Sometime during the night he had found a bed in the south wing. Eusebio reconnoitered. He reported that Prowers was in Steve's room, sleeping soundly.

They ate breakfast without him. Outside the snow still fell, persistently. It was more than a foot deep. Elsie looked dismally out at it. Across the creek she could see the cattle hugging around a stack pen, bawling for feed.

"Maybe no can get hay wagon out," Eusebio said.

"Do what you suggested the other day, then," Elsie directed. "Open a gate of one of the stack yards and let the cows in. You can take a saddle horse out, can't you?"

Eusebio said that he could. Today, but not after today if it continued to snow.

"That's just what worries me, Eusebio. The snow may pen us up for a week or more with Prowers on our hands. How far is it to the nearest neighbor?"

He said that the Tolliver brothers lived nearest, over on the San Isidro.

"All right. After you open the stack-pen gate, keep on going east. Ride to the Tolliver ranch. Ask one of the Tollivers to come over here and stay until Prowers is gone. Tell them that Prowers has made no threats, but we're a little afraid of him."

Eusebio went out, plunging through snow to the barn.

Any one of the three Tolliver men, Elsie thought, would do in this emergency. Especially Frank, the oldest brother. She knew that the Tollivers respected women. They might cheat a neighbor on a horse trade, but she never heard of anything more serious being charged against them. Bert and Bill were less intelligent than Frank, but either one of them would serve for the present purpose. There was a black sheep of a younger brother, too, Joe Tolliver. But Joe had been away from home for several years.

From a window she saw Eusebio cross the creek and ride toward a stack pen. The snow was knee-deep to his horse. She saw him open the stack-yard gate. Cattle crowded in around each of three stacks. That load was off her mind, anyway. Much hay would be trampled, but the cows would be well fed.

She saw Eusebio proceed on east, his horse plunging awkwardly. Soon he disappeared over a rise toward the San Isidro.

All morning she expected Prowers to appear in the kitchen, but he didn't. He failed to appear until she was eating a late midday meal. He came in with the look of a man who has been on an all-night spree. His eyes were bloodshot. His jowls were bluish and unshaven; his mood was morose. He poured himself a tall drink before greeting his hostess.

Then, without an invitation, he sat down opposite her at the table.

"You'll be starting to town now?" she suggested hopefully.

He answered with a shrug, and waved a hand toward the snow-caked windowpane. "In that?" he derided.

Magnolia served him bacon and eggs.

After he had eaten, he became more agreeable. "I'll take my hat off to you on that colt deal, Miss Claiborne. You could have knocked my eyes off with a stick when LeFever showed me that pedigree. He was wise, too. He got my certified check first."

To keep him in that humor, she bantered him. "After all, what's a pedigree? The colt won the race, didn't he?"

"He did. You haven't heard me squeal, have you? Listen, Miss Claiborne; I'm no busted bookie any more. Last couple o' years I've cleaned up. I could afford to pay thirty thousand dollars for a good three-year-old stud racer, and I paid it! I'll make it back off him in one season."

"I'm glad you're satisfied, Mr. Prowers. I am."

The man continued to be reasonably companionable. He drank moderately this morning. Elsie, to keep him friendly until the arrival of Frank, Bill, or Bert Tolliver, talked horses and told him something of her father's career as a turfman. All the while she was keeping an eye out the window for the return of Eusebio.

After a while she went to the parlor and sat there, sewing. Prowers followed, still talking horses. He lighted a cigar. He talked droningly for an hour.

Then he was silent for almost as long. Elsie looked up from her work. The man's chin had drooped on his chest and he was asleep.

She left him. When next she saw him, he had been to Steve's room and shaved. But his eyes were still bloodshot.

"Look here," he said suddenly, "what do you want to hang around a broke-down cow ranch for? This is no place for a girl like you."

She said coldly, "It suits me very well. I'm a partner here with Stanley Cogswell. All I have is invested in this ranch."

"You and Cogswell aiming to get married?" She knew he had been drinking again. His lips were curling in a sneer.

"That is no concern of yours," she said.

"Listen. Why wait around for that busted tenderfoot? He's nobody. He's got nothing. And it looks like he ditched you. Or maybe you're waiting on Steve Lacey. But Steve crossed you. He skipped with a purse of money and you'll never see him again. On the other hand, look at me! I'm—"

"Yes, look at you, you big stiff! I been tryin' to look at you for a long time."

The intruding voice was shrill. Elsie turned and saw Eusebio peering in from the hall. At his elbow was a slight sharp-featured man with an oval red spot on his left cheek.

He was the ne'er-do-well of the Tolliver clan, Joe.

Sight of him dismayed Elsie. She knew the reputation of Joe Tolliver. Joe was reputed to be a crook himself. Or worse; people said that he was a pawn of crooks, a shifty, shystery little hand-servant of thieves. Eusebio must have brought him in by the kitchen door and then forward through the house to the parlor.

Elsie saw no hope that Joe Tolliver would in any way prove competent to deal with Prowers.

Prowers himself evidently shared that opinion. He glared at the intruder for a moment, then blustered, "Look who's here! What jail turned you loose, Joe?"

Joe's eyes darted shiftily from Prowers to Elsie, then back to Prowers. His mouth smirked crookedly. "I ain't been in no jail, Milt. I got home a week ago, an' been bachin' there ever since. Don't know where Frank and them are. I guess they're off aswap-pin' horses."

"What," Prowers demanded, "did you come hopping over here for?"

"I'd hop a long way to see you, Milt; been lookin' fer you fer three year. I come to get mine, Milt."

"Your what?" Prowers's voice was less overbearing now. It carried a note of caution. His small eyes were hard and dangerous.

"Don't stall, you big stiff!" Joe challenged. "I want mine, and you can dang well afford to slip me. You're lousy with coin, they tell me. And look at me. I'm a bum. I'm broke. And who helped you get your start? I did. You promised me a thousand, three year ago, to send that tel—"

"Shut your cheap, blackmailing mouth!" Prowers roared at him, advancing in a blaze of temper.

Joe gave a step back into the corridor. But he was stubborn. His voice changed to a whine. "If you want me to shut up, you put up, Milt Prowers. Now that you've made me wait this long, you'll put up plenty. Ten grand'll do right now. I done your dirty work and I want my split. If I don't get it, I'll squeal to this dame."

Prowers towered over him in a black rage. His right fist was clenched. Tall and fat, he was like an infuriated buffalo bull about to toss overhead a yapping coyote pup. "I told you to shut your trap, Joe."

"Put up and I'll shut up," Joe whined doggedly. "Or if you want to do ten year on a rock pile, go ahead. That wire I sent ain't half of it, either. I could sing a song that'd hang you a mile high. Remember the time you and Bert Pauly dry-gulched the goatherder? He wasn't even trespassin'. He was on government—"

Prowers swung the fist. It caught Joe's right temple with crushing force. The impact of it cracked like the snapping of a bone. Joe's slight body was catapulted back across the corridor. His head struck a doorknob of the south wing.

He slipped inertly to the floor there. His eyes had a glazed look as they stared at Prowers.

"Don't you believe a word of it," Prowers said to Elsie. "Boy, toss some snow on him and bring him to."

Elsie was too horrified for words. Eusebio and Magnolia, standing by, were likewise stricken dumb. Prowers strode past them to the kitchen. In the silence of the next moment, they could hear him fill a glass with whisky.

Eusebio went to the front door and opened it. He stooped there, coming back with his sombrero full of snow. He applied the snow to the face of Joe Tolliver.

"Is he daid?" moaned Magnolia.

Eusebio didn't know whether he was or not.

"Let's get him on a bed," Elsie said.

She opened the door at which Joe Tolliver had fallen. It was the door of Steve's room. The three of them dragged the inert form in and raised it to a cot. Joe's eyes still had the glazed look. He was as limp as a bag of salt. A ribbon of blood trailed from his temple.

Suddenly he stiffened. A new horror gripped Elsie. Those eyes were like glass now. She felt of his heart. Then she reeled away dizzily. She steadied herself on Magnolia's thick, black arm and whispered, "I think he's—dead!"

Joe Tolliver was dead.

When she was sure of it, Elsie Claiborne crossed the corridor to her own bedroom. Magnolia and the boy followed her. They closed the corridor door and bolted it.

Elsie sat on the couch and stared at the bolted door. Two facts faced her. First, Prowers had murdered Joe Tolliver. It may have been the blow of his fist or the impact against a doorknob which had caused death; in either case Prowers had killed Tolliver. Second, the killer was as yet unaware of his crime.

He was drinking in the kitchen now, presuming that he had merely knocked Joe senseless. In time he would learn the truth. What would he do then?

What would he do when he became aware that he had dealt death in the presence of three witnesses?

If he could, she reasoned, he would flee away. But if deep snow kept him from running away, what then? Would he wait around in this snowbound ranch house, like a trapped rat, to be found, confronted, and accused?

Elsie went drearily to her window. Down, down, down, inexorably down the snow fell. Across the road she could see only the top two wires of a four-wire fence. A saddle horse might plunge through that, but not far or fast.

In a little while she heard Prowers call thickly from the kitchen, "Hey, Joe, come in here. Let's talk things over."

Silence. Would the silence tell a story to. Prowers?

He called again. Then his chair rasped as he pushed it back; Elsie heard the tramp of his feet as he came up the corridor.

She heard him enter Steve's room, across the hall. Then more stifling silence. It told her that Prowers was looking upon the cold, lifeless product of his violence.

"Barricade the door," she said to Eusebio.

The three began tugging at the furniture. They dragged the couch against the bolted door. Upon the couch they heaped the dressing-table and all chairs. Then they waited breathlessly.

At last they heard Prowers emerge from the room over there. His steps stopped in mid-hall. They could feel him thinking. They could sense the terrible menace of his thoughts. In a dead silence they waited for his voice.

Yet without a word he retreated. They heard him in the kitchen. Again a chair rasped as he sat down at the table there. They heard the trickle as he poured liquor. Then his voice came harshly.

"The cheap squirt of a squealer! What else could I do?"

A bottle fell. They could hear it roll across the kitchen floor. Then a chair rasped, and they hear Prowers pacing to and fro.

"We'll stay right here," Elsie whispered. "Let's pray he'll decide to get his horse and ride away."

But Milton Prowers did not leave the house. Night fell with snow still falling in thick, dense flakes. Three immured ones huddled all night in the upturned bedroom, sleepless. They were snowbound with a murderer, on a blighted Ranch of the Roses.

CHAPTER TWENTY-ONE
BLIND BULLETS

B Y DAWN IT HAD STOPPED SNOWING. The house was quite still. The stillness of it bred a hope that Prowers had left them.

"You better get some sleep, honey chile," Magnolia said. She made a pallet on the floor and forced the girl to lie on it.

Through sheer exhaustion Elsie fell asleep. When she awoke, her room was bright. She sat up and saw that the sun was shining brilliantly out of doors.

"Magnolia! Eusebio!" she called. They were both gone. The barricade had been removed and the corridor door stood open.

With infinite relief she saw that it had not been battered in. The door had been properly unlatched from the inside. The furniture had been restored to orderly positions. Therefore her companions had gone of their own accords.

It meant, she reasoned, that Prowers had evacuated the premises. Why not? The sun was shining. The sky was clear and blue. There was no wind. The snow was three feet deep, but melting in a glitter under the rays of an early May sun. The white expanse of it seemed studded with a million diamond beads. As the girl looked at it from her window, the sheen of it dazzled her eyes.

The storm over, Prowers must have made good his escape. No doubt Magnolia and Eusebio, upon discovering this, had gone to fire the kitchen stove and prepare breakfast.

So Elsie went out into the corridor. No sound came from the kitchen, whose door stood open. The house was like a tomb. Puzzled and a little afraid, she called again, "Magnolia! Eusebio!"

No voice answered her. She summoned her courage and went down the hall. What she saw in the kitchen made her gasp. There, seated at the table, was Prowers. His drooping jowls were purple. He was haggard and disheveled. There was no sign of the Negress or the boy.

"Come in," Prowers said hoarsely. "I won't hurt you."

"Magnolia—Eusebio, where are they?" she faltered.

Prowers thumbed downward toward the floor. His broad shoulders shrugged. "What else could I do?" he challenged.

Elsie now heard low moans of distress from the cellar. She looked down and saw that a stick of stove wood was thrust through the iron rings once used as a padlock hasp to secure the floor door.

"What else could I do?" Prowers repeated hoarsely. "They came in here this morning—I guess they thought I was gone. So I chucked them in the cellar."

Elsie stood poised for flight. He read her thought accurately, and said, "Don't run away. I won't hurt you. I could take an ax and chop down any door in the house, couldn't I? I could have broken in on you folks last night. But I didn't, did I?"

She was forced to admit that he hadn't. Now quite distinctly she could hear the complaints of prisoners beneath the floor.

"I didn't, because it wouldn't have got me anywhere. My cue is to get free of this deadfall, Miss Claiborne. The sun's out; the snow's melting fast. I'll be out of your way soon as I get something to eat. I'm hungry like a wolf."

His wry, forced grin was without mirth, showing white rows of teeth. It made him look not unlike a wolf, a fat, bloated wolf confronting the surviving sheep of the fold.

"What about breakfast, Miss Claiborne? Then, if you'll be good enough to walk down into the bull pen, I'll blow the ranch. I won't touch you, you understand. That's fair, isn't it?"

"You mean you'll lock me down there, too?"

He spread his palms helplessly. "What else can I do? Put yourself in my place. I didn't go to kill Joe Tolliver, but I did. He's dead. There were three witnesses. You know what that means."

With another forced grin he put thumbs and index fingers in a circle around his throat.

"Suppose I leave without locking you up! The first thing you do is let out the nigger and the Mex. The Mex rides for help, and a posse's after me in no time at all. This other way I may get a week's start."

"A week! Why, in a week we'd starve or freeze or smother."

Again the broad shoulders shrugged. "Tell me any other way I can save my skin, and I'll do it."

The thought of being confined in that dark hole for an indefinite period, perhaps to perish, at any rate to remain there until released by chance rescue, was ghastly. Yet the logic of it was clear; it was the only scheme of escape possible for Milton Prowers.

"Something to eat?" he said again. There was no malice or meanness in his voice, only desperation.

She went dumbly to the stove. It was hot. He had kept up a fire all night. She broke four eggs in a frying-pan with as many strips of bacon. Cold coffee was left from yesterday. She put the pot on to warm.

Prowers did not move from his seat.

She served him with food and coffee. Then in a stupor of dejection she moved to the front of the house.

Looking out through the glass pane of the front door, she saw sun-bathed snow glittering like as much mica. It was melting. Yet it was deep yet, deeper than any snow she had ever seen.

She pressed her face against the glass and looked wistfully up the trail toward town.

Only by the fences could she tell exactly where that trail was. It was laned, the tops of posts on either side protruding from hip-deep snow. Only the top wire of four on either fence could be seen.

Suddenly, far up that lane, she made out a tiny speck. It was a black speck on white, far away, and seemed to be jumping along with a peculiar gait close to one of the fence rows. At first she thought it was a rabbit.

The bobbing dot came nearer. It was following, with an odd exactness, that line of post tops. It brought a thrill of hope to her; for she saw now that it was a man. A man was plunging afoot, through hip-deep snow toward the house.

She pulled open the door. A wall of snow fell into the hall. She floundered out with the white bank of it deep about her skirt. Was it Steve? Was it Stanley? Surely it was one of them who came now! Who else but one of those two would defy the hazard of this storm?

Her eyes strained eagerly, until the dazzling glare made her cover them with her hands. It was blinding. But she had seen that bobbing speck again, nearer. It was a man. He was guiding himself by fence tops and floundering doggedly toward the house.

Her heart was near to bursting. It was bound to be Steve or Stanley. One of the two who loved her was coming home. Again her eyes braved the glitter. He who came, she saw, wore a brown felt hat and a plaid mackinaw coat.

Steve, she was sure. He wasn't tall enough for Stanley Cogswell. "Steve!" she cried shrilly. "Steve! Steve!"

Then a heavy hand was clapped over her mouth. Milton Prowers thrust her back and stepped to the edge of the porch. She saw him standing there with an automatic pistol in his hand. He was staring up the lane. He looked haggard and tired and old. Still there was no malice or meanness in his face, only desperation.

"Steve, look out for Prowers!" she warned shrilly. She lunged forward to dart past Prowers. He caught her arm and hurled her back. She fell in a lump near the door.

She saw him train the pistol on the man who approached, and who now was almost within range. It wasn't Steve, after all, she thought; it was more like Stanley Cogswell. She had judged by his height; now she realized that a man wading in hip-deep snow loses height. The set of his shoulders and the shape of his head, seen against the glitter, more nearly suggested Cogswell than Lacey.

Prowers, she thought frantically, would shoot him down. "Go back; go away!" she screamed. But he came nearer.

When she repeated the warning, Prowers, without looking around, said harshly, "Shut up." He stood at the edge of the porch, knee-deep, holding his aim.

He who came was still beyond pistol range, but not too far for the girl to discern a detail which chilled her with a new terror. The man's hand was sliding along the only exposed wire of the fence. He came slowly. At each post top, he groped. His progress was pitifully uncertain. Then Elsie saw that the upper part of his face was black.

Grotesque circles ringed his eyes. They disguised him, made it harder to distinguish even at this near range whether he was Cogswell or Lacey. Yet the disfigurement caused her to reclaim the first guess. Steve Lacey!

And snow-blind! His eyes were tightly shut. Hours on the glittering snow had blinded him. Evidently he had resorted too late to the old plainsman's trick of burning the end of a stick, cooling it in the snow, and then using the charcoal to daub black circles around the eyes. The ruse gave relief like that of smoked glasses.

Lacey had once told her that trick. Lacey knew it. But would Cogswell?

The man came on. He was only fifty yards away now. "Steve!" she cried wretchedly. All of the glittering scene swayed dizzily. Even now she wasn't quite sure who it was that came blindly toward Prowers.

Then she heard his voice. "Elsie, where are you?"

It was the voice of Stanley Cogswell. Hearing it, a paralyzing dread swept through her. "Go away," she shrieked. "It's Prowers, he's going to shoot you."

"He'd better," Prowers shouted hoarsely, and fired.

The bullet struck the oncomer's felt hat and tilted it to an oblique angle. The high forehead exposed was Stanley Cogswell's. "Get in the house, Elsie," he yelled. He left the fence and came plunging blindly on toward the gate. Sound guided him now. His right hand came from his coat pocket with a pistol.

Prowers moved forward to meet him. His second bullet plowed snow near Cogswell. Cogswell aimed unsteadily and fired at the sound of the shot. He missed by ten feet, breaking a windowpane that far to the left. "Go in the house, Elsie," he shouted.

He fired again, wildly. It was evident that he could see nothing. The man who could went to meet him, aiming deliberately. Shooting into the glitter, he missed. But only by inches. Cogswell was missing by feet and yards. He fired at each sound of the other gun. They stood hip-deep at twenty paces—a wild, crazy duel between the blind and the quick.

Prowers, confident, lunged forward to close the gap. But at ten paces he reeled drunkenly with his hand to breast. His knees sagged. He collapsed there, midway to the gate. Cogswell dropped his gun, its heat and weight boring a hole in the snow.

His stinging eyes were closed tightly. Again he heard Elsie's voice, nearer. He heard her plowing toward him. Then he could feel her hands on his shoulders.

"I heard you calling Steve."

"It was you I wanted most," she said. Then he felt her cheek against his. "You won't ever leave me again?" She was crying.

"I'll never leave you again." He couldn't see her. She kissed first one of his eyes, then the other.

The sun shone brilliantly around them, a sheen of dancing diamonds on the snow.

CHAPTER TWENTY-TWO
THE ROUNDUP

T HEY WERE MARRIED, a week later, at the courthouse.

"This is the place where all the trouble started," Cogswell said jubilantly as they came out. Elsie's arm was linked snugly to his own. He couldn't see her as clearly as he wanted to, through the dark glasses, although his eyes were almost healed.

On the train to California they spoke often of Steve.

"I supposed he was there with you," Cogswell repeated, "until he wrote me from Texas."

"Saying he had received thirty thousand dollars from Bud LeFever?"

"Yes, that was all he said."

"You don't believe ill of Steve, do you?" An earnest, anxious plea was in her voice. Insistent faith was there, impelling his own.

"Not for a minute, Elsie. Steve's square, in spite of the evidence. He simply couldn't be any other way. True, months later I paid him cash for that back pay. It's hard to figure out. But—we both know Steve Lacey."

She kissed him for that.

"And Prowers, of course," she offered in a little while, "was fibbing about Steve finding the purse in the meadow. Steve couldn't have, because he was looking for the purse until the last minute. Why, even after supper that last night he was out there sifting through his windrows with a fork."

"Prowers was maligning him," Cogswell agreed. "You can imagine how I felt upon learning that he'd ridden out to the ranch."

He told her again about how he had hurried West on receipt of Steve's letter, only to be assured that no horse could make it through the storm to Rincon Creek. The last rider who went that way, Greenstead said, was Milton Prowers.

Which made Cogswell only the more desperately determined to attempt the trip himself. In a drift near the Frijoli his horse foundered. Then the glitter of sun on snow, as he pressed forward afoot, had blinded him.

"I remembered a tip from Steve and charcoaled my eyes. It helped a little. But by the time I reached the ranch lane I couldn't see a thing."

"The snow will be gone when we get back, don't you think?"

"Yes, and the cattle fat. I sent Uncle Jack out to help Eusebio take care of them."

California sunshine greeted them. The Stanley Cogswells spent a month in a cabin by the sea.

June, and they were back. The big snow was gone. As they drove over Frijoli Hill, the range was never greener. Magpies chattered in the piñons. The high air was like wine.

One hand was enough to drive with. Elsie sat close, her head comfortably on his shoulder. Distantly ahead she could see the bowed rimrock of Rincon Mesa. Bright parks of quaking asp dripped from it, merging into black banks of spruce. Below these, the vega benches shone like polished silver in the sun. Below all the bulbous arm of a cottonwood creek thrust out upon the plain.

Elsie loved the sight of it. Her heart wanted to burst.

Soon they turned through a gate and drove smartly down the lane toward the house, the barn, the mud corrals and the hamlet of huts built years ago by Don Ramon Estabal.

"See, the roses are in bloom! They're gorgeous!" Her ecstasy was breathless. The big race-track circle was vivid, now, with pink and white blossoms.

"I see Eusebio and Uncle Jack!" Cogswell said. "There on the corral fence."

The livery-barn wrangler and the chore boy were shouting and waving hats.

Then came another chorus of welcome. It awed them for a while. It held them in a spell of overwhelming wonder.

Wonder gave way to rapture. Another field of red and white, broad and beautiful, was spread before them. The corrals were packed with lowing life.

"Why, it—it looks just like the stockyards!" Cogswell was too confounded to say more.

"They're gorgeous!" Elsie marveled. This time she didn't mean the wild roses.

She saw white heads, silken white necks, creamy dewlaps, curly manes, broad red backs. A glow filled and thrilled her. Blooded stock! The love of it was in her veins. A thousand head of purebred heifers lowed a welcome, like a triumphant roll of drums.

Uncle Jack came running. "Don't look fer no brands." He grinned. "They don't brand them kind of fancy stuff. Steve, he had a little zinc tag put in the left ears, with CC and a register number. Me an' Eusebio was just about to turn 'em out to pasture."

"Steve!" Elsie cried. "Has Steve been here?"

"Been here and gone. He went back to the Bar 37, down Texas way, where they made him foreman at sixty a month."

Uncle Jack handed a letter to Elsie. Her eyes grew moist as she read it. Her husband took it and read:

Dear Miss Elsie,

In my last windrow I found the wallet. For once in his life Prowers told the truth—there was just three hundred dollars in it. Also there was a receipt for a hotel bill, a hotel in San Antone. The date was the same as the one on the fake forged contract with your father. Prowers couldn't have been in San Antone and Denver on the same day, so I figured if I could get him to identify and claim the wallet I'd have him where the wool was short.

I located him in New Orleans. When I called there, they told me he was out to the track, where a jamboree called the Old Planters' Sweepstakes was being pulled off that afternoon.

He was right in front of a booking-cage when I found him. I showed him the wallet. "There's evidence in it to put you on the rock pile for life," I said, "not counting what Vera Grady told me." That last was a bluff. But him being rich, I figured he'd offer to pay back the swindle money to keep out of jail.

He outsmarted me. Knowing there was only three hundred dollars in the wallet, he refused to claim it. Said it wasn't his. That queered my play. He walked off, leaving me with a three-hundred-dollar purse on my hands, right in front of a booking-cage.

They were calling a race. I saw the list of entries. The last name on it was Gold Brick. I looked out at the starting-line and saw your colt. He looked great. Still, he was unknown, with the class of the country lined against him. That made him the rankest outsider at the wire.

I saw his odds, a hundred to one to win. On a hunch I took the three hundred dollars from the purse Prowers wouldn't claim, and slammed it through the wicket. Got it on Gold Brick's nose to win, just as they closed the books.

He romped home, and I romped back to Texas to buy thirty thousand dollars' worth of registered ballies for the CC, five hundred at sixty a head. But when I got to Texas I found another thirty thousand. Milt Prowers had bought *that colt. All of which made the price of an even thousand of the prettiest, curliest-maned bally heifers between Kansas and the Gulf.*

So it works out slick all around. I wanted to plow up that circle, you recollect, to locate the sixty thousand. It wasn't there, but it turns up, anyway, and you still got your pet roses. Don't never plow up that patch, Miss Elsie. I reckon every woman wants a rose garden. If any man or crittur ever tromples on yours, just call on

Stephen Lacey.